"I'm a maste ~~all downhill~~ **rom here, I promise..."**

"It's a good thing that everyone's left, then," Joanna said.

Jack's eyes widened in mock horror. "Except you're still here! And I'm running out of charming one-liners."

Joanna laughed, and she felt a warm shiver go up her spine.

And he's funny, too.

"In all seriousness, the speech you made back there was quite insightful. Sometimes I forget that words aren't the only way to communicate." Jack had a thoughtful look in his eyes.

"Thank you for saying that," Joanna said, "and for listening. I really didn't think anyone was paying attention to me at all."

"Hey, us new kids have to stick together, right?" Jack held the door open for her as they stepped into the hall.

"Thanks, Mr. Sun. By the way, what did you say at the end of your Mandarin speech that made everyone giggle?"

Jack looked at Joanna right in the eye. "I said, 'Maybe I'll find a reason to stay longer.'"

Dear Reader,

I'm so thrilled to share with you my debut romance novel, *The Teacher's Match*. I was inspired to write this book having faced my own struggles in finding the right career for myself.

In the book, Joanna and Jack, both teachers, meet at a Mandarin immersion elementary school on the first day of spring. Joanna is starting over in a new career and is determined not to let a relationship—especially a work one—get in the way of her success. Jack is about to move back to Taiwan to work for his family's business, despite having a gratifying teaching career in the US.

The Teacher's Match is set in western Michigan and features some beautiful backdrops, including gorgeous sunsets on Lake Michigan and the annual tulip festival in Holland, MI. I also met my husband in western Michigan, so it holds a very special place in my heart!

I hope you enjoy reading *The Teacher's Match* as much as I did writing it!

Sincerely,

Kristi Hong

THE TEACHER'S MATCH

KRISTI HONG

HEARTWARMING

Harlequin®
HEARTWARMING™

ISBN-13: 978-1-335-05146-2

The Teacher's Match

Copyright © 2025 by Kristi Hong

Recycling programs for this product may not exist in your area.

Harlequin Enterprises ULC
22 Adelaide St. West, 41st Floor
Toronto, Ontario M5H 4E3, Canada
www.Harlequin.com

Printed in U.S.A.

Born to immigrants from Taiwan, **Kristi Hong** grew up in Michigan, and while she's lived in many different places around the world, she's a Midwestern girl at heart. After a career on Wall Street, Kristi fulfilled her middle school dreams by becoming a published author, with a goal of writing books featuring diverse characters, particularly Asian Americans.

Kristi worked at an ice cream shop and a florist shop as a teenager and has loved all things dessert- and floral-related ever since. When not writing, Kristi can be found reading a book, taking a long afternoon nap or munching on a pan-fried dumpling.

Visit the Author Profile page at Harlequin.com

For my parents

Acknowledgments

Huge thank-yous go out to:

—Eunice Shin, for putting out the original call for a "G-rated Asian American romance" and setting this all in motion;

—Cecilia, for being my expert consultant on all things romance;

—Samantha, Sarah and Ben, for providing writing critique but also (perhaps more importantly!) moral support;

—Love, for all the Mandarin immersion school and dragon boat rowing material;

—Kellee and Audrey, for all of their fun and creative plot suggestions;

—Dana Grimaldi, my amazing editor, for all her work and guidance;

and

—My husband and children, for the constant support.

CHAPTER ONE

TODAY'S ARRIVED. It's really here.

Joanna Lin drove down the pretty, tree-lined street that led to Lakeland Elementary School. She pulled into the staff lot and parked her car in the first space facing the entrance of the one-story, red-brick building, which looked just as charming as its photos online. Joanna wondered which of the windows might belong to her new classroom. She pictured the miniature chairs soon to be occupied with little bodies, the neat stacks of fresh crayon boxes waiting to be opened, the bulletin boards ready to be filled with drawings and art projects—*art projects taught by ME, eek!*

Getting out of her car, Joanna quickly checked her reflection in the driver's side window. She had splurged and gone shopping the day she received the official offer for her new job, picking out a patterned flutter-sleeve belted dress and a pair of espadrille wedges. It was the complete opposite of the outfits that were acceptable at her old job, where a stiff pantsuit and sensible shoes were the firm's unspoken uniform, and Joanna's colorful ensembles had stuck out like a peacock in a penguin colony.

Goodbye, boring outfits, forever!

As she took a few steps toward her car's trunk, Joanna paused for a moment to admire the lilac bushes planted on both sides of the school's front doors. Though their buds were still small and dark, like bunches of tiny purple grapes, she could practically smell the sweet fragrance that would fill the air as soon as they burst open.

And it's the first day of spring, too. A perfect day for a new beginning.

She unloaded a large box filled with paint-brushes, tempera paints and other art materials that she had packed over the weekend, unsure what supplies the school would have, and not wanting to be caught shorthanded on her first day.

Her mind went back twenty years, to when she was just a little girl. Joanna had always looked forward to the first day of school. She loved it all—new classroom, new teacher, new books and materials, endless possibilities for the year ahead. Every year, she prepped her backpack weeks in advance, making sure all her pencils and pens were arranged inside just so, then set it right by the front door so it was ready to go on the ap-pointed day.

This time, she was quite a bit older, and she

was starting in March, not September, but it was just as exciting.

The biggest difference, of course, was that today she wasn't a student, but a teacher!

Carrying the box of art supplies, her handbag and travel coffee mug, Joanna strode up the sidewalk to the school's entrance. Fumbling, she managed to free a hand to open one of the double doors.

"Oof!" Joanna yelped as her arm met resistance and her head whiplashed back, just as a ray of sunlight shone straight into her eyes. She scrambled to set all her things on the ground and then tried the other door, but to no avail, as it, too, didn't budge.

Glancing around, she realized that hers was the only car in the entire parking lot.

Oh no. Could I have gotten the date wrong?

After checking her email to confirm that she had, indeed, arrived on the correct start date of her new position, Joanna called the number for the main office while peering into one of the windowed doors, in the hopes that someone might already be inside to let her in. Hearing the automated message that the school's open hours didn't start for another thirty minutes, and seeing no one inside, Joanna was about to just take a seat on the front steps to wait, when a gust of wind blew toward her. She pulled her coat tighter around herself, but the wind ruffled up the skirt of her new dress and reminded her that while the calendar might have said it was the first day of spring, winter in western Michigan had not yet completely departed.

Resigned, Joanna walked back to her car and got in, her eyes peeled for any sign of life in or around the school. The morning sunlight, which had been softly streaming through the windshield just a few minutes ago, now felt harsh and penetrating, and her excitement for the day ahead was rapidly turning into apprehension.

She took a deep breath to calm her nerves. *Better early than late*, she tried to reassure herself.

Flipping the sun visor down, she checked her appearance in the mirror. Earlier that morning, she had applied a bit of blush on both her cheekbones. Now, thinking she looked pale in the bright spring sun, she reached for her makeup bag and added a few more dabs of blush on each side.

Today is the first day of the rest of your life. It's going to be amazing.

Her stomach tightened, then turned.

Okay, so you're nervous, but who wouldn't be? Starting a new career in a new town—this is a big deal.

After a few minutes of restless fidgeting with her phone to confirm once again that she had the right date and location—*hopefully there wasn't another Lakeland Elementary somewhere else nearby!*—Joanna decided she might as well eat breakfast, an exquisite, glazed fruit tart she had picked up from the Swiss Bakery on her drive into work. Temporarily distracted from her current predicament, Joanna took a bite of the chocolate-dusted berries and custard filling, through to the flaky crust, sighing at how delicious it was, never mind that she was eating in her car.

TEN MINUTES LATER, as she was lifting the lid off her coffee mug, Joanna perked up at the sound of another car pulling into the lot. A chic-looking woman wearing a white trench coat and patent leather heels emerged from it.

Thank goodness.

Joanna shoved the half-eaten tart back into its white bakery bag and rushed to gather up her things, fearing the woman might enter the building and leave the doors locked behind her. Thankfully, though, as Joanna approached the school's double doors for the second time laden with all her items, the other woman rushed ahead to open one of the doors for her.

"Good morning! Welcome! You must be Jacky Sun," the woman said, smiling warmly. "I'm Mindy Perez, the school guidance counselor." She had dark hair, a beautifully made-up face—smoky eyes and gorgeous contouring—and a swanky air about her. "Have you taught fifth grade before?"

"Thank you," Joanna said gratefully, turning

sideways to wedge her box through the doorway. "But I'm not supposed to be teaching fifth grade, at least I hope I'm not. I'm Joanna Lin, the new art teacher...?" She trailed off uncertainly, her jitters from earlier returning.

Mindy's face reddened. "Oh no, I did *not* just do that. Of course, you're the new art teacher." She motioned to the box of art supplies and said, "Please, let me help you with that. I'm *so* sorry! There's a new fifth grade teacher starting today, too, and she speaks Mandarin—obviously, as we're a Mandarin immersion school—and I saw that you looked Asian, and well, I just assumed." She shot Joanna an embarrassed grimace.

Joanna put out a hand to reassure the other woman. "No problem. An honest mistake. I'm just glad I'm not expected to teach fifth grade today, because I definitely didn't go back to school for that! And yes, my parents were born in Taiwan, but they both left when they were quite young, and I was born and raised here in the US."

"I'm so mortified," Mindy said, shaking her head. "I'm a mix of ethnicities myself—Latina, Black, German and Irish—and hate when anyone assumes anything about me. Not to mention I'm also the school guidance counselor. I should have known better."

"Please, don't worry about it. But maybe you can show me to my classroom?"

"Yes, I can definitely do that. Right this way," Mindy answered, leading Joanna down the hall.

They walked into the main atrium of the school, which was bright and airy and smelled lemon fresh, and where a large red banner was strung up with the words *Welcome to Lakeland Elementary School* in large block letters, followed by a set of elegant, brushstroked Chinese characters.

"You probably already know this from when you interviewed," Mindy explained, gesturing to the banner as they passed by, "but our principal had a vision that children can absorb multiple languages early in life, so he founded this Mandarin immersion school five years ago."

"It's really incredible," Joanna replied, seeing schoolwork done in Chinese characters displayed outside the classrooms as they made their way down the hall. *I wonder if Mom and Dad ever wanted to teach me Taiwanese or Mandarin.* It wasn't something they'd talked about much. All she knew was that her parents were proud Americans, and while it was becoming more diverse, the small eastern Michigan town that Joanna had grown up in hadn't had any Asian families other than the Lins. Besides a few years of high school French, English was the only language Joanna had ever learned.

"Do the students find it hard?" Joanna asked. "Especially if they don't have someone at home who speaks Mandarin?"

"Most adjust really quickly," Mindy replied. "Principal Malik was right—children's brains really are extraordinary. You should see my boys— twins in the second grade here—they chatter away to each other in Mandarin when they don't want me or my husband to know what they're talking about. I'm studying it, too, but I can't keep up with them!"

"That's remarkable. And how much English instruction do the students get?" Joanna asked.

"Hardly any. Immersion really is the best way to learn a language. The only parts of their day the students hear English are the single subjects. PE, music and art—" Mindy stopped in front of a windowed door. "And here you are."

They walked into the classroom, which had a large, wide window facing the blacktop, and several large round tables grouped in the middle of the room, each surrounded by small student chairs. Cabinets and counters lined the walls, with bulletin boards mounted a few feet above the counters. Joanna drew in a short breath.

And here I am. I can't believe it. My very own art classroom.

Joanna set her box down on one of the round tables and took a long sweep around the room. "This is fantastic. I didn't expect it to be so big." Her mouth stretched into a giddy grin.

"I have to admit, the walls look a little bare to me," Mindy said, as she, too, glanced around.

"Ms. Rani, the prior art teacher, cleared out all the student artwork when she left just before spring break."

"I don't mind," Joanna responded, her voice chipper. "They'll be full in no time with new projects. But the way you just described the last art teacher's departure—it sounded kind of, I don't know, abrupt?"

Mindy's expression remained neutral as she said, "It wasn't expected, that's true. But, she was very young, it was her first job out of college, and well, let's just say this job isn't for everyone. In addition to having to deal with all the kids, our school has a unique culture. It can be a lot to handle."

Joanna's heartbeat sped up a touch at the guidance counselor's words.

Uh-oh. Maybe I'm really not prepared for this at all.

Mindy must have sensed Joanna's worry, as she quickly added, "There I go again—putting my foot in my mouth. I'm sure you're going to do fine. You even brought your own supplies! I shouldn't have mentioned the prior teacher at all."

Joanna didn't feel reassured but tried not to show it. "Thanks for showing me to my classroom, and for all the background on the school."

"It was my pleasure. The teachers' lounge is the room next door to the right. At today's morning meeting, Principal Malik will introduce you and the new fifth grade teacher. Who is not you! Because you're the new *art* teacher," Mindy said, emphasizing her words with a dramatic gesture toward Joanna. "I'm so sorry again. See you there?"

"Sounds great," Joanna replied, happy to have met such a friendly colleague already, notwithstanding the mix-up over her identity.

MINDY DEPARTED, and as Joanna was taking inventory of the cabinets and getting out materials for her first class, she caught sight of a photo frame tucked in between two paint bottles in her box. She recognized it immediately and smiled as she wondered how her mother had managed to sneak it into her supplies before she left the house last week for her big move across the state. Joanna reached over and pulled the frame out and brought it closer so she could see the photo. Taken a few autumns before her father had gotten sick, it showed her parents in front of their big dogwood tree, her cheery, round-faced dad carrying a rake, and thin but sturdy mom wearing a canvas sunhat.

Joanna blew one kiss to the photo, then looked through the front window to the sky and blew another one.

I'm finally doing what you said I should do, Dad—following my dreams. I wish you could be here to see it.

Her journey hadn't been easy. It had taken a

lot more years than Joanna had planned to get her life on track. After college, she'd spent a few years trudging along as a paralegal in a big law firm before she discovered that she really didn't enjoy legal work, and no amount of experience was going to change her mind. But by then she had started dating an attorney at the firm, which kept her in that unfulfilling career even longer still. It wasn't until after her father had passed away that she found the courage to quit the job and go back to school for the career that she really wanted.

A year and a half later, armed with the proper qualifications and a heart full of determination, Joanna had started her search. After months of applications and follow-up calls and emails, she saw an urgent job posting from a school on the other side of the state looking for an art teacher to start right after spring break. A handful of interviews and a two-hundred-mile drive later, she had finally achieved it: Joanna Lin, a few weeks past her twenty-ninth birthday, was starting her new career today.

Miss Joanna, elementary school art teacher.

As if responding to her thoughts, the handbag on her desk started vibrating. Joanna put the frame down and drew out her phone, giving the screen a tap to answer the call. "Hi, Mom!"

Her mother's voice rang through the speakerphone. "Good morning, Joanna, did I wake you?"

"Nope! I'm at work already," Joanna answered, sitting down at her desk chair.

"Oh, does school start so early?"

Joanna bit her lip at her mother's unintentional dig. "Actually, no... I was a little early, but thankfully the school's guidance counselor was, too, and she let me in. How are you? Everything okay there?" Joanna worried about her mother being all alone in their family home. It had been hard enough when her father had passed away two years ago, but Joanna had moved back in with her. Now, however, her mother was really on her own.

"I'm fine. Don't worry about me, dear. Have you eaten breakfast yet?"

"Oh, I started to. Thanks for the reminder," Joanna answered, retrieving her tart from earlier. "I picked something up from the bakery around the corner. I'll take you there when you come visit."

"Sounds wonderful. I can't wait. I just wanted to call and send you good wishes on your first day. Congratulations on starting your new career, honey. Your dad would have been so proud."

Joanna imagined what it would have been like to have her dad there on the phone. "We miss you a lot, Jo Jo!" she could hear him saying. "The house isn't the same without you."

All the way up to the end, his heart was working just fine, Joanna thought, her eyes welling up with tears. *Even if everything else wasn't.*

"Thanks, Mom, that means a lot." Joanna felt a

wave of gratitude flow through her as she glanced at the photo of her parents again. Her mother had been unbelievably supportive of her career transition. And before that, it had been her father, very nearly on his last breaths, who had encouraged Joanna to leave the job she didn't love and the man who went along with it.

"You've been a paralegal long enough to know you don't want to be a lawyer. And you've been with Tim long enough to know you don't love him. Don't spend another day in that law firm," he had said. "There is something else out there that will bring you real joy. You just have to go for it. Follow your heart, Jo Jo."

Just then, Joanna noticed the photo of her parents had slipped from the mat inside the frame. She put her tart down and opened the backing to move the photo into place, and realized there was a picture underneath of her and Tim at a company holiday party. She had apparently overlooked it when she'd purged her belongings of everything related to him after they broke up. A dark cloud entered her thoughts, but she swatted it away as quickly as she did the actual photo, crumpling it up and shoving it deep into the now-empty bakery bag.

Definitely don't want memories of Tim and the law firm ruining my first day.

Snapping Joanna out of her thoughts, her mother's voice sang out, "By the way, honey, I heard from my friend Tracy—remember her? We used to work together before she retired—that her nephew's old college roommate recently moved to western Michigan, right near where you are, I think. He's just a few years older than you and she said he's single. You could explore the area together. What do you think? I can get his number, or give Tracy your number to pass to him?"

Joanna inwardly groaned. Carol Lin was their community's self-anointed matchmaker, always an ear to the ground on who was eligible and looking for love (or not looking, she didn't care!). Joanna did have to admit that her mother had a knack for it; the evidence of her successful matchups—dozens of wedding invitations—were prominently displayed all around their home.

Apparently, Mom's reach extends clear across the state, too. That's actually pretty impressive, she thought with a twinge of pride, but not enough to give in.

"Mom, it's literally the very first day of my new job," she said. "I don't want a relationship to get in the way of figuring out my life, like what happened with Tim."

"I know, I know. I left you alone while you were back in school, and then looking for this job, didn't I? But now you've found your new career! Don't you think it's time you got back out there?"

Joanna knew her mother meant well, but she had to push back. "Remember what I told you?

That my position is still probationary? I have to perform well to get an offer for a permanent position next school year."

"You're sure to get an offer," her mother said encouragingly. "I just can't see how you wouldn't. You were made to be an art teacher. I remember when you used to play school with all your dolls and stuffed animals. It wasn't ABC's you were teaching them, it was basic color theory! I still remember you asking 'And what color does red and blue make, Teddy?'"

"I appreciate your confidence, Mom, but I can't afford to mess this up. A position like this is so hard to find—you know that public school funding for elementary art is declining every year—so I really have to focus. Please, don't give out my number to anyone, okay?"

"Alright, I won't," her mother answered cheerily. "Will you at least think about it, though? This man sounds like he'd be a good match for you."

Joanna cut her mother off as gently as possible. "Sorry, Mom, I gotta let you go. I have my first staff meeting soon. Can I talk to you later?"

"Sure, honey. Message me when you free up again," her mom answered. "Have a wonderful day, dear."

Joanna imagined her dad saying, "Bye, Jo Jo! Have a good day at school. We love you!" And to this, she had to smile, as he'd called out the same thing every single school day without fail, from the first day of kindergarten until high school graduation.

"Bye, Mom." Joanna ended the call and tucked her phone back into her handbag as she finished off the last buttery bit of her fruit tart. As she wiped the edges of her mouth with a napkin, she spotted on her desk a small scrap of the photo of Tim, apparently having ripped off as she was discarding it.

Her mother's urging played through her mind. *Don't you think it's time you got back out there?*

Shaking her head, Joanna used her thumb and forefinger to pick the piece up and drop it into the bakery bag, then folded the top over twice to ensure the scrap, along with the rest of the photo, would make it to its intended destination—a garbage can.

Sorry, Mom. I need to make sure I succeed at this job first. My love life will just have to wait.

CHAPTER TWO

SEEING SHE STILL had plenty of time before the staff meeting, Joanna tied on an apron and started squeezing out different colors of paint, using paper plates as palettes. While she was setting the plates out on the round tables, two women entered her classroom chatting animatedly in, what Joanna assumed was, Mandarin.

It didn't take long to realize that they, like Mindy Perez, the guidance counselor, had also mistaken Joanna for the new fifth grade teacher. The taller Caucasian woman, her strawberry blond hair in a stylish, asymmetric cut, smiled at Joanna and extended a hand, while enthusiastically saying something, and then the shorter Asian woman, who wore dark-rimmed glasses and had a small, heart-shaped mouth, added something else, while bowing her head slightly.

For a moment Joanna wished she could pretend to be this new teacher, as they both seemed so delightfully eager to meet her. Not being able to speak Mandarin, though, prevented her from doing so; instead, she simply shook her head, saying in English, "I'm so sorry, I'm not the new fifth grade teacher. I'm the new art teacher." She pointed at the yellow paint bottle she was holding.

"Oh! So sorry," the petite one said, covering her mouth. She introduced herself as Miss Wei-Wei and her colleague as Miss Alex, both fourth grade teachers. "I didn't know we had a new art teacher. Did Ms. Rani leave? We saw you from the hallway and were asking if you were lost, since this is the art classroom. We thought you were the new fifth grade teacher, Jacky Sun, because, well, you look Chinese—"

"Which we shouldn't have done, obviously," Alex said, her voice deep and raspy. "*Huge* fail on our part—much apologies about that." She flashed Joanna a gritted teeth, sheepish expression, not unlike the one Mindy had displayed earlier.

"It's okay," Joanna said. "To be honest, I wouldn't have guessed that *you* spoke Mandarin." Then she caught herself. "Ack, I probably shouldn't have said that, either."

Alex gestured at her own pale face. "I know, right? You're probably wondering, how did this whitest of white girls learn Chinese?"

Now it was Joanna's turn to be embarrassed. "Oh no, I wasn't thinking about how white you were—I mean, um…"

"No worries—I'm used to it. You should see

when parents meet me. Shock and awe everywhere. I had one mom last year who literally stopped dead in her tracks, like, *paralyzed*, when I introduced myself in Mandarin at the school's open house." Alex's manner of speaking was so cool and casual that Joanna immediately felt at ease.

Wei-Wei laughed, covering her mouth again, then said to Alex, "I admit, I was very surprised when I met you that you were a Chinese teacher."

"No, Miss Wei-Wei, you, too?" Alex teased, and then turned back to Joanna, explaining, "I grew up in Beijing, where my parents are both English teachers."

Joanna nodded. "Got it. My parents are originally from Taiwan—"

"The new fifth grade teacher is also from Taiwan!" Wei-Wei exclaimed. "She moved to the US, went to Yale for college, then Harvard for her master's degree. She was Teacher of the Year at her last district. Everyone is very excited that she's able to join us, especially considering it's the middle of the year."

Alex put her hands on her cheeks in mock admiration. "Can you imagine? Yale! *And* Harvard!" she repeated.

"It's very impressive," Wei-Wei said earnestly. "Wait, are you making fun of me?"

Alex laughed and gave Wei-Wei a little nudge with her shoulder. "Yes. No, but seriously, Teacher of the Year? That *is* impressive. I'm looking forward to meeting her, for sure. Actually, Principal Malik is supposed to introduce her and, I assume, you, too—" she nodded at Joanna "—in just a few minutes. Shall we head over to the lounge together?"

"You two go on ahead. I just have to wash my hands," Joanna answered. "I'll be right behind you." As she watched the two women walk out of her classroom, she found that their excitement was contagious; suddenly, Joanna was eager to meet this new star teacher, too.

I wonder what a Teacher of the Year looks like?

A few minutes later, Joanna arrived at the lounge, where most of the teachers and staff were gathered in a huddle near the center of the room, their backs toward her.

"Joanna," a voice called out, and she saw Mindy Perez sitting at a table, waving her over. "Over here! I saved you a seat."

"Thanks. But just so you know, I'm not the new fifth grade teacher," Joanna said with a wink.

"Good one," Mindy said. "But I knew that, because Jacky's already arrived." Both of Mindy's eyebrows went up as she pointed her chin to the center of the room.

"Is that right?" Joanna asked. "And is she everything that you expected?"

Mindy chuckled. "I'll admit that Jacky Sun is *definitely not* what I expected."

"Wait, is she not Asian?" Joanna asked, thinking of what Miss Alex had said about parents being surprised she spoke Mandarin.

Mindy gave her a mischievous look. "Just go and see for yourself."

Joanna turned to catch a glimpse of the new teacher, and when she did, she actually gasped.

Mindy was right; Jacky Sun was definitely not what Joanna had expected, either. As the crowd parted and Jacky came into view, Joanna saw that the hotshot, went-to-Yale-*and*-Harvard new Teacher of the Year wasn't an Asian woman at all.

Joanna's mouth nearly fell open at the sight of the chiseled-jawline, movie-star-good-looking Asian *man*.

TALL AND LEAN with an athletic build, he wore a fitted light blue button-down shirt, its sleeves rolled up to his forearms in a casual-yet-polished way, and his hair was styled in similar fashion—offhandedly mussed, but without a strand out of place.

Joanna felt her face heating up as she looked toward Mindy then back at the new teacher.

Definitely didn't need that extra blush today.

He paused for just a second before displaying a dazzling, double-dimpled smile and extending his hand for her to shake. "Hi, I'm Jack Sun, the new fifth grade teacher." His voice was deep and strong, and Joanna felt a warm stir through her body as she took his hand.

Trying to maintain her composure, she stammered, "H-hi! I'm Joanna. Joanna Lin. I've been hearing about you all morning. Your reputation precedes you, it seems."

"Is that so?" Jack's dimples appeared again as he reacted to her statement. "It's nice to meet you, Joanna. You must be our art teacher."

Joanna was taken aback. "Yes, I am. Have people been talking about me, too?"

"Well, no," Jack admitted, shaking his head. "But you're wearing a painter's apron and you've got a little speck of paint on your cheek, and some on your dress, too." He pointed to her face, then her shoulder, where Joanna could now see a small yellow streak on her sleeve.

"Darn it." Joanna wrinkled her brow slightly as she lifted her arm to inspect the mark, trying to wipe her face at the same time. "Must have gotten on me while I was setting up for my first class. Or maybe it was custard from the car," she blurted out.

Jack looked slightly confused. "I'm sorry?"

"Oh, er, nothing," Joanna said, feeling inexplicably flustered. "I got here too early this morning and had to eat breakfast in my car. I had a fruit tart and maybe some of it got on my dress? I'm not really sure…um, just forget I said anything!"

Gosh, what is wrong with me?

"I see. Don't worry, it's hardly noticeable," Jack assured her, reaching over to the sink and pulling out a paper towel from the dispenser. "Here, use this. I'm sorry I pointed it out. You look like you're ready for a lively—and hopefully lovely—day teaching art."

Joanna blushed again as they made eye contact when she took the paper towel from him and started gently dabbing her sleeve. "Thank you. It's actually my first day here, too. And yes, I'm hoping it will be lovely. It's nice to meet you. Although I was expecting someone who looked a little, um, different?"

"Ah, yes, some of the other teachers told me that Principal Malik did not mention any pronouns in his introductory email to the staff. And what can I say, when it came to choosing an English name, my mother really liked Jacky Cheung." Seeing the blank look on Joanna's face, he added, "You know, the mega pop star?"

"Oh, my mom loves Jacky Cheung, too!" an excited voice interjected. It was Miss Wei-Wei; she had been standing just behind Joanna and now squeezed in to join the conversation. Wei-Wei said something to Jack in Mandarin, to which he responded with a light chuckle.

"Actually, just *Jack* is fine," Jack clarified, in English. He continued in Mandarin, saying something that made Wei-Wei laugh.

Jack realized that Joanna wasn't following the

conversation and said, "I'm so sorry, you don't speak Mandarin, do you?" After she shook her head, he translated. "Miss Wei-Wei asked me if I could sing like Jacky. And I'm sad to say that, unfortunately, my singing voice didn't quite get to professional level, so my mother's dream of me becoming his protégé will never be achieved."

Jack and Wei-Wei speaking in Mandarin and discussing this unfamiliar pop star made Joanna's face redden yet again. "Sorry, I don't know who that is," she said, clarifying, "I was born and raised here in the US."

"Of course, I'm sorry," Jack responded. "Sometimes I forget everyone's not like me, with a foot in two countries separated by the vast Pacific Ocean."

Joanna inspected him carefully. Jack seemed pretty American to her, but after this morning, she knew better than to assume. "I heard you're originally from Taiwan?"

"I was born there, yes, but my parents sent me here in middle school to get an American education. And get one I did, including intense speech coaching to perfect my American accent. Of course, whenever I go back to Taiwan, I get teased mercilessly for my lack of knowledge of the latest slang and pop culture!"

The offhand way he said this gave Joanna the sense that his self-esteem was completely intact, and she said, coyly, "I'm guessing you manage just fine."

Jack shot her a half smile, and seemed to be about to ask her something, but their conversation was cut short as Principal Malik appeared at the door of the lounge. He was a big man, with a full, dark beard, and he wore a red Lakeland T-shirt over a collared button-down tucked into khaki pants. Clearing his throat, he drew the attention of the room.

"Welcome back, everyone. Hope you all had a restful spring break. The only thing on the agenda this morning is for me to introduce the two new teachers who are joining Lakeland Elementary today. First, I'm very honored to welcome a new Mandarin teacher, Jacky Sun, who is here all the way from the east coast to cover Jessica Zhang's fifth grade class while she is on maternity leave.

"You may have seen from, ahem, *his* résumé that he attended Harvard and Yale, and he also told me during his interview that he did some rowing in college, so I'm definitely looking forward to having more muscle on our team come June for the Dragon Boat Festival."

Cheers resounded from the audience, and Joanna made a mental note to ask Mindy about this event, as it seemed like the entire staff was fired up about it. Then the principal turned to Jack. "Now, I know this particular assignment is only temporary, but I'm hoping that it's a good fit for both you and us. We can always use another good Mandarin teacher, so maybe you'll decide to stay in our little town longer. What do you say?"

There was some light clapping as Jack stepped forward to stand next to Principal Malik.

"Thank you, Principal Malik," Jack started, dimples appearing again.

Joanna exchanged a look with Mindy, who was now standing next to her.

"Now that's one good-looking man," Mindy whispered, elbowing Joanna as Jack continued speaking.

"Didn't you say you have a husband?" Joanna said out of the side of her mouth.

"All I said was that he's good-looking. But the way you were talking to him just now tells me you *don't* have a husband," Mindy tittered.

"I was just being friendly!" Joanna elbowed Mindy back good-naturedly.

"As Principal Malik said, my name is Jacky Sun, but you can call me Jack. I was born in Taiwan, but have lived in the US for over half my life, and have been teaching Chinese for the past ten years. I'm thrilled to be able to share not only my first language, but my culture as well with the children of Lakeland. I truly believe that language exchange can build bridges and bring the world together. It is only when we can speak the same language that we can truly communicate."

"Wow." Mindy started shaking her head and

clapping enthusiastically along with the rest of the room. "I can't tell what I like more about him, his smile or that speech."

Then Jack raised a hand, signaling he wasn't done. As soon as the room was quiet again, he started speaking once more, this time in Mandarin.

Joanna couldn't understand a single word Jack was saying, but Alex, Wei-Wei and all the other Mandarin teachers were rapt with attention, completely captivated by Jack. Even Principal Malik looked awestruck.

"That man should be giving regular speeches behind a podium," Mindy reiterated, nodding appreciatively.

Jack finished up by saying a final sentence, to which Wei-Wei, Alex and a few other teachers clapped and giggled.

I wonder what that was? Joanna tried to remember if there was a joke at the end of his English speech.

The room erupted into applause again as Jack yielded the floor back to Principal Malik.

"Thank you, Jack. What a wonderful sentiment, and an excellent display of the bilingualism and biculturalism we hope to instill in all our students. Next, I'm very pleased to present Ms. Joanna Lin, our new art teacher, who miraculously was able to start today on very short notice. I apologize that I didn't have a chance to email her intro to everyone. We hope she will stay, ahem, a little longer than our previous art teacher." He nodded at Joanna, clearly expecting her to say a few words, too.

Why didn't anyone tell me I'd have to give a speech?

She gave an awkward wave at the crowd, not sure what to say.

Then she remembered how hard she had worked to get here.

Come on, Joanna. You can do this.

"Hi, everyone. I'm Joanna Lin," she started shakily. "I'm not sure how I'm going to beat that speech. But for those that might be wondering, this speech will be in English only," she deadpanned.

Mindy let out a loud guffaw, and Joanna immediately relaxed a little.

Thanks, Mindy.

"I'm very happy to be here as well. And yes, I hope to make this a long-term position." She paused and glanced at Principal Malik, who thankfully gave her a reassuring nod. "I don't have quite the résumé as Jack, but I've been painting and drawing all my life, and I love working with children. I like what Jack said about language exchange helping to bring the world together, but I also believe that art is its own kind of language. And I can't wait to start using art to communicate with the students of Lakeland Elementary, and all of you, as well."

She gave a small smile as everyone clapped for her, too, although perhaps not quite as loudly as they had for Jack. She stepped aside to let Principal Malik wrap up with a few parting words. After he was done, a few teachers came up to say hello and introduce themselves to her, but it seemed that a much bigger crowd formed around Jack.

"Well, that was…interesting," Joanna commented as she returned to Mindy.

"I'll say," Mindy said, craning her neck, clearly trying to get another look at Jack.

"I'm not much of a public speaker," Joanna said, "as you probably could tell."

"What's that?" Mindy asked, eyes still focused on Jack.

"Oh, nothing," Joanna said, wondering if Mindy had even been paying attention to the rest of her speech.

I bet no one was, not with Jack Sun in the room!

Just then, the bell rang and everyone quickly started dispersing. Realizing she was still holding the paper towel that Jack had passed her earlier, Joanna walked to the trash can near the sink to throw it away. When she turned around, she saw that, besides her, Jack was the only one left in the lounge.

Joanna suddenly felt even more nervous being

alone with Jack than she had in front of the entire staff just a few moments ago. She felt her face getting hot as he approached her.

"And with that, it looks like they've left us to fend for ourselves," Jack said.

"Uh, yeah, ha, looks like it."

"By the way, that was a really insightful speech, Ms. Lin—is that what you prefer your students call you?"

His perfect hair and dark eyes gave off a sparkle that made him look straight out of a magazine ad. *Well, I can't disagree with Mindy. He is one good-looking man.*

Joanna tried to keep her cool, saying, "*Miss Joanna* works, thanks for asking. But my speech was nothing compared to yours, Mr. Sun. It seemed so effortless for you."

Jack shrugged modestly. "Please, call me Jack. And I admit it, my mother put me in a lot of public speaking contests when I was a kid."

"She was determined to get you on stage somehow, huh?" Joanna said. "Even after the singing didn't work out?"

"Something like that, yes. Also, I'm the master of first impressions. It's all downhill from here, I promise."

"It's a good thing that everyone's left then."

Jack's eyes widened in mock horror. "Except you're still here! And I'm running out of charming one-liners."

Joanna laughed, and she felt a warm shiver go up her spine.

And he's funny, too.

"In all seriousness, the speech you made back there was quite insightful. Sometimes I forget that words aren't the only way to communicate." Jack had a thoughtful look in his eyes.

"Thank you for saying that," Joanna said, "and for listening. I really didn't think anyone was paying attention to me at all."

"Hey, us new kids have to stick together, right?" Jack held the door open for her as they stepped into the hall. "Can I walk you to your classroom?"

Joanna pointed to the door just ahead on the left. "Thanks, you just did."

Jack chuckled, shaking his head. "Ahem, well then. Enjoy the rest of your day, Miss Joanna." He bowed his head and made a grand gesture with his arms to usher Joanna into her classroom.

"Thanks, Mr. Sun. By the way, what did you say at the end of your Mandarin speech that made everyone giggle?"

Jack looked at Joanna straight in the eyes. "I said, 'Maybe I'll find a reason to stay longer.'"

CHAPTER THREE

WELL, THAT WAS NICE, Jack thought as he returned to his own classroom. He knew he should be focusing on his new students, but there was something about Joanna's hair, her dress, the bit of paint on her cheek, the shy confidence she exuded—he was definitely intrigued with Lakeland Elementary's new art teacher.

Just then, Jack's phone vibrated with an incoming video call from his mother. Checking the clock and confirming he still had a few minutes before the first bell, he held up his phone and accepted the call. His mother's face appeared, her background the tidy home office that his parents had once shared but was now hers alone.

"Hi, Jack," his mother said in Mandarin. "Have you eaten yet?" The lines around his mother's mouth seemed more stark than usual, and she had dark circles beneath her eyes.

"Hi, Ma. Yes, I've eaten." Jack looked at the clock again and did the quick time conversion.

"Shouldn't you be headed to bed soon? It's late over there."

His mother ignored his concern, saying, "You didn't answer my email from yesterday so I thought I'd give you a call."

"Sorry, I didn't get a chance to check my email before leaving for my first day at this new school." Jack tried to lighten the mood, saying, "You know, Ma, I could be teaching right now."

His mother raised an eyebrow. "I figured you wouldn't answer if you were, right?"

"True, I do have a few free minutes."

"How did the move go?"

Jack hesitated before answering. As innocuous as the question sounded, what his mother really meant was "How much longer are you going to stall before coming home?"

It had always been expected that after Jack finished his schooling, he would return to Taiwan to help manage Sun Textiles, the company founded by his great-grandfather. But after graduating with a degree in education, not business like his parents wanted, Jack started teaching, and before he knew it, ten years had gone by, and he was happy and thriving in his career in the US.

Then, last summer, his father passed away without warning. When Jack rushed back to attend the funeral, he understood without his mother saying anything that he had better start wrapping up his life to prepare to return to Taiwan. He had dutifully submitted his resignation at his school in New York, helped pick his replacement so his students were left in good hands and finished his last day at the semester break in late January.

But then Jack got a call from an old classmate who was teaching at a Mandarin immersion school in Michigan and scheduled to go on maternity leave in March. "I'm desperate to find someone good to cover my class," she had said. "These kids are incredible and I don't want to leave them hanging right at the end of fifth grade."

Jack sympathized with her situation, and though he hadn't spent much time in the Midwest, when he looked up the town of Lakeland, the photo that appeared first on the list of search results—of a gorgeous sunset on Lake Michigan—convinced him to take the job, despite his father's invisible hand beckoning him home. He called his mother and told her that a school really needed him (*which they did*, he insisted to himself) and that he was moving to Michigan for a temporary assignment. He'd been grateful it wasn't a video call, so he didn't have to see the disappointed expression on his mother's face.

"The move went fine," Jack said finally. "My apartment has a great view of the lake."

"That's nice," she replied. "And how's your class? It's been a while since you've taught elementary school."

"I haven't met them yet, but in looking through their work, their Chinese level is really high, better than some of my high schoolers. Remarkable how in this small Midwestern town, thousands of miles away from where I was born, all these children are learning our native language."

"That is quite incredible," his mother agreed, then quickly shifted topics. "I emailed over the company's operating budget and strategic plan for the next fiscal year. Can you take a look before the board approves it at next month's meeting?"

Jack hoped his sense of dread wasn't noticeable as he asked, "Sure. Has Jonathan already looked at the…" He struggled to repeat the words for *operating budget* and *strategic plan*, his business Mandarin not quite up to par. "…materials?" he finished.

His mother nodded curtly. "Yes, your brother signed off on them already. But I'd like you to review them, as well, since it's your company, too."

Swallowing hard, Jack answered, "Right, got it. I'll get to it as soon as possible."

"Good, thank you," his mother said, her features softening a touch. "Enjoy the springtime in the Midwest. Years ago, before you and your younger brother were born, your father went to that area to visit a customer and couldn't stop talking about it for months after. He kept saying he wanted to take me to see all the beautiful trees and flowers in bloom."

His mother's eyes stayed dry, but Jack knew she must have been weeping inside at the memory. The sight of his mother not crying was somehow worse than if she actually were. A lump formed in his throat, and he found himself at a loss for words.

His mother filled in the silence. "Well, I should let you go. We're all looking forward to you coming home soon, son."

Jack said goodbye and set his phone down on his desk. He understood the deeper meaning in his mother's last statement, could even hear her saying it: *You've had ten years to enjoy being a teacher in the US. It's time that you returned, for good.*

I know, Ma. It's time.

He opened up the weekly lesson plan that his old friend Jessica had left for him, flipping through the pages to the first week of June, the end of the school year.

Two and a half months. Better make the most of it.

He turned back to this week's lesson plans and saw that his class had art on Tuesday mornings. The knowledge that he would be seeing the lovely new art teacher the next morning made Jack's heart rate pick up a few beats. He thought back to meeting Joanna in the teachers' lounge just now and couldn't help but smile.

"Why are you smiling?" A student had appeared at Jack's desk, the first of the day to arrive. Tall, with two flaxen plaits framing her face, she had an intense look in her eyes.

Slightly embarrassed for being caught in a daydream by one of his students, Jack quickly replied in Mandarin, hoping to divert her attention. "*Ni hao*, I'm Sun *Laoshi*, your new teacher. May I ask your name? And can you ask that again, but in Chinese?"

The student switched to Mandarin without so much as a blink. "My name is Maja Andresson. Mei-Ya is my Chinese name. Why are you smiling?" the student repeated. "What were you thinking about?"

Jack tried to hide his shock, and scrambled to explain himself. "I—I was just thinking of…my mother," he said.

"Your mother," Maja echoed. "Where is she?"

"She's in Taiwan," Jack answered, admiring both the boldness and fluency of the student's conversational Mandarin.

"Oh! We're going to Taiwan after the end of the school year, on our fifth grade graduation trip."

"Really?" Jack was surprised yet again. Not only were these kids learning his mother tongue, but they had a trip planned to his homeland as well!

"Yes, the entire fifth grade is going. We've been planning and…" Maja paused. "How do you say *fundraising*?" she asked in English.

Jack translated the word, and she continued in Mandarin. "...*fundraising* for two years already. Zhang *Laoshi* was supposed to go, but then she had a baby. Are you going to come with us instead?"

"Actually, I'm already planning to be back there in June," Jack said.

"Good. So you'll be happy then?"

His eyebrows drew together at her question. "Why do you say that?"

"Because you'll get to see your mother. Weren't you just thinking about her?"

"Oh right, my mother." Jack could see this Maja was a sharp one. "Of course I'll be happy to see her."

JOANNA HAD JUST finished placing paintbrushes at each seat when she looked up to see her very first set of students entering her classroom, a first grade class of about twenty students led by a teacher who introduced herself to Joanna as Ms. Yang, or Yang *Laoshi*.

"Welcome to Lakeland," Ms. Yang said in English as the students took their seats. "I'll be back at the end of the period. Thank you!"

"Um, okay, sure, see you later," Joanna answered, jarred by the teacher's quick departure. She turned to face the entire classroom of kids, a sea of wiggling bodies and bright eyes, all looking at her expectantly. "Welcome, students!" she said, her voice shaking slightly. "Today—"

Splat!

A dark-haired boy in a hooded sweatshirt had just knocked one of the paper plates of paint off a table, and it was now lying face down on the floor next to him.

"Oh, sorry!" the little boy exclaimed, his eyes as big as golf balls and bottom lip quivering.

"It's okay!" Joanna hurried to fetch a rag to mop up the mess, the smell of paint mixing with lavender soap hitting her nostrils as she wiped. "What's your name?" she asked the boy, who had frozen in place, hands clasped at his chest.

"Asher," he replied quietly. "I didn't mean to drop the plate."

"Of course you didn't." She motioned for him to sit back down in his chair. "Don't you worry for even a second." After cleaning the floor and consoling Asher a few moments more, Joanna finally got all the kids settled with their smocks on and ready to get started.

"Let's try that again. Good morning, students! I'm Miss Joanna, your new art teacher, and today, we're going to paint a sunset over a lake."

She showed the class the sample painting that she had done over the weekend. The sky was a blend of purples and reds, and the sun and its reflection a brilliant amber.

"Wow, did you paint that?" asked a little girl

sitting near the front. She had a sprinkle of freckles across her nose and cheeks. "All by yourself?"

"Yes," Joanna answered. "I was so inspired by the sunset over Lake Michigan as I drove into town last week, that I pulled over on the side of the road just to watch it. I also took a bunch of photos, and when I got home, I sat down right at my kitchen table to paint it."

"I don't think I'll be able to do that," Asher said.

"I think *I* can!" the freckled girl declared.

"Let's all give it a try," Joanna said, and she demonstrated how to make big, gentle brush strokes across their large sheets of paper. "Come on, Asher, I know you can do it."

Asher didn't answer aloud, instead biting his lip as he tentatively dipped his brush into the yellow paint.

There you go! Joanna gave a silent cheer.

The class was completely captivated for the full period, but unfortunately, the sunsets didn't turn out exactly like Joanna had planned.

Oops. Maybe we should have gone over basic color theory first.

"Miss Joanna, why is my sunset brown?" a student asked, raising her hand.

"Mine is, too," another said.

"Me, too!"

The freckled girl in the front said, "It kind of looks like—"

"A murky day?" Joanna interjected, afraid of where the description might be heading. "It's okay," she continued cheerily as she surveyed everyone's paintings. "I think you all did a fantastic job with blending the paints together. Maybe *too* good of a job. Bring them over to me and we'll hang them up to dry. It's a good lesson in color mixing, right? If you mix all the colors together, you get…brown."

When Ms. Yang came back to collect her class, she thankfully didn't say anything about the color of the paintings. Instead, she applauded them, saying some obviously encouraging words in Mandarin. Then the students all turned to Joanna and, in unison, said something that she didn't understand.

"Does that mean *thank you*?" Joanna was slightly embarrassed she had to ask.

"Yes," the freckled girl answered. "And Yang *Laoshi* also said she thought our paintings are very beautiful. But I don't think mine is. It looks yucky."

"I don't like mine, either," another boy said.

Oh no. Joanna wanted to cry. But before she could conjure up some encouraging words, Asher called out, "Miss Joanna, I loved painting today. Even though mine kinda looks like mud, this was still the best class ever."

"Oh, thank you," Joanna replied, happy that at

least one student had enjoyed the class. "How do you say *you're welcome*?" she asked Ms. Yang.

The teacher called on another student, who confidently said words that sounded like "*boo kuh chee*."

"Well then, *boo kuh chee*," Joanna said, stumbling over the words, sure she was mispronouncing them, but smiling in spite of herself. "You all did brilliantly. See you next week."

The day passed quickly, with four more classes coming into Joanna's classroom. The students were as adorable as ever, but despite Joanna changing the setup at her lunch break and putting the colors onto separate plates, very few of the children were able to resist mixing all the colors together.

"So, HOW'D YOUR first day go?" Mindy appeared at Joanna's classroom shortly after the dismissal bell rang, her heels rapping on the floor as she walked in. "The farmers market at the waterfront is opening today. My boys have Chinese calligraphy after school so I have about an hour before I need to swing back and pick them up. Wanna walk down with me?"

"Well," Joanna started, managing a tight smile, "unfortunately, I discovered that when given several paint colors, the vast majority of elementary-aged students will mix them all together, resulting in a sunset scene of one singular hue." She motioned to the set of paintings from her last class that she was in the middle of hanging on a clothesline that stretched across the classroom. "Even the third graders couldn't stop themselves from combining everything. So, thanks for the invitation, but I think I need to hang back and rework my lesson plans for tomorrow."

Mindy glanced around and waved a hand. "I think these paintings are great! And I also think a walk down to the lake would do you some good. Here, let me help," Mindy offered, grabbing a clothespin and helping Joanna clip one of the sunsets to the line. "This is nothing compared to Ms. Rani's first day. She couldn't even get the kids to sit down, much less do an entire painting. Oops, I'm sorry for mentioning her again."

"Well, since you have, maybe I need to get some tips from you on how I can avoid Ms. Rani's fate," Joanna said, feeling uneasy again.

"I don't think you need to worry about following in her footsteps. These paintings really are very good," Mindy assured her. "Even if they are a bit…monotone? But look at *your* painting! Now *you're* an incredible artist." She stepped over to Joanna's model canvas, bobbing her head at the landscape with wide eyes and obvious admiration.

"I feel comfortable with painting myself, yes," Joanna said. "But there are so many kids, with so many different needs. My student teaching didn't prepare me nearly enough. And, with the added component of Chinese here… I'm not sure if I'm communicating well at all. During my third grade class after lunch, no one seemed to be listening to me! I wondered if they understood anything I was saying—were they expecting I speak in Chinese? Is this normal?"

"Before I became a guidance counselor, I started as a classroom teacher," Mindy said. "My entire first year teaching was a battle. I remember thinking of throwing in the towel many times. Then someone told me that something like fifty percent of teachers quit in the first five years."

"Oh gosh." Hearing this made Joanna feel even more anxious. "I've already left one career. I can't fail at this one," she said earnestly.

Mindy nodded, seeming to understand her concern. "I can share some classroom management tips, if you like? Sometimes just a few tricks here and there really make a big difference. And feel free to call my extension anytime if you feel like you've lost control of a class. I'm happy to pop over. The art, though—that's all you."

Grateful for the support, Joanna accepted her offer. "I would love any tips you have. That would be so great, Mindy, thank you. And I'm sorry, I didn't even ask how your day was!"

"Can't complain," Mindy said. "Everything went fairly smoothly. Jack's arrival was a nice pick-me-up, too." She pumped her eyebrows up and down a few times.

Joanna pictured Jack's dimpled smile as she lifted a student chair and placed it on top of a table. She found him handsome, sure, but she didn't need to admit that to Mindy.

"And when he made that speech in English and Mandarin," Mindy continued, putting up a chair as well. "I mean, seriously?"

"Yes, that was cool," Joanna agreed, keeping her tone light. "I didn't understand any of the second part, but it sounded impressive."

Mindy peeked out from behind the last chair. "Right? I do love a multilingual man. Tell me you're going to make a move. Also, come to the farmers market with me! Pretty please?" She put her hands together in a prayer pose.

"Okay, okay! Yes to the farmers market," Joanna said, laughing. "But sadly, Mindy, I don't think making a move on Jack is in the cards for me. And do we even know that he's available? And don't you have antifraternization rules here?" Back at the law firm, dating among colleagues wasn't prohibited, but it definitely wasn't encouraged.

"I heard Mrs. Wooten, our music teacher, ask him if he moved here with anyone and he told her that he was single. And, no, there aren't any rules against teachers dating each other. So why not get to know him a little better, huh? Is there someone special in your life already?"

"Definitely not." Joanna shook her head vigorously as she put on her coat. As they left her classroom and walked down the hall toward the school exit, Joanna gave Mindy a quick summary of her past, and the resolution she had committed to earlier that day. "I just really want to do well at this job, get an offer for a permanent position, and work on me for a little while."

"Fair enough," Mindy responded, raising both hands in surrender. "We'll just have to admire Jack together from afar."

As if Mindy had timed the delivery of that line for precisely that instant, the two women pushed the double doors open to see, standing just a few yards in front of them at the student pickup zone, the aforementioned Jack, smartly dressed in a fitted jacket and lit up by the afternoon sun. He was helping load students into the steady stream of cars proceeding slowly through the pickup line. Alex and Wei-Wei were positioned on either side of him.

"Principal Malik's got you on pickup duty on your first day, Mr. Sun?" Mindy called out as she and Joanna approached the three teachers. "That's harsh!"

"I've been a newbie before. Gotta pay my dues!" Jack called back pleasantly as he waved, but then he quickly returned to helping a small boy into the back of a dark SUV. After retrieving a water bottle that had fallen out of the student's backpack and putting it in the back seat, Jack said to Mindy, "Thankfully, Miss Alex and Miss Wei-Wei offered to show me the ropes."

The two teachers standing next to him both nodded cheerfully.

"We are very happy to do so," Wei-Wei said.

Alex gave two thumbs up. "Yup, it's no problem at all."

"We're headed to the farmers market down at the shoreline," Mindy said. "Wei-Wei, I know you have calligraphy class, but Alex, Jack, would you like to come with us? We can wait until pickup is all finished."

"Unfortunately, I can't make it today, but you definitely should go, Jack!" Alex encouraged.

Jack's eyes twinkled in the sunlight as he looked at Joanna. "Sounds great. I'd love to check it out. But I'm not sure how long this usually takes." He looked to Alex and Wei-Wei.

Wei-Wei responded, "Often one or two parents are late and we have to escort the students to the main office and wait with them until they're picked up. We should show you the process we have to follow."

Jack nodded. "Of course, let's do that." He turned back to Mindy and Joanna. "Why don't you two go on ahead and I'll meet you there when we're done here?"

"Sure, sounds good," Joanna said, trying to sound breezy even as she felt her palms start to sweat. Between that and the shivers up her backbone, she was starting to feel a little out of sorts.

Joanna, pull yourself together! He's just another fellow teacher. So what if he's handsome, bilingual and obviously brilliant at his job? This is NOT going to turn into another Tim situation.

"Great," Jack said, flashing her a charming half smile, this time with only one dimple appearing. "Looking forward to it."

"See you later!" Joanna couldn't stop a silly grin of her own from popping on her face, and it remained there as she and Mindy walked off toward the lake.

Mindy caught her expression and cast a suggestive look over to Joanna. "Rethinking your earlier stance, hmm?"

Joanna covered her mouth in mild embarrassment. She stole a quick look back toward the school and saw Jack, standing tall and confident as he continued to direct traffic.

"I do *not* want to start anything," she insisted. "And even if I did," she said, glancing again at the mini crowd of teachers surrounding Jack, "it seems like I'd have to get in line!"

CHAPTER FOUR

JOANNA AND MINDY walked the few short blocks to the waterfront, where, despite it being still fairly chilly, the rays of the afternoon sun reflected gloriously off Lake Michigan, taking the edge off her shaky first day.

"Isn't the lake just spectacular?" Mindy said, as if reading Joanna's thoughts.

"Unreal," Joanna agreed, soaking in the view, which included a picturesque pier to the north that led out to a stately lighthouse. "It looks like a postcard." She took out her phone to snap a few photos.

"Wait until spring really arrives," Mindy said. "Then you'll definitely want to have your camera ready."

They arrived at the market, which was positively humming, with booths and stalls lined up on both sides of the shoreline path selling fruits and vegetables, flowers, baked goods, and a plethora of other foods and wares.

"Looks like this is the place to be!" Joanna

commented as she saw people walking in both directions, their arms full of purchases from the market.

"Yes, we've been waiting all winter for it to open." Mindy gestured to one of the flower stalls. "Let's stop here." As they both surveyed the wide selection of freshly cut flowers and potted plants, Mindy asked, "So, is Lakeland Elementary everything you expected it to be?"

"I guess I didn't quite know what to expect," Joanna answered, leaning down to admire a dainty African violet. "Being in front of the classroom, all by myself—it's a lot. Nothing can quite prepare you for that, do you know what I mean?"

"I do," Mindy said, and she patted Joanna's arm encouragingly. "I've been in this profession almost fifteen years and it can still be stressful sometimes, of course, but every day I'm grateful that I get to do a job that I love. It will get easier, I promise."

Just then Joanna pulled out her phone to take a close-up photo of a container of snowdrops, their white flowers hanging down from their stems like tiny bells. "I just had a vision of a great paper cutout project I could do using these snowdrops as a theme."

"You really do seem to be in your element," Mindy said. She paused too, scanning the table and selecting two pots from the Easter lily section. "For you," she said, after she paid and thanked the vendor. She handed one earthen pot over to Joanna. "A welcome gift from me."

"Oh, thank you, Mindy, that's so nice of you," Joanna said, accepting the gift. "I can't wait to watch it bloom. You'll have to tell me when yours starts to open so we can compare."

Mindy gave her a wink. "Oh, this one isn't for me."

"It isn't?" Joanna asked.

"No, it's for Lakeland's other new teacher," Mindy said.

"Oh, I see. And what would your *husband* say about that?" Joanna teased.

"I'm just being friendly!" Mindy said, clearly mocking the words Joanna had said to her earlier in the teachers' lounge. "Here, can I trust you to give it to him from me?"

"I see what you're trying to do and it isn't going to work. But sure," Joanna said as she took the second plant and carefully placed both pots side by side in a shopping bag.

As they continued on the path and approached another stall, Joanna heard the sound of a deep voice that she immediately recognized even before seeing its speaker. It was Jack, and he was chatting with the stall vendor, a jovial young Asian man holding tongs and tending to a large, steaming pan full of plump buns snuggled all together.

"Well, look who made it," Mindy said quietly to Joanna. "Wonder why he's here, hmm?"

"He's obviously here to get some of these delicious-looking buns," Joanna answered, breathing in the fragrant aroma of fried dough, but also sneaking a look over to Jack. "They smell *so* good," she gushed, perhaps a little too loudly.

"Mrs. Perez and Miss Joanna," Jack said, holding Joanna's gaze for a second. "I was just coming to find you when I also caught the scent of these fried pork buns. I'm in shock. Have you ever had one before? They're called *sheng jian bao*, and very popular in Taiwan. I don't often see them in the US—but here they are, right here in Lakeland."

The vendor smiled broadly at Joanna and Mindy, making crinkles around both his eyes. "Can I offer you two a sample?" he asked, gesturing to the buns with his tongs.

"Yes, I'd love one," Mindy said.

Joanna raised her hand. "Me, too," she said, further enticed by Jack's excitement.

The vendor placed two buns into small paper bags and passed them over to Mindy and Joanna. "Please, enjoy."

"Xie xie," Mindy said as she accepted one of the bags. Joanna recognized the phrase from her first class that morning.

At least I know that means thank you, Joanna thought.

The man's eyes widened as he looked at Mindy. "You speak Chinese?" he said.

"A little bit," Mindy answered, nodding. "We all work at the Mandarin immersion school up the street, and I've also been studying it for a couple of years."

"Ah, that's wonderful," the man said. "Mr. Sun here was just telling me about his new job at the school. When my son gets old enough, I'm definitely sending him there. My wife and I are from Shanghai. Mr. Sun just told me he thinks that Taipei has the best *sheng jian bao*, but really, the best can be found only in Shanghai!"

"Let's just call it a draw, shall we?" Jack joked. Turning to Mindy and Joanna, he urged, "You both really need to taste them. I've already placed a regular order with Mr. Chen here."

"Please, just Danny is fine," the vendor said.

Joanna brought the bun, which was sprinkled with sesame seeds, to her mouth, then took a big bite. It was soft and doughy at the top, fried at the bottom, and inside, juicy and simply delicious. "Mmm, you two weren't kidding," she said to Jack and Danny. "This is so tasty. I'll take a half dozen. And a business card!"

Mindy was already on the last bite of hers. "I'll take a box, too," Mindy said. "And I'll be sure to stop by every week from now on."

"I'm so glad to hear that," Danny responded. "Please also visit my restaurant, The Dumpling Spot, where I usually am. This is actually the first time I've set up at the market."

"Looks like we're not the only ones who are glad you did," Mindy said. Indeed, Joanna looked around and saw that a long line had formed behind them.

"We should let you get to your customers," Jack offered, saying a few more words in Chinese, including *xie xie*.

Joanna stood by, watching Jack chat animatedly with Danny, wishing she could understand more of what he was saying.

"Ooh, look at the time," Mindy said, not looking at her wrist or phone but raising an eyebrow at Joanna. "I gotta head back to the school and pick up the boys. See you both tomorrow!"

Joanna barely had a chance to wave goodbye before Mindy disappeared into the crowd.

"Wow, *sheng jian bao*," Jack said as he and Joanna continued on down the market. "I'm still in shock. I may have found my reason to stay." He looked over at Joanna and grinned.

Caught for a moment by Jack's smile, Joanna quickly averted her eyes and looked down at her bun. Completely tongue-tied, she spurted out, "These really are delicious!"

Really? That's the best I could come up with— a comment about the buns?

Joanna was still feeling sheepish, and scrambling to find something to say that wasn't about the bun, when she heard a voice coming from somewhere up ahead.

"Sun *Laoshi*! Sun *Laoshi*!"

Joanna looked up to see a tall, spindly girl with sandy blond hair standing with two adults with identical coloring in a stall full of beautiful pies, cakes, bread and other baked goods.

"Mei-Ya," Jack said, followed by something in Chinese, as he and Joanna approached the stall.

The young girl responded in Chinese, then turned to the two adults and switched to English, saying, "Mom, Dad, this is my new teacher, Mr. Sun."

They both greeted Jack, and the girl's father, a hearty man who stuck out his hand immediately for Jack to shake, said, "So nice to meet you. Maja's been telling us all about her new teacher since she arrived here from school."

"Very nice to meet you as well, Mr. and Mrs. Andresson," Jack said. "And this is Joanna Lin, our school's new art teacher." He turned to Joanna, adding, "This is Mei-Ya—Maja, in English—one of my fifth graders."

After Joanna and Maja's parents exchanged pleasantries, Jack said, "I'm so impressed with Maja's Chinese. I think she could run the class. She's also been helping me figure out everything I need to know at Lakeland. She even had to show me to my classroom after lunch, didn't you, Maja?"

"Actually, I think I showed you to the staff restrooms," Maja said, her expression neutral. When everyone laughed, she looked around and said, "What, it's true!"

Mrs. Andresson, a tall and stern-looking woman, patted her daughter on the shoulder. "Lakeland has been truly wonderful for Maja. At her old school, she was bored and had trouble making friends. Then we moved her over to Lakeland two years ago, and it's been a real transformation. The school's really brought out something in her."

"That's so great," Joanna said.

I hope Lakeland can do the same for me.

"Mei-Ya," Jack said, "I believe you'll see Miss Joanna tomorrow at nine o'clock, right?"

Maja shook her head. "No, we have art every Tuesday at *ten* o'clock, not nine."

"What'd I say, she could run the class," Jack said, as everyone laughed again, and Joanna couldn't help but be drawn in by Jack's palpable magnetism.

Forcing herself to pull away, she said, "All these pastries look amazing." She gestured around the stall.

"Thank you. We also run the Swiss Bakery over on Main Street," Mrs. Andresson said. "We close early on Mondays and sell here when the farmers market is open."

"Oh, I live right around the corner from there," Joanna said brightly. "I just had one of your fruit tarts for breakfast today!"

"Wonderful, I hope you enjoyed it. We actually tried a new recipe on that batch—one that Maja came up with." Mrs. Andresson nodded toward her daughter, who had moved over to the other side of the stall and appeared to be rearranging one of the tables.

"How long have you been in the bakery business, Mr. and Mrs. Andresson?" Jack asked.

"The bakery's been in our family three generations now," Maja's father said. "My maternal grandfather arrived here in Michigan in 1945 and started the bakery, in the same building we're still in today. My mom took over in the late seventies, and she handed over the oven mitts to me a few years ago." He stopped and smiled, adding, "Although she's still there most mornings, checking up on me."

"Looks like a nice family business you've got here," Jack commented, pausing for a beat before adding, "and sounds like Maja's quite knowledgeable as well."

They all looked over to see Maja talking to a customer while pointing to a loaf of bread and miming rolling out dough.

Mr. Andresson chuckled. "Yes, as you said, Maja could definitely run our store!"

"EVERYTHING OKAY?" Joanna started by treading lightly after she and Jack had left the Andressons' stall. She barely knew him, but the change in Jack's demeanor was quite apparent—his face was no longer as bright, and his step seemed to have lost some of its spring.

Jack turned his head to her sharply. "Was it that obvious?" he asked.

Her arms loaded with potted plants and baked goods, Joanna tilted her head to one side. "It just seemed like something affected you back there."

Jack nodded, his lips turning slightly down. "You got me, Miss Joanna. That conversation I just had with Maja's father, about running a family business…it made me think about my own family's company, which was started by my great-grandfather." He told Joanna about being sent to the US first to learn English and then study business in college, before he ended up becoming a teacher instead.

"What kind of business is it?" Joanna asked.

"Textiles. But to be honest, besides picking out what I'm going to wear in the morning, I don't know a thing about textiles."

Joanna smiled sympathetically. "But it sounds like you do know a lot about the career you chose? Teacher of the Year at your old district, so I've heard?"

Jack hung his head good-naturedly. "Okay, I regret including the award in my résumé. I'm really never going to hear the end of it, will I? Miss Alex has already started calling me that instead of my name. But in all seriousness, when Maja's father said she could run their store… I know he was just joking, but, well…"

"Are your parents asking you to quit teaching and work at the company instead?" Joanna guessed. She remembered her own fear when she'd quit her job and faced the daunting challenge of starting all over in a brand-new career, but she didn't want to tell Jack about it, in case he thought less of her teaching abilities.

"It's just my mother now—"

"I'm so sorry," Joanna said, leaving space for a moment. "I lost my father recently, too."

"Oh, I'm sorry for your loss, as well," Jack said. "It's so hard, isn't it?"

"Impossibly so," Joanna agreed, blinking back tears.

"But yes, I'm planning on returning to Taiwan to help run the business at the end of the school year. And my mother has been texting me non-stop since I arrived here." Jack drew his phone out from his pocket and showed her all the messages from his mother. "Not to mention it's the middle of the night over there!"

The messages were all in Chinese, but Joanna chuckled at the sight of them. "Looks like we have something in common. Mine's only on the other side of the state, but she's been texting me all day, too." She held up her own phone, where there were a dozen texts from her mother that Joanna hadn't had a chance to respond to yet.

"It sounds like our mothers would get along well," Jack said. "Anyway, that's probably more information about me than you wanted to know."

Joanna glanced up at Jack's face; the sun was shining from behind him so she could only make out the silhouette of his well-defined jawline, but she blushed yet again, the umpteenth time that day.

Okay, I admit it, Handsome Jack. I'd like to know more.

CHAPTER FIVE

THE NEXT MORNING, Jack stopped for a moment at the door to Joanna's classroom as he led his students in for art class. She'd worn her hair down today, the fine, dark strands falling gently around her oval face and past her shoulders.

"Good morning," he said, and Joanna flashed him a soft smile.

"Don't you mean *zao an*?" Maja said from behind him, translating *good morning* into Mandarin. "We're not supposed to speak English, remember?"

"Ah, right," Jack said. "*Zao an*, Lin *Laoshi*." Then he lowered his voice and leaned in closer to Joanna, who had approached him when he had stepped into the room. "These fifth graders are serious with the Mandarin immersion, let me tell you."

"Getting schooled by your students already, Mr. Sun?" Joanna's tone was friendly, but she was already turning away from him. She greeted his class and began giving instructions, asking several students to go gather the materials they would need for today's lesson.

A table at the front of the classroom held an assortment of pastries, including a fruit tart, several small square cakes, a long eclair, a cookie and a Swiss roll all spaced out evenly on a tray. A photo of the items was projected onto a large screen.

"What's all this?" he asked Joanna, pointing at the table. "Breakfast?"

"Ha," she said, then explained, "It's a still life composition for the students to work on shapes and shading."

Jack nodded, then noticed a large drawing pad sitting on Joanna's desk. "Did you draw that?"

"Yes, last night! So the students would have a model," she answered.

"Wow," he said, blinking in amazement. *This is fantastic*. It looked so much like a black-and-white photograph of the pastries that Jack had to inspect it closely to confirm it wasn't. "You really just drew that last night?" he said. "That's incredible. How long have you been drawing?"

"Thanks," Joanna said, a strand of hair falling in front of her eyes. Jack wanted to brush it away for her. "I've loved sketching and painting since I was little. It really just takes practice. And what can I say, I was really inspired by the Andressons' bakery, and the farmers market, and, well, this whole town, actually!"

"I'm really captured by Lakeland, too," Jack

agreed. "You may not believe this, but I basically took this job after seeing a photo of the sunset on Lake Michigan." *Although it probably wouldn't have taken much to convince me.*

"Wow, really?" Joanna shook her head, seemingly amused. "I do believe it, as the sunsets have been pretty spectacular. Combined with the Swiss Bakery—" she gestured at the pastry tray "—I may never leave!"

"Looking at all these makes me wish I had stopped by this morning for breakfast on my way in. Hey, wait a minute."

"Hmm?" Joanna asked, a faint line appearing between her eyes. "Is something wrong?"

"What happened to this one?" He pointed at Joanna's sketch, which had a croissant in the top corner, then the corresponding space on the actual tray, which was empty.

"All right, you caught me," Joanna laughed. "That was *my* breakfast."

"Ah," Jack said, chuckling along with her.

He continued to admire her sketch, perhaps a bit too long, as Joanna asked, "Do you want to stay and try your hand at drawing? You can pull up a chair with the kids." She pointed to an empty seat at the front table.

Jack couldn't tell if she was serious, but answered, "I'd love to, but I've got this morning's test to grade and they'll want those back ASAP. And, well…"

"Yes?" Joanna bent an ear toward him.

"Remember when I said I wasn't such a good singer? I'm an even worse artist," Jack admitted. "I'm really terrible. I can't even draw a straight line."

"I'm sure that's not true," Joanna responded, shaking her head. "You just haven't had the right teacher."

"Trust me. Even my stick figures look awful."

"But what about Chinese characters? Aren't they like drawings? They look so artistic to me."

Jack was about to tell her that the way he learned to write Chinese was about as unartistic as he could imagine—rows and rows of characters written over and over again—but their conversation was cut short by Maja, who stuck up her hand from the back of the room and asked, "Miss Joanna? Should we start drawing those pastries?"

Joanna turned her attention back to her class. "Yes, Maja. You can all start by lightly drawing the outline of each object. Have you done basic 3D shapes already?"

"Yes, can we get started right now?" Maja asked, her pencil already on her page.

"I think that's my cue," Jack said, turning to head out the door. "Sorry for keeping you."

"Not at all. See you later," Joanna responded. "Oh wait, I forgot. Mindy got us both Easter lilies yesterday as welcome gifts and she wanted me to give you one." She went to the window, where two matching clay pots were sitting on the counter, absorbing the morning sunlight. Carrying one back to him, she inhaled audibly. "And it looks like this one sprouted overnight!"

Jack looked closer and saw the tiny tip of a bright green leaf poking out from the dirt. "That was so nice of her. Are you sure you don't want this one?"

"I'm sure mine isn't far behind, hopefully," Joanna answered, frowning slightly. "The vendor said they should bloom in about a month, so if you leave yours at your window, we can follow their progress together."

"Sounds great. I'll thank Mindy when I see her next," Jack said. As he was about to turn away, he noticed some charcoal on Joanna's forehead. "Miss Joanna, you've just got a little bit of something on your—" He pointed at his own forehead.

"Sheesh, not again," Joanna said, blushing and rubbing her forehead with her fingers. "Did I get it?"

"Yes," he said, feeling his own face flush as her eyes met his. "I'll see you in an hour."

JOANNA MANAGED TO make it through the rest of the week staining only one dress—fortunately, an old one that probably should have found its way to the donation bin long ago—and not needing to call Mindy for any classroom emergencies.

By Friday afternoon, she was exhausted, but in

a good way. Instead of wanting to go home and binge-watch a television series while eating ice cream all night, like she had at the end of many days at the law firm, Joanna found herself looking forward to working on next week's lesson plans.

I actually WANT to prepare for work! Now that's a first, for sure!

"Knock, knock!" Mindy walked into her classroom, her dangly earrings casting triangles of light all around. "Can I interest you in our weekly Friday happy hour?" Mindy asked. "Alex and Wei-Wei are usuals, Coach Clay, and, oh, I also invited *Jack.*" Mindy made her hands into the shape of a heart in front of her chest.

"What are you, twelve?" Joanna laughed. She'd been busy the rest of the week, even taking her lunch at her desk every day to prep, so she hadn't talked to Jack much since his class had come in on Tuesday morning. But now she wondered how his first week had gone, too. "Sure, I'd love to join," she said, then added, "to see *everyone*, not just Jack."

They met the rest of the teachers at the school's entrance after pickup and the group walked up Main Street together. Joanna tried to say hello to Jack, but he quickly fell in line with Alex and Wei-Wei; between Alex giving Jack local restaurant recommendations and Wei-Wei asking him about his family lineage, Joanna couldn't get in a word edgewise.

Stopping in front of an Irish pub called Patrick's, its name written in bold, cursive letters on a big green awning, the group was met with a sign hanging on the door that stated Closed Today for a Private Event.

"Aw man, that's a bummer," Coach Clay said. A muscular man well over six feet tall, he wore a Lakeland Elementary baseball cap and a T-shirt with the words PE Rocks! across the front.

"You've got to be kidding me." Mindy threw her hands up. "This is our place every Friday! How could they just close without asking us? Don't they know us teachers get thirsty after a long week of running after all of Lakeland's children?"

"What about the Tap House over on Lincoln?" Coach suggested.

As the group discussed a few other possible choices, Jack suddenly piped up. "I wonder if the private event is actually going on right now, or just starts later. Let me go in and see what the situation is." He tried the door, which was unlocked, then quickly disappeared into the bar.

"Did I tell you how much I like Jack?" Mindy asked, and the others agreed, especially, it seemed, Wei-Wei.

"He's really a man of action, a good character trait," Wei-Wei said, causing Alex to laugh out loud.

"He had her at Harvard," Alex joked in her raspy voice.

About two minutes later, Jack reappeared at the entrance.

"We're good," he announced, holding open the door for everyone. "They said we just have to leave by six. Is that enough time for a thirsty teacher to get rehydrated?"

"I'll tell you in two hours," Mindy laughed, giving Jack a high five as she walked into the bar. "Thanks, Mr. Sun!"

After being seated—Coach Clay at the head of the table and Jack right next to him—everyone was happily sipping on drinks and munching on appetizers. Coach Clay asked Jack and Joanna, who was seated on Jack's other side, if they'd had a chance to explore the area yet.

"Mindy brought us to the farmers market on Monday," Joanna answered. "Which was great, and I'm definitely planning to make that a regular thing. Let's see, the botanical gardens is high on my list, too. I'd love to get more ideas for the students based on local plants and flowers. Any other recommendations?"

"The botanical gardens are a must-see, for sure," Mindy said. "And it'll be even more beautiful in a few weeks—it surprises me every year how stunning it all becomes."

Alex jumped in, saying, "The lake, of course, is also a big attraction."

"Yes, there's a string of lighthouses up and down the coast that would make a fantastic day or overnight trip," Wei-Wei added, from farther down the table.

"Oh, that sounds very cool," Jack said. "I'd love to check those out. When I was a kid, my parents used to take my brother and me to lighthouses all the time around Taiwan."

"Ah, yes, I've visited the one down at Eluanbi, the southernmost point," Wei-Wei said. "It was quite lovely."

Jack and Wei-Wei continued talking about lighthouses, and Joanna bristled slightly. She couldn't find a way into the conversation since she had never actually visited a lighthouse before.

"Speaking of the lake," Coach Clay broke in, "who's up for doing the annual jump with me next month?" His eyes searched around the table.

"Not me," Mindy said, hugging herself and shuddering. "It might be spring, but Lake Michigan is still *frigid*!"

"True," Coach agreed. "But come on, it's always a fun event!" He turned to Jack and Joanna, saying, "It's an annual tradition for Lakeland. Local businesses make donations, restaurants and shops sponsor booths and food, all to support a local organization. This year, we're raising money to upgrade the children's section of the Lakeland Library."

"Ooh, yeah, I was there the other day and the

Chinese book selection is downright grim," Alex said. "Can we get some more Chinese books in there, Coach?"

Coach nodded. "Yes, that was on their grant request!"

"Sounds like a great event," Joanna said. "But just looking at Mindy *thinking* about how cold it'll be is making me cold." The guidance counselor still had her arms wrapped around herself.

"What about you, Mr. Sun?" Coach asked. "You seem like a guy who can handle tough conditions, eh?" He flexed both his arms up and down.

"How cold are we talking, Coach?" Jack asked, narrowing his eyes but also smiling. "Like, below freezing? Remember I'm from Taiwan, a subtropical island!"

"Come on, it's for the children," Coach urged. "Don't make me beg, Jack."

Jack laughed and said, "How about this? I'll do it if Joanna does."

"Me?" Joanna said. She was surprised, and truthfully a little flattered, that Jack would single her out.

"Yes!" Mindy encouraged. "Joanna! Joanna!" she started, and everyone around the table joined in.

"How did this suddenly come down to me?" she said in amusement. She turned to Jack. "Didn't I hear Principal Malik say that you were a rower out east? So you should be used to cold water!"

"On the water, not in it!" Jack clarified.

"I'll tell you what," Coach Clay said, his eyes perking up when Joanna said the word *rower*.

"I might be willing to give you a pass on the lake jump, but we'll *definitely* need you on the school's dragon boat team come June."

"Oh, yes!" Wei-Wei exclaimed. "I'm tired of being beat at our own event! How did Beverly Harbor's team get so skilled at dragon boat racing?"

"I heard they train year-round and compete all over the country," Alex offered. "They've come in first place every year since we started our big Dragon Boat Festival four years ago," she explained to Joanna and Jack.

"Your natural athleticism would surely help us win," Wei-Wei said, admiring Jack's physique.

"You got it, Coach, I'm definitely in for rowing," Jack said, patting Coach Clay on the back. "But I've actually never rowed in a dragon boat before. What's the format?"

"Yes!" Coach said, then started explaining the setup. "The biggest difference you'll find is that we *paddle* a dragon boat, not *row*. Instead of facing backward, we all sit forward, and it's two to a row, so you really have to work as partners. Each dragon boat needs twenty paddlers, a drummer—that's Miss Wei-Wei here—and a steerer—that's me. There are multiple events, so we can always use more paddlers!" He looked over to Joanna. "Can I count on you, too?"

Alex, Wei-Wei and Mindy were all staring at her, as well.

"This one, you're not getting out of," Mindy said. "The Dragon Boat Festival is the school's marquee event. The entire community is involved, including our PTA, and people come from all over—even teams from other states. And yes, it would be so great to finally win this year!"

"Okay, I guess I'm in," Joanna answered, eliciting a fist pump from Coach Clay.

"Excellent, I have a good feeling about you two," he said to Jack and Joanna. "You guys are going to bring us a victory, I know it." He was already strategizing where to put the two new teachers in the boat, murmuring, "Front or center?"

"I think front," Wei-Wei said, with both Mindy and Alex nodding in agreement.

"I don't know," Coach deliberated, "they might be good in the center. Jack looks like he's got some serious strength-to-weight ratio." He reached for a napkin to start drawing out configurations.

As the others huddled around Coach, Jack got up from the table and asked Joanna if she wanted to join him in checking out the pool table.

"Well done diverting attention away from

the lake jump back there," Joanna joked as they walked away from the table. "Oh, and getting us into the bar in the first place! Is there anything you can't talk your way out of, Mr. Sun?"

Just then Jack's phone buzzed. Apologizing, he glanced at the screen, and said, "Unfortunately, it seems there are some things that cannot be talked out of."

"Let me guess, a message from your mother?" Joanna asked.

"How did you know?" Jack laughed. "I swear, it's as if she's not twelve time zones away at all! My mother really never seems to sleep."

"Everything okay?" Joanna asked. Though Jack was smiling, his eyebrows furrowed as he scrolled through his messages.

"Yes, she just wants me to review something and I haven't had a chance to get to it yet, with settling in and everything—so much to do, right?"

"Totally," Joanna agreed.

"But hey, are you free this weekend?" Jack asked, tucking away his phone. "Maybe we could check out the botanical gardens together, say Sunday morning? Everyone seems to agree that it's a must-see. You can get some more lesson ideas, like you mentioned."

Joanna's heart fluttered. *Is he asking me on a date? Or just being friendly?*

Then a warning sounded in her head. *Remem-*

*ber what happened with Tim. No dating col-
leagues.*

"Great," Joanna said, trying to act indifferent
as they exchanged phone numbers, "sounds like
a plan."

"What plan?" Mindy asked, wandering over
from their table.

"Joanna and I were just talking about checking
out the botanical gardens on Sunday," Jack said.
"Would you like to join?"

Joanna's heart stopped fluttering. *Okay, so obviously he didn't mean it as a date.*

Which is good, she reminded herself.

Jack's phone buzzed a second time, and he
apologized again as he started to step away, saying, "I'm so sorry. If I don't respond, she's just
going to keep messaging me."

"No worries," Joanna said. "Please, go ahead."

"So, he asked you on a date already?" Mindy
asked, her eyebrows wagging.

"It's not a date," Joanna whispered, after confirming Jack was out of earshot.

Mindy shot her a knowing glance. "Sure, whatever you say!"

CHAPTER SIX

ON SATURDAY MORNING, Joanna woke to the sound of both her doorbell ringing and cell phone buzzing at the same time.

"Joanna? Joanna!" a muffled voice from outside called.

Is that Mom?

Joanna groggily rose from her bed as the ringing and buzzing continued. She pattered over to the window and drew open the curtain to look out to her building's doorstep. Sure enough, her mother was standing there, several grocery bags on the ground next to her, holding her cell phone to an ear with one hand, and pressing forcefully on Joanna's doorbell with the other.

"Mom? I'm up—you can stop the calling and ringing!" Joanna yelled out to her after opening the window. "Did you tell me that you were coming to visit?"

"Good morning!" Carol hollered back, waving. "I woke up at five a.m. to make the drive. I brought food!" She held up the bags.

Well, she did bring food. I guess I'll allow it, Joanna grumbled to herself as she went down to let her mother in. "I'm glad to see you," she said, and gave her a hug. "But maybe next time give me a little heads-up? It's a long drive, especially on your own."

"Sorry, didn't I tell you I was coming?" her mother asked, as she brought all the bags into the kitchen and started unloading them onto the counter. "I did message you, didn't I? Well, I thought I did. Anyways, be right back—there's a lot more in the car. I just want you to be able to focus on your job and not worry about cooking!" She disappeared out the front door.

"Thanks," Joanna called after her as she turned on her coffee maker.

A few minutes later, Carol reentered the apartment, carrying more bags and dragging a large cooler behind her.

"Goodness, Mom, did you really need to bring a cooler?"

Carol shrugged. "Sometimes you don't know how long you'll be stuck in traffic! Now, how did the rest of your first week go?"

"The kids are wonderful, and the other teachers and staff are all really great."

"But…?"

"But, I definitely have a lot more to learn, that's all," Joanna said lightly. She had already told her mother about the ruined sunsets on her first day, and didn't want to worry her further. "The school guidance counselor, Mindy, gave me some classroom management tips that I'm hoping to try next week."

"That sounds great, honey," Carol said, giving her a pat on the back. "I know you can do anything if you put your mind to it."

Joanna appreciated her mom's support, but she also knew Carol would say encouraging words for almost anything she tried. "How are you doing? Anything interesting happen at home?"

Her mother's face perked up. "Well, since you asked, remember Amita, the woman who just moved in a few doors down?"

"Uh-huh…" Joanna said, suspecting she was walking into a trap, but she wasn't quite sure what it was yet. "Let me guess, you set her up with someone?"

"Yes, a couple of months ago, Mr. Bruce—"

"Our mailman?" Joanna interrupted. "Isn't he married? With, like, a bunch of grandkids?"

Carol tsk-tsked her daughter. "Let me finish! A couple of months ago, Mr. Bruce mentioned that his much younger cousin had recently moved nearby from upstate, and was single and enjoyed playing tennis. At the time, I didn't think much of it—"

"I doubt that," Joanna teased. "I'm sure you filed it away."

"Right, *at the time*, I didn't think much of it, but

last week, when I went over to welcome Amita to the neighborhood, I saw a racket and a basket of tennis balls in the garage, and I just got this feeling."

Joanna knew where this was going. "Let me guess, you immediately pounced?"

"Yes, I planned a dinner party for this past weekend so they could meet."

"And...did they?" Joanna asked.

"Oh, they did," Carol said smugly. "And they've been out twice this week already. First for some tennis, and then last night, dinner downtown!"

"Wow, two dates already? Well done, Mom."

"I'm telling you, I just had this feeling!" Carol said. "You know, honey—"

Before her mother could continue, Joanna interrupted again. "Mom, I'm gonna stop you right there."

"What, I wasn't going to say anything about *you*!" Carol said innocently. "Or the man who happens to live nearby..."

"Mom," Joanna warned. "I told you already, I need some time to settle into the job."

"I gave you a whole week," her mother responded.

Joanna snorted. "A week? That's not enough!"

"How long do you want? Just give me a date and I'll put it in my calendar." Carol whipped out her phone.

Joanna knew her mother wasn't going to let up.

I can only push off the inevitable blitz, not prevent it, she thought, as she tossed out a random day. "How about in a few weeks? I'm supposed to have a check-in with Principal Malik after my first month, on April 22, during parent-teacher conferences week. If that goes well, then—"

This time her mother cut in, fingers tapping on her phone. "April 22, I've got it marked. Spring should be in full swing by then. It'll be perfect!"

Joanna could only shake her head as her mother, apparently satisfied, turned back to organizing all the food.

"What have I done?" she groaned.

LATER THAT AFTERNOON, Joanna received a message from Jack:

Jack: Still up for the botanical gardens tomorrow?

Darn it! Joanna thought, grumbling at her mother again for Carol's "I thought I messaged you" drop-in.

Joanna: I'm so sorry about this but my mom made a surprise visit and she'll be here until tomorrow afternoon. Rain check?

Jack: Why don't you bring her?

Joanna: Are you really sure you want to spend a morning with my mother?

Jack: I make a great first impression, remember?

Reading Jack's message, Joanna shook her head. *His enthusiasm is cute, but he doesn't know my mother.*

She quickly started a new message to Mindy.

Joanna: So...my mom dropped by unexpectedly and now Jack wants me to bring her to the botanical gardens tomorrow

Mindy: You mean for your "non-date"?

Joanna: No time for jokes! What do I do? The minute my mother meets Jack and finds out he's single, she'll go into full-on Cupid Mode trying to get us together.

Mindy: I say let her work her magic! Are you thinking black tie or just formal for the wedding?

Joanna: Mindy! Stop it! This is serious!

Mindy: Alright, alright! Just tell Jack you can't make it, he'll understand.

Mindy: After all, it wasn't a date, right? He'll probably ask Alex or Wei-Wei to go instead...

Joanna: MINDY!!!

Actually Mom's arrival is a good reminder. Going to the botanical gardens alone with a co-worker is definitely too chummy. Returning to Jack's message, Joanna quickly typed out a reply.

Joanna: Apologies, but my mom wants to make some minor repairs around my apartment so we'll be heading to the hardware store tomorrow.

Joanna: Feel free to go without me!

This wasn't technically a lie. "Want me to re-caulk your tub?" Carol had asked, offhandedly, just a few minutes ago, but still, Joanna felt a little bad about canceling on Jack, especially when she read his response.

Jack: No worries, I guess it'll just be me exploring the 100-acre gardens on my own...

JACK SCROLLED BACK through his messages with Joanna, wondering if he had made a mistake asking her to go to the botanical gardens. Back at the bar, he'd realized it sounded like he was asking her out on a date, when he just wanted to get to know her better.

We're just two new kids in town exploring the area together, right?

After sending what he hoped was a light, no-big-deal kind of message, he hoped for a response. Seeing none, Jack looked over to his desk, where his laptop sat closed. He knew he should get to reviewing the board materials his mother had sent over, but he just couldn't bring himself to open the files.

Tomorrow. I'll look at it all tomorrow, he told himself.

So on Sunday morning, Jack sat at his desk, reviewing the Sun Textiles board documents. He read through each line item of the budget and forced himself to try to appreciate its importance, but nothing was sinking in. Revenue and gross margins, sales and marketing expenses—these were things that just didn't move Jack, although he was loathe to admit this to his mother.

After a couple of hours, Jack stretched and yawned, then pushed his laptop to the side. He reached over to his school satchel and pulled out a stack of student work he had brought home on Friday, feeling much more eager to review these documents. Starting to grade the writing assignment Teach Me How to Do Something, he stopped after reading Maja's.

This girl really gets it.

Her short paragraph describing how to make bread was both informative and entertaining, and her Chinese characters flawless. *She could definitely draw a straight line*, he thought as he examined her script. She also incorporated a few very sophisticated Chinese idioms, a proficiency even high school students often struggled with. Jack was certain the advanced phrases were not part of Lakeland's fifth grade curriculum.

I wonder how she learned these?

Jack finished the rest of the essays—making a few grammar corrections and finding a few sloppy strokes but mostly thoroughly impressed with his new class—then reorganized the pages and put them back in his bag.

He reached for his phone, clicking on his messages, and thought about Joanna. He hadn't heard from her since last night, but her mother was in town, so he couldn't blame her for being out of touch, or for canceling on their planned visit to the botanical gardens—no doubt he would have done the same if his own mother had shown up without warning.

Just as he was wondering what Joanna might be thinking, a message popped up from her:

Joanna: Sorry again for missing this morning. How many acres did you get through?

Jack: No apologies necessary. Sadly, I did not make it through any of the acres! Spent the day appeasing my mother's requests.

Joanna: I think I have you beat. I bet your mom hasn't ever sent you two months' worth of food?

Then a photo came in, showing a fridge stuffed to the brim with containers and bags of food.

Jack: You got me, my mother has not managed to do that from across the ocean!

He typed out Let me know if you need any help eating it, but then paused before hitting Send, unsure if it would seem too forward.

Before he could internally debate it any further, another message came in.

Joanna: I'll bring some in for all the teachers and staff to share!

Okay, Jack thought, as he deleted the words he had written. *Message received. Let's keep it professional.*

Jack: Sounds great!

BACK IN HER APARTMENT, Joanna tried to read between the lines of Jack's texts.

So he didn't end up going to the botanical gardens with anyone else.

She thought back to his introductory speech,

and the last statement he had translated for her:
Maybe I'll find a reason to stay longer.

*What did he mean by that? And why did he only
say it in Mandarin and not in English? Was he
flirting with just the Chinese teachers?*

Why do I care anyways?

Get a hold of yourself, Joanna!

Just then her phone buzzed with several messages from her mother.

Mom: I arrived home safely!

Mom: I know you said to give you a month, but
Tracy just asked me again if you wanted the number of that man her nephew knows.

Mom: She says he's very successful. He runs his
own company, managing hundreds of people.

*Hmm, an expert in managing people? Not ex-
actly what I'm looking for right now, Mom!*

Mom: It can't hurt, right? She says she saw a
photo of him and he's VERY handsome.

Seeing the word *handsome* made Joanna blush-
ingly think of Jack. But then she remembered
what Mindy had said about the last art teacher not
being able to handle the job, and how she had left
abruptly, leaving her classroom barren.

I have to make sure this job works out first. I can't afford to mess this up. I already spent two years switching careers.

Her memory went back to Tim, who had been her supervising attorney at the law firm. They had dated for over three years, and Joanna had been expecting a marriage proposal that never came. Thank goodness it didn't, because she would have said yes and where would she be now? By the end of the relationship, she'd been completely lost, kept in a career she didn't love with no identity of her own and, perhaps worst of all, no respect from her colleagues, who had treated her like Tim's shadow.

The day they broke up, her mother had met her at the doorway of their family home, ready to embrace her.

"It's just like your dad said," Carol said, "he wasn't the one for you. This is a good thing. Just you wait and see, honey. You just have to figure out who you are."

And that's exactly what I'm doing, Mom.

Joanna thought about all the time and effort she had invested in this new career, and how her mom had supported her the whole way. But just when Joanna was feeling warm and fuzzy about her mother, another text came in.

Mom: So what do you think? Can I tell Tracy that you're ready to be set up?

In a flurry of thumbs, Joanna started typing back a message.

Joanna: Mom, please. I've got enough going on with the new job. You know how important this is to me and how hard I've worked to get here.

Joanna: I don't want to be in a relationship right now, whether I find one on my own, or you set me up.

Joanna: I'm working on me right now.

Joanna: No dating.

Joanna: Period.

CHAPTER SEVEN

JOANNA BEGAN HER second week of school with new resolve, starting by implementing as many of Mindy's classroom management tips as she could.

Okay, first order of business—greet each student at the door.

"Good morning!" Joanna said cheerily to the dark-haired boy whom she recognized from the prior week. "Asher, right?"

Nodding, he mumbled back, "Mmm-hmm. Good morning."

"Nice to see you again! We're going to be drawing today, how does that sound?"

"Um, good, I guess?"

"Great!" Joanna responded. She looked to the next student in line. "Good morning! Remind me your name?"

By the time Joanna got to the end of the line, over ten minutes had gone by, and most of the students had already seated themselves haphazardly, which meant she had to ask everyone to stand up again as she tried to execute Mindy's second tip: assigned seating.

Over the weekend, Joanna had carefully written out the names of her class lists onto seating charts. It seemed like a cinch to put in place, but when Joanna started pointing out where everyone should sit, the freckled girl named Cara called out, "Do we *have* to move seats? Ms. Rani always let us sit wherever we wanted!"

When Joanna encouraged the class to try her system, telling them that sitting alphabetically would help her learn their names more quickly, Cara immediately pointed out that she had mixed up the two Dylans. "Dylan A should be at that table, and Dylan O in the back," she corrected Joanna loudly.

"Right, sorry about that," Joanna said sheepishly. She helped the two boys to switch seats while trying to keep a positive look on her face, despite feeling quite the opposite inside. When she finally got everyone in their assigned seats and ready to get started, nearly half of their instruction time had already been wasted.

Unfortunately, the day didn't get much better from there. With her rowdy third grade class, Joanna tried allowing them Mindy's suggested five minutes of "settling time" at the beginning of the period. But this did nothing to actually settle them—if anything, they seemed to get even more riled up as each minute passed—and she had to resort to sending two of the more disruptive students down to Principal Malik's office.

By the end of the week, she was utterly spent.

What am I doing wrong? she thought as she sluggishly started putting the chairs on the tables on Friday afternoon.

"Uh-oh, tough week?" Mindy asked, her sweet perfume raising Joanna's spirits a little as the guidance counselor walked into Joanna's classroom.

"Yes," Joanna said, "but don't worry, I'm not throwing in the towel yet. It has been a process, though!"

Mindy smiled at her sympathetically. "My classroom management tips aren't a magic wand. They can take time to take effect, but stick with them. I know you'll get the hang of it. And look at these walls—they're already filled!" Mindy gazed around the room, clearly admiring the colorful paintings, drawings and other projects that covered nearly all of the walls, which had been completely bare only two weeks ago.

"True," Joanna agreed, although it felt a little like a consolation prize.

"Shall we head to happy hour?" Mindy asked. "Jack called over to Patrick's and confirmed they were open for business—no negotiating needed today."

Hearing Jack's name, Joanna stiffened. After her no-dating resolution, she had managed to keep

things friendly with him, but not *too* friendly—
basically instituting her own antifraternization
policy. She said hello when he dropped off his
class and when she saw him in the teachers'
lounge or hallway, but did not engage in much
conversation beyond that.

*Last time I went to happy hour, I accepted his
invitation for an almost-date...*

"I think I'm going to pass on happy hour today.
I want to study my seating charts and commit
them to memory," she answered Mindy truthfully, not mentioning that she didn't want to risk
socializing with her handsome colleague.

THE WEEKS PASSED QUICKLY, and while there were
still plenty of hiccups, with each class, Joanna
could feel herself getting into a rhythm with her
students. She began learning their names and
each of their personalities: Asher, the dark-haired
boy who had spilled his paint on her first day,
often needed a little extra support to get going,
whereas his freckled classmate, Cara, could be
counted on to jump in immediately and assist
others when she was done. Joanna's third grade
class was still a handful, but at least she hadn't
had to send any more students down to the principal's office.

One morning in mid-April, Joanna woke to the
sounds of birds chirping and the sun feeling a lot
warmer as it broke through her curtains. When

she opened her kitchen window while brewing her morning coffee, the sweet, heady scent of the lilac shrubs just outside wafted into her apartment. Leaning out, she saw with delight that the pointed bunches of exquisite lavender flowers had opened.

Joanna hurried out to her building's front door and took a barefoot step outside; flowers all along the street had opened as well, sturdy tulip stems standing tall among beds of dainty tricolor crocuses with their distinct bands of lilac, white and yellow.

Looks like spring has finally sprung in Lakeland!

Donning a powder-pink A-line dress with a scooped neckline and capped sleeves, and tying a ribbon in her hair, Joanna decided to leave her apartment a little early and walk the two miles to school. She was nearly late as she'd stopped to admire the delicate star-shaped blue hyacinths that lined Main Street, their fragrant scent following her as she walked on.

At the entrance to the school, groups of daffodils had changed from stems and tight buds looking like a pack of new paintbrushes to full-on sun-yellow blooms, standing stick-straight like a brigade of trumpeters welcoming her into work.

Everything's exploded!

When she arrived at her classroom, Joanna went over to her window ledge to check on her plant.

Except for my Easter lily...it seems to be a late bloomer.

Although the plant had sprouted, the leaves a lush, sap green color, its flower buds were still tiny, barely discernible until she leaned in to really inspect it.

Before lunch, Mindy dropped in to see the lily as well, commenting, "Your lily's growing nicely!" She, too, was wearing an outfit fitting of the day, a lovely floral blouse with a ruffled neckline and cuffs.

"Is it?" Joanna asked, glancing at it again. "On my walk over this morning, the entire town seemed to be in bloom! But this one's barely in its bud phase. Do you think it needs more water? Or sun?" She looked around the classroom to see if there was a different place she should move it.

"Nah, it's perfect where it is! You just have to be patient. Some flowers take longer to bloom. But it'll get there, trust me!"

"I wonder how Jack's lily is doing?" Joanna said absently.

"Interesting question. Maybe you should stop by his classroom and check?"

"Maybe I will," Joanna answered.

"What's that, now?" Mindy asked. "That's the first time you haven't pushed away a suggestion about you and Jack! Is this the same Joanna Lin? Or has she been replaced by someone else who's actually open to a possible romantic relationship?"

Joanna waved her off. "Please, my interest is purely botanical. No work romances for me, remember?"

THE WEEKS HAD flown by for Jack, too. His students were doing well; they were an excellent class, with homework always turned in on time, and virtually no disciplinary issues. Jack didn't even have to remind them to put up their chairs at the end of each day. And Maja, especially, continued to impress him day after day.

After reviewing the budget his mother had sent over and giving her some scant comments—he really didn't have anything to add—she had given him some breathing room, at least until the company board meeting next month.

Since he was on borrowed time, Jack knew he should be content with simply enjoying spring in Lakeland. Running on the shoreline was now a regular evening activity for him, and Jack cherished every sunset on the lake, knowing that he didn't have many left.

Today, Jack's mind was on parent-teacher conferences. Maja's parents had just arrived for their meeting, and Jack had prepared a folder to show them what an outstanding Chinese student their daughter was.

"Mr. and Mrs. Andresson, thank you both for

coming in today. I know it's probably not easy to get away from the store," Jack said as he shook their hands.

They nodded, Mr. Andresson responding, "Please, call me Luca, and my wife, Hanna. And of course, when you emailed asking if we both would attend today's conference, it sounded like it was important."

"I hope I didn't alarm you," Jack said. "But it is important, in that Maja is quite exceptional. She's one of the best students I've had in my ten years of teaching." He pulled out one of Maja's essays. "This essay is easily at a high school level. Not only the grammar and sentence construction, but the concepts are way beyond even an advanced Chinese learner. She really *thinks* like a native speaker."

Maja's mother smiled proudly. "I think it's helping out Mr. Chen, which she started doing late last year. Do you know him? His restaurant, The Dumpling Spot, is just opposite us. She's been minding his son around the restaurant while he works."

Her husband agreed. "His house is filled with Chinese books that he's always lending to her, and both his parents were scholars back in China. They also chat with Maja all the time in Mandarin."

"Ah, that makes sense," Jack said. "I was wondering where she was picking up all her extra knowledge. The reason I asked you both to come in today is because I wanted to discuss possibilities to continue her Chinese studies after she leaves elementary school. Unfortunately, the district isn't currently offering Chinese in middle school, but I'd like to find some resources she could use next year after school or on weekends."

Suddenly, the smiles on Maja's parents' faces faded, and Jack feared what would come next.

"Well," Luca started, "we really appreciate your support of Maja, but she is getting to the age where she can start working at the store…"

"She really loves making buns and bread," Hanna added.

"Yes, actually one of her essays explored that," Jack commented, remembering the details she had provided.

"…and I'm just not sure there's going to be much extra time next year in middle school," Luca Andresson said.

Jack's heart sank. *There's nothing worse than telling a teacher that his student can no longer continue learning.*

"I understand," Jack said, trying to think on his feet. "What about Danny Chen? Will she continue to babysit his son? Perhaps she can maintain Mandarin exposure with them."

Maja's parents looked at each other, expressions strained.

"Unfortunately," Luca said, "Mr. Chen's son

will be starting elementary school next year, and Hanna and I think it's time for Maja to transition from babysitting to working at the store. Again, we so appreciate this, Mr. Sun. But I just don't see how she'll have the time to continue studying Chinese."

"Of course, I understand," Jack said again, trying not to show how disappointed he felt. "We'll try to make the most of the rest of the school year, then."

"Thank you," Hanna said. "We're all really looking forward to the Dragon Boat Festival and, of course, their big graduation trip to Taiwan after school lets out."

"Right, I've been hearing a lot about the trip from all the students," Jack said. "It'll be a nice, er—" he cringed inside "—ending to cap off their Chinese studies."

"Thank you again, Mr. Sun," Luca said, standing up and offering his hand. "And please, do come by the bakery any time."

Shaking their hands, Jack said goodbye to Maja's parents and attempted to turn his attention to his next student's folder. Unable to focus, Jack decided to refresh his cup of coffee before his next conference. When he got to the teachers' lounge, mug in hand, Miss Wei-Wei was sitting at one of the back tables, close to the counter where the coffee maker sat.

"Hi, Sun *Laoshi*. Looks like we have the same

idea," she said in Mandarin, pointing to her own empty mug in front of her. "I was just making a fresh pot." The coffee maker was indeed giving off a gentle gurgle as the water started to heat up. "It seems to work on its own time, though, so perhaps you want to take a seat," she added, holding out a hand toward the chair across from her.

"Got it. Thank you, Miss Wei-Wei," Jack said, setting his mug on the table and sitting down as directed.

"Parent-teacher conferences are never easy, right?" Miss Wei-Wei said amiably.

"Right," Jack agreed. Then he thought of something. "Did you by any chance have Maja Andresson in your class last year?"

Wei-Wei nodded. "I did. She is a very special student."

"She is, isn't she?" Jack said. "I'd like to find a way for her to continue her Chinese studies after she leaves Lakeland. But her parents don't think she'll have the time. And it's really a shame that the middle school doesn't offer continued Chinese classes."

"Yes, sadly the district has been slow to carry on the success we've had here at the elementary level. And it would definitely be a big loss if Maja stopped studying Chinese completely," Wei-Wei said. "Maybe we can offer some concrete options for her to consider, like online classes or self-study?"

"That's a great idea. With a set plan in front of them, maybe they would reconsider."

"Of course. Let me do some research and compile a list for you."

"That would be really helpful, thank you so much," Jack said. After talking to another teacher he felt a little better. Perhaps there was still some hope for Maja.

Wei-Wei stood up and stepped over to the back counter, saying, "Looks like the coffee may finally be ready." As she offered to fill his mug, she asked, "It's great of you to make all this extra effort for Maja. Do you want children of your own?"

Jack accepted the coffee and answered, "Yes, for sure, someday." Looking at his watch, he realized he had to run. "Apologies, Miss Wei-Wei, but I have another conference in a few minutes. Thanks again for your help with Maja."

JOANNA HEADED OVER to Jack's classroom with a bounce in her step.

He might be in a conference, she thought, but when she got to his classroom, the door was open, lights on, but no Jack. Figuring he'd be back any minute, Joanna strolled in and checked on his Easter lily, which was sitting on the corner of his desk.

Wow!

The flower buds on Jack's plant were much bigger than the ones on hers, and though they were still tightly closed, they looked like they were going to burst open at any moment.

After a few minutes of admiring his lily and Jack still not returning, Joanna wandered down the hall to the teachers' lounge to see if he was there. As she walked in, she saw him standing by the counter, his back toward her. She was about to call out and tell him about the Easter lilies, when she realized that standing right next to him, pouring coffee into his mug, was the lovely Miss Wei-Wei, her dainty mouth turned up at both sides.

"...do you want children of your own?" Wei-Wei was saying.

"Yes, for sure, someday," Jack responded.

They're discussing whether or not he wants children? Joanna felt a twinge in her stomach that she recognized as jealousy.

But I don't even want a relationship right now, especially a work one, she reminded herself as she quickly turned to leave the teachers' lounge without being seen.

Back at her own desk, Joanna tried to focus on preparing for her meeting with Principal Malik later that afternoon, but she couldn't stop thinking about Jack and Wei-Wei.

Maybe it's just because I saw him with her that I'm suddenly interested. Wanting what I can't have?

But she knew it wasn't just that. Jack was really incredible with his students; unlike her, he had taken over his class seamlessly, and every time she saw him with them, he was engaged in energetic discussion. He made it look so effortless. And he helped out with so many other things— taking on pickup duty when another teacher couldn't make it, clearing tables after lunch or holding the door for a line of students coming in from recess. The other teachers all loved and respected him; even Coach Clay couldn't stop bragging about how they were sure to beat Beverly Harbor in this year's dragon boat race, given Jack's participation on the Lakeland team.

Maybe there's nothing going on between Jack and Wei-Wei. They could have just been having a friendly conversation.

Or maybe they're an item now and she's his "reason to stay..."

CHAPTER EIGHT

"JACK, HOW ARE YOU? Your first month has gone great, by all accounts." Principal Malik looked up from the folder he was holding. "You are universally loved—by your fellow teachers, students, parents, staff, everyone! Lakeland Elementary is lucky to have you."

"Thank you, Principal Malik," Jack responded, a bit distractedly, as his mind was still on the conference he'd had earlier with Maja Andresson's parents.

"Please, call me Omar. And seems like you have something on your mind," Principal Malik observed, taking off his reading glasses.

"I'm sorry. You're right, there is something on my mind. But first let me say I'm really loving it here. The students and staff are truly wonderful." He then relayed what had occurred in the conference with Maja's parents, asking, "Have you thought about the learning path for studying Chinese beyond Lakeland Elementary? We do a fantastic job of teaching all these kids Mandarin, but when they leave here, then what? From what I've researched, it doesn't look like any of the middle schools or high schools in the area offer even introductory Chinese."

Omar leaned forward in his chair and nodded. "I've been pushing hard for the middle school in our district to offer advanced Chinese, now that our first immersion class will be finishing up fifth grade. But it's been a tough go, unfortunately. Not necessarily surprising, but still tough."

"How were you able to start Mandarin immersion here at Lakeland in the first place?" Jack asked.

"I've always believed that we can learn so much from other cultures, and the earlier, the better. Convincing the school board to convert Lakeland Elementary to an immersion school wasn't without its challenges, but at the time, the school was struggling—test scores were low and attendance waning. Now, five years later, we have to do a lottery at kindergarten because there are so many students who want to enroll here—can you believe that?"

Jack leaned in, putting a hand to his chin. "Remarkable. So why is it so hard to convince the school board to add Chinese to the middle and, eventually, high school curriculum?"

Omar let out a breath and shook his head. "Unfortunately, Jack, these things just take time. I think we'll get there eventually, but there might be a one- or two-year gap before they get it up and running in the middle school."

Jack shook his head, too. "That is really a shame, boss."

"It is, but I'm not giving up," the principal said emphatically. "With each year that goes by, Lakeland keeps growing and I know eventually the tides will rise for us. We just have to keep at it, keep doing what we're doing, show the community how wonderful our students are. I'm hoping we'll get a Chinese class in the middle school very soon."

But that'll be too late for Maja, Jack thought, feeling like he had failed as Maja's teacher. He had to do something to prove—even if it was just to himself—that he still provided value as a teacher. "Is there anything more I can do for the school while I'm still here?"

Omar leaned back in his desk chair. "Well, it's certainly not a secret that I'd be thrilled if you would consider staying on permanently, even after Jessica Zhang returns in the fall. It's looking like we'll have enough demand to add a new kindergarten class next year. What do you say? We could also move some people around, if kindergarten wasn't your thing."

"Hmm," Jack said, thinking out loud. "I do enjoy teaching beginners—introducing them to Chinese language and culture. It's gratifying to watch them go from seed to flower." He thought back to his early years in New York, where he had started teaching Beginning Chinese to middle schoolers. There was definitely a learning curve, but seeing it click for the students was incredibly rewarding. "Although," he continued, "I've never taught kindergarten before. It would present a new challenge for me, teaching little ones."

But I won't be able to do it. The realization hit Jack like a gust of wind to his face.

"I'm so sorry," he said, wanting to be upfront with his boss. "I think I let my mind wander too much just now. Unfortunately, I've already committed to something else following my stint here." He sighed. "As you know, I had planned on this being only temporary."

The big man sighed as well. "I know, and I can't say I'm not disappointed. I thought for a minute there I had you, but looks like we're just going to have to work harder at convincing you to stay! How many months do we have left?"

Jack glanced over at the calendar propped up on the principal's desk. "Less than two? And of course I'm fully committed to the job while I'm here. Are you sure there isn't anything more I can do, anything at all?"

Omar looked down at the folder in front of him. "Well, let's see, it looks like you've already done a month of pickup duty. And Coach Clay's got you on the dragon boat racing team…"

"Yes, he passed out the training schedule yesterday. He seems quite intense about it."

"Indeed!" Principal Malik shuffled a few papers on his desk, opened another folder and glanced through it. "Actually, there is one thing—if you're open to it, that is. It's teaching-related, and I'd be appreciative of the help, if you can spare the time."

"Of course," Jack said. "Name it."

JOANNA SAT, tapping her foot, on the other side of Principal Malik's desk. Just before starting her meeting, he'd been called out to deal with something, leaving her to wait anxiously in his office. Spotting a folder on his desk with her name on the tab, she resisted the urge to peek inside.

Would there be something in the folder about all the brown paintings?

Or the rowdy class that I still can't get to follow instructions?

Argh, what's taking him so long?

Her foot-tapping had progressed to a full leg shake by the time her boss came back.

"So sorry about that, Joanna," Principal Malik said, as he settled back into his chair. "Never a dull day here at Lakeland Elementary, that's for sure!"

"No problem, Mr.—er—Principal Malik," Joanna said, trying to stay calm as he opened the folder with her name on it, moving in painfully slow motion.

"Please, call me Omar," he responded. "Everyone's so formal today!"

Joanna wasn't sure who else he was referring to, since she was seemingly the only person in the room, but she didn't want to distract him from giving her review. "Sure, no problem," she said again, adding, "Omar."

"All righty…let's see here…" He put on his reading glasses and squinted through them, appearing to have trouble deciphering the words on the pages.

If you're not going to hire me full-time, just come out and say it already.

Joanna's knee started bouncing, and she had to use her hand to stop it.

Omar looked up. "Everything okay?"

"Er-er, yes," Joanna stammered. "I'm just really nervous. This is my first review as a teacher."

"Ah," he responded kindly, "there's no need to be nervous. Now, how do *you* think things are going?"

His question caught her off-guard. "How do *I* think things are going?"

Omar set down the folder. "I think it's important for you to reflect on how your first month has gone, and see if there's anything I can do to help you."

Joanna had certainly not been expecting this.

Her reviews at the law firm had always been given by two stern-faced superiors in suits, and usually started with a couple of things she did well, but then progressed to a dreaded list of things she should work on. "Um, it was a bit shaky at the beginning, but I think I've started to find my footing. This past week went very well, and the kids seem to be really enjoying art and learning a lot, too."

"And you?" Principal Malik asked. "How are *you* doing?"

Joanna smiled as she thought about how happy she had felt this morning walking to school. "Good," she said. "I'm doing really good!"

"That's great to hear." Her boss smiled back at her. "I've heard only positive things about you from all the students and staff. You're a wonderful addition to Lakeland, Joanna."

Whew! "Now *that's* great to hear!" Joanna said. "Why didn't you start with that?"

"I'm sorry, I should have," the principal apologized. "I didn't mean to keep you in suspense. And please do let me know if there's anything I can do to assist you in any way."

"Of course I will. Mindy Perez, and so many of the teachers, have already been a huge help."

"Glad to hear everyone is helping each other out," he said, nodding. "That's the Lakeland spirit."

"Yes, it's really fantastic how supportive everyone is of one another. I wasn't sure what I was expecting, but Lakeland really is an amazing community. I'd love to be a more, well, *permanent* part of it." Joanna bit her lip, hoping the mention of a permanent position wasn't too forward.

"It is quite a special community, and I'm glad you mentioned that. There *is* something, Joanna, that I wanted to discuss with you."

Joanna's smile quickly faded. *Oh no, here it comes. The dreaded "items for improvement" list.*

"Yes?" She braced for impact.

"I wanted to give you some time to get settled before telling you. As you may have heard, the prior art teacher left rather abruptly. Without going into specific details—and truthfully we don't know all her reasons—I believe she had trouble fitting into the culture of the school."

"You mean not speaking Mandarin?" Joanna guessed, thinking of the times she had walked into the teachers' lounge and everyone had to switch from Chinese to English solely for her benefit.

"I believe that might have been part of it, yes," the principal said, then continued a bit more slowly, "and I am wondering if this might be an issue for you, too? I'm concerned that you are not engaging much with the rest of the staff. I would hate for you to feel like an outsider."

Oh no. My self-imposed antifraternization policy with Jack is backfiring, big time.

"Not at all!" Joanna said. *I was just trying to avoid starting a workplace romance!* "I feel very welcomed! And I'd like to engage more! Pickup duty, maybe?" she asked. "I'm happy to, of course. I'm surprised I hadn't been assigned yet."

Her boss shook his head. "No, it's not pickup duty. We're covered on that front through the end of the year—"

"Morning drop-off duty? Lunch recess? Power-washing the blacktop? I'll do anything!" Joanna offered desperately.

"Thankfully we're covered on all of those things, too," Principal Malik chuckled. "Although maybe not the power-washing—I'll keep that in mind! Anyways, it's not a task for the school per se, it's more for you."

"Oh, for me? What is it?"

"I believe it's vitally important that all the staff and teachers immerse themselves in the culture and ethos of the school, including learning Mandarin. The Chinese teachers, of course, already are fluent, but the rest of the English-only staff— including Coach Clay, Mindy Perez, Mrs. Wooten and even myself—are all in various stages of learning. I consider it professional development, specific for the needs of our school. Usually, I let my teachers settle in a little, but unfortunately with our last art teacher, I think not starting Mandarin studies early on added to her difficulty in fitting in, which, ultimately, led to her departure."

Joanna felt a pang of sympathy for Ms. Rani. "It sounds like it was pretty rough for her here," she said.

"Evidently, and I feel partially responsible," Principal Malik said. "I don't want to repeat that with you. Given you're doing so well on the teaching front, I think you should get started on your Mandarin learning right away. We use the official Chinese Proficiency Test for non-native speakers, which has six levels. I'd like to see you pass the first level by the end of the school year in June, which, as I'm sure you're aware, is also when I'll be considering you for a permanent position come next school year."

At the mention of a permanent position, Joanna froze, her legs stiffening.

Wait, I need to learn Mandarin to get a permanent offer? I can't even say ni hao *without half the teachers giggling at me.*

"Joanna?" Principal Malik tapped on his desk. "Did I lose you?"

"Sorry!" Joanna said, snapping herself back.

"The level one CPT is fairly simple. You'll only need to learn a hundred and fifty characters." He looked over at his desk calendar. "Let's see, I'll schedule you to sit for the test on June 8. That's the Monday of the last week of school."

Joanna nodded, scribbling down the date and

trying to remain calm as she counted the weeks in her head. "Sure… I didn't expect this, but it does make sense. I admit I've felt a little left out on a conversation or two around school. Are there, um, study materials available?"

"I'll do you one better," Principal Malik said. "The Chinese teachers here take turns leading weekly evening Mandarin classes for us English-only folks. For you, though, since you're just starting out, I thought it would be good to have one-on-one attention given you don't have much time. I was thinking three sessions a week, if that works for you?"

"Um, sure," Joanna said. "That sounds great. But are there teachers that can offer that much of their time?"

"Yep, in fact, I just lined it up. One of our teachers was gracious enough to volunteer to help with all of your lessons."

"Oh, that's so nice! Which teacher?"

"Jack Sun."

CHAPTER NINE

JOANNA LEFT SCHOOL, regretting that she'd decided to walk to work that morning.

Not even halfway home, the skies darkened and it started to rain, first a light drizzle but then quickly turning heavier. Also regretting that she hadn't checked the weather that morning, and resigned that her dress would undoubtedly get drenched, Joanna put on her jacket hood and quickened her pace toward her apartment. Passing the just-opened flowers lining the streets, she felt even more distressed that many were now drooping, weighed down by the fat droplets of water dripping on them.

I feel rained on, too!

Her boss had just told her that she'd have to learn a whole new language in less than two months!

Calm down, Joanna. It's just a hundred and fifty characters.

Still, as easy as the kids at Lakeland made it seem, Joanna had heard that Chinese was one of the hardest languages for an English speaker to learn. Though she had tried to ask most of the teachers to teach her a few words when they dropped off their classes, she hadn't retained much more than *hello*, *bye*, *thank you*, and *you're welcome*.

And my Asian face isn't gonna help me learn it any faster, she thought forlornly.

The rain turned into a full-on downpour, soaking through her hood and dribbling all over her face. She broke into a sprint, and when she finally arrived at her front door, she saw that pools of water had formed all around the bed of crocuses just outside her building's entrance.

I hope they don't drown, she thought, feeling helpless as she walked into her apartment.

After changing out of her sopping-wet dress and starting to towel off her hair, Joanna picked up her phone to text Mindy to commiserate about her new job hurdle, but she stopped before sending the message.

Mindy'll probably just make some suggestive comment about spending time with Jack.

Instead, she called the only person who would make her feel better.

"Hi, Mom," she started, as soon as Carol's cheery face showed up on the screen.

"Hi, Joanna! Why is your hair all wet? Did you just take a shower?"

"No, it started raining as I was walking home today."

Her mother caught on right away. "What's wrong, honey? Did something happen at school? How was your meeting with the principal?"

Joanna gave her mother a quick summary of Principal Malik's review of her first month at Lakeland.

"That all sounds quite good," Carol said brightly. "Why the glum face then?"

"I didn't tell you the bad part yet," Joanna said. "He said I have to learn Mandarin and pass a proficiency test before the end of the school year for him to even consider me for a permanent position."

"Oh, honey."

"This is a disaster! There's only, like, six more weeks of school," Joanna moaned.

"I guess Dad and I should have taught you some Chinese growing up. We never imagined you might need it! I'm so sorry, Joanna."

Joanna was touched that her mother was feeling somehow responsible for all of this. "I wasn't blaming you, Mom. How could you have known this would happen to me? It's just such a huge task."

"I can help, at least," Carol offered. "Tell me what to do."

"That's really nice of you, but actually Principal Malik has already arranged for one of the Chinese teachers to tutor me three times a week."

"Three times a week, in addition to your regular teaching schedule? You'll have a lot on your plate."

"Yes, and there's also our school's big Dragon Boat Festival happening the Sunday before the last week of school, and I already volunteered to lead the decorations and art activities for it." Joanna squeezed her eyes shut and started rubbing her temple.

"You'll pull it off, I know you can," Carol said. "I have confidence in you. I wish Dad could be here to give you a pep talk."

"Yeah, me too." Joanna said.

Then Carol offered, "He'd probably say 'Only a hundred and fifty characters? That'll be duck soup for you.'"

Joanna smiled. "Thanks, Mom." She looked out the window and saw that the rain had stopped, and her mood improved, just a smidgen.

"Are you sure there isn't anything I can actually do, besides a bad imitation of your father?"

Joanna was about to say no, but then she thought of something. "Yes, there is one thing. Can we postpone any setups? I know your calendar reminder probably went off this morning and you're itching to call that Tracy person."

"I was just waiting for the green light," Carol

said, looking hopeful. "But I understand after today if you want some more time."

"Yes, I do. Thank you, Mom," Joanna replied.

THE NEXT DAY, Jack walked into Joanna's classroom right after dismissal holding a few workbooks. "*Ni hao*, Lin *Laoshi*. I hear we're going to be spending some time together."

Jack had been more than happy to help when Principal Malik asked him to take on Chinese tutoring—anything to keep him at school rather than home alone, looking at financial statements and textile designs.

But when he found out the student was Joanna Lin, Jack couldn't stop thinking about her lovely face and fine hair, her infectious laugh and sweet way with her students. And now, walking into her classroom and seeing her in person with her hair dotted with tiny specks of paint, well, Jack felt like the luckiest man alive.

"Ni hao," Joanna said back to him, slowly. "Did I say that right?"

"Don't worry, we'll work on it," he answered, realizing how anxious she was by her tentativeness.

"That bad, huh?" Joanna asked, wincing. "Just when I thought I had found my groove, Principal Malik springs this on me."

"No, you weren't bad at all, really! And I was surprised, too, given it's so close to the end of the school year," Jack said. "But it sounds like they got burned from their last art teacher's departure. Something about her having issues with fitting in, I believe he said?"

"Yes, he mentioned that to me as well." Joanna wrung her hands.

"Are you alright?" he asked.

"F-fine. I'm just nervous."

"Don't be," Jack said, trying to reassure her. "This is going to be a piece of cake, I promise. A tasty one too, like from the Swiss Bakery, got it?"

Joanna cracked a smile. "Well, if it's from the Swiss Bakery, then okay."

"Alright, let's get started. Just confirming, you haven't studied Chinese at all, right?"

"Right. My parents came to the US when they were young adults, and even they rarely spoke Mandarin with each other. I only learned English, and never had a need for anything else. And honestly, never really thought about it, until I applied for the job at Lakeland Elementary and saw that it was a Mandarin immersion school."

"Sure." Jack nodded. "That makes perfect sense."

"But to be honest," Joanna continued, "and maybe this is why I'm extra nervous, I've been feeling self-conscious about not being able to speak Chinese since the first day I arrived at school. It seems like everyone expects me to speak it, because of what I look like. Even though

I didn't have parent-teacher conferences, a lot of parents visited my classroom, and I could tell many of them thought I would speak Chinese."

Jack shook his head sympathetically, his heart aching for her. "I'm so, so sorry to hear that. It's really hard and unfair when people make assumptions about you. And here's what I think. You should definitely not feel like you have to learn Chinese to fit some ignorant person's assumptions. You should do it because you want to."

Joanna stuck out her tongue. "Or because I have to, to keep my job."

"I guess that's a good reason, too," Jack chuckled.

"I have a confession to make," she said.

Jack's heart skipped a beat. What was she going to confess? "Yes?" he asked.

"I'm not sure if anyone told you already, but this is actually my first teaching job. I just went through a big career change." Her eyes flicked down to the table.

"Really? I would not have guessed. You're such a natural in the classroom," Jack responded genuinely. He really was surprised at her confession.

"Thank you for saying that," she said. "I really need to pass this test."

"Don't worry, I haven't had a single student fail on me yet," Jack said. "Let's get down to business, shall we?" He put down two workbooks and a syllabus he had prepared that laid out the planned schedule. "These books cover the level one CPT. There are fifteen lessons, and you'll need to learn to read and write a hundred and fifty characters, so ten characters per lesson. There are corresponding audio files, which I'll play in class, and also email to you. I'll supplement with additional material as necessary, and also introduce some topics I think would be relevant for you that aren't covered in the books. This schedule has us doing three lessons a week to finish the material in five weeks, leaving one week for review before the Dragon Boat Festival, and the test the day after that."

"Whoa, Mr. Sun," Joanna said, clearly taken aback at the detailed plans he had just outlined. "You're really not messing around."

"I do take my teaching responsibilities very seriously," Jack answered, slipping into teacher mode, a role he was very comfortable with. "So please, open up your workbook to lesson one. We'll start with tones and basic character strokes."

LATER THAT WEEK, on his regular run along the shoreline, Jack stopped to watch the sunset on Lake Michigan, something he truly believed he could never get tired of. Joanna had been on his mind since their first lesson. He had felt invigorated taking her on as a student, and he was grateful to Principal Malik for giving him the opportunity to tutor Joanna.

Time really flew when he was with her, and Jack knew it wasn't just being needed as a teacher. It was the way Joanna had looked a little scared when he had showed her the schedule, but then her determination took over once they had started the lesson. How his heart beat faster every time they made eye contact.

But what could he do about it? Laying out the syllabus really put it in black-and-white that his time was up in six weeks. Joanna would take the test, school would let out and he'd be on his way back to Taiwan.

If Ba were still alive, maybe it would be different.

But he knew that kind of thinking was useless.

Ma and Jonathan need me. I have to go back. That's all there is to it.

He wondered if Joanna even cared that he was leaving.

It probably doesn't matter to her at all. She just needs my help to pass her test.

As he made his way back to his apartment, he reflected on her learning so far.

Her comprehension was good, better than she believed. *She's picked up more than she realized, being in the immersive environment of our school.*

Her character recall was strong, and written

strokes very confident. *Her art background and skills help a lot, I think.*

But when she spoke aloud, she held herself back, afraid to make a mistake. He needed to get her to shed that fear.

AFTER HER FIRST two lessons—tones, strokes and basic greetings—Joanna could see how Jack had won Teacher of the Year. He was patient, present in every moment and never appeared bored, even though he'd undoubtedly taught the same lesson hundreds of times. She really believed that he wanted to help her understand everything in the lesson.

She studied every night, reviewing her workbook while listening to the audio files Jack had emailed her and filling blank pages with characters. She found an immediate affection for writing; it was as if each character was a picture, and she internalized each one, making memorization a cinch. Of course, it didn't hurt that the first few sets of characters she had to learn were all pretty simple.

But she felt incredibly self-conscious when speaking, uncertain every time she opened her mouth, even though Jack assured her that her tones were spot-on.

"I'm not that verbal of a person. I communicate through art, remember?" she reminded him near the end of their third lesson, a Friday afternoon at the end of April. She'd been struggling to say "My name is Joanna Lin. I'm American."

"We need to work on that. You can't learn anything without making some mistakes," Jack said encouragingly. "Tomorrow morning, we're going to take the lessons out of the classroom and dive into the real world using Mandarin. How does that sound?"

At the prospect of spending time with Jack outside of the classroom, Joanna thought for a moment before answering. *This is definitely not a date.* "Sure," she said. "What do you have in mind?"

"Be ready at eight thirty and you'll find out!"

CHAPTER TEN

THE NEXT MORNING, Joanna woke to a message from Jack.

Jack: See you in about half an hour. Oh, and bring a towel!

What? Bring a towel? Joanna had a feeling she'd gotten roped into something terrible, and indeed, Jack's next message confirmed it.

Jack: We're going to do Coach Clay's LAKE JUMP!

An hour later, Joanna found herself with about a hundred other people, shivering in the brisk morning breeze on a long pier over—what she was certain was—a freezing Lake Michigan. While the pale blue sky was clear and cloudless, and the bright sun was sure to warm up the water as the day progressed, it was still at least twenty degrees colder than what Joanna would have considered an acceptable temperature to dip her feet in the water, much less her whole body.

In the crowd at the pier were quite a few teachers from Lakeland Elementary, including Alex and Wei-Wei. She and Jack waved at them; when they both waved fervently back, Joanna suspected their excitement was directed more at Jack than herself, which then made her worry they would think she and Jack were on a date. She didn't have much time to dwell on this, however, as just then the wind picked up, reminding her what they were all about to do.

"So how, exactly, is this going to help me with my Mandarin?" Joanna asked Jack, her teeth chattering. He stood straight-backed next to her and somehow didn't appear to be affected by the weather at all. "Also, how are you not cold?" She stole a glance at his broad chest, which was covered by a tight, long-sleeve rashguard. "What was all that you said to Coach when he first brought this up, about growing up on a subtropical island?"

Jack shot her a one-dimpled half smile. "Trust me, I'm shivering inside! And don't worry, this is all part of my larger plan."

"And that plan is?" Joanna inquired, bobbing her knees to try to warm up. "I'm dying to know how this fits in with our syllabus!"

"Afterward, we're going to head over to The Dumpling Spot and enjoy a nice, hot bowl of soup, which you are going to order for us—in Chinese, of course," Jack said.

"Jack, Joanna!" Joanna looked up to see Coach Clay yelling through a bullhorn from the beach. He stood among a large group of observers, including Mindy and her family, Principal Malik and even a local news crew. "So glad you could make it! Thank you for your support!"

"You owe us one!" Joanna called back. It dawned on her that Coach was fully clothed, even wearing a fleece jacket, zipped all the way up to his chin. "Hey, wait a minute, Coach! Are you not doing the jump yourself?"

"Someone's gotta supervise!" Coach blared the siren of his bullhorn for a few seconds, and everyone turned their attention to him. "Good morning, Lakeland jumpers! Thank you so much for joining us on this gorgeous spring morning!"

The crowd on the pier responded with a loud cheer and Coach started introducing and thanking all the sponsors and donors of the event. He also welcomed and pointed out the main librarian of the Lakeland Library, who was enveloped in a full wet suit and swimming cap and positioned farther down the pier from Jack and Joanna. She waved with both hands when Coach Clay announced her name and shouted out, "Thank you so much to everyone for coming out!"

After all the introductions and thank-yous, Coach announced, "Our lovely Lake Michigan is a balmy thirty-six degrees this morning."

The crowd responded with an even louder

cheer, as Joanna shook her head at Jack. "How did I let myself get talked into doing this?" she asked him.

He gave her a playful bump with his shoulder. "Just think how good that bowl of soup is going to feel warming up your belly."

Back on the bullhorn, Coach reviewed the rules. "Feetfirst jumps only. No pushing or shoving!"

"You heard him, right?" Jack teased. "I know you want to be first in the water, but don't you dare try to push me aside!"

"Believe me," Joanna responded, "I'm not going to be pushing or shoving anyone to get into the water!"

"Alright, that's it! Have fun! Let's count it down, folks!" Coach Clay and the observers on the beach started counting down from ten.

As they got to one, Joanna took a breath and squeezed her eyes shut. She heard shuffling and splashing all around her.

On second thought, maybe I don't have to do this?

She opened her eyes. She was still standing on the pier. Everyone else had jumped in, and most were swimming toward shore already.

"Come on in, Joanna! The water's fine!" Jack called out, treading water below her.

That couldn't possibly be true, but Jack was making a good show of it, turning onto his back and putting his hands together at his chest like a sea otter. "Argh! I really don't want to!" she yelled back. "Can I just walk back to the beach?"

"No way! We didn't come all this way for you not to jump!"

"It was only like a ten-minute drive," Joanna said.

Jack flipped upright again. "It's really not that bad! Come on! This is an important symbolic step in your Mandarin learning!"

"Pfffft!" Joanna stuck her tongue out at him.

"If you don't jump, I'm going to start singing," Jack warned. "And that's definitely not something you want to hear, I'll guarantee you."

The first of the jumpers had already made it to the beach, stripping off their swimwear and wrapping themselves in towels and coats. Joanna looked enviously over at them.

"Okay, Joanna," Jack called from the water. "It's alright if you don't want to do it. But I have to get out of this lake. Because you're right, it's *freezing* in here!"

"I knew it!" Joanna said. She watched as Jack started swimming toward the shore, his smooth strokes cutting through the water and leaving ripples behind him.

I've come too far to quit now. Let's just do this.

"Aaaaaaaaah!" Joanna screamed as she took another deep breath, closed her eyes again, and this time, jumped.

YIKES!

The lake felt like an ice bath, sending a shock from her toes all the way to the top of her head as she broke through the surface of the water and immediately started breaststroking to the beach. Not stopping until she was completely out of the water and onto dry sand, Joanna spotted Jack, his black hair slicked back and face glistening.

"Congratulations! You did it!" Jack said, walking toward her and carrying her towel. "How do you feel?"

"Frigid!" Joanna said, her entire body trembling.

"Aw. For real, it wasn't so bad, was it? Don't you feel like you can do anything now?"

"Hmm…" As Jack wrapped the towel around her, Joanna felt his hands pause on her shoulders. Worried someone from school might see them, Joanna quickly took a step away and said, "You're right, I survived! Now where's that hot soup you promised me?"

AFTER CHANGING INTO dry clothes, Jack and Joanna went over to The Dumpling Spot, where they were seated near the front window. While she had gotten takeout a few times, and eaten many of Danny Chen's buns from the farmers market, it was the first time Joanna had actually eaten inside the restaurant. The decor was modern yet cozy, with subdued pendant lights hanging over sleek long tables, and plush, upholstered chairs with arms that made Joanna want to kick off her shoes and curl her feet under her when she sat down.

"Alright, Joanna, here's your second challenge of the day," Jack said. "I'm going to go to the restroom, and you're going to order us lunch using only Mandarin. You can point and gesture, but no English, okay?" He took a quick glance at the menu. "I'll take a bowl of wonton noodle soup." He said the name in Chinese for her.

Joanna quickly grabbed a pen from her handbag, and asked Jack to repeat himself, so she could write down phonetically what he had just said.

Okay, Joanna, you can do this. At least it's warm in here.

Biting her bottom lip as Jack disappeared, Joanna studied the menu. She realized she couldn't read any of the Chinese characters, nor did she know how to say the names of any of the dishes in Chinese besides the one Jack had just translated for her.

I guess I'll be having the same thing as Jack.

She took a deep breath and called the waiter over, pointing at the menu while slowly pronouncing the words. "Two wonton noodle soups," she stuttered in Chinese, while also holding up fingers to confirm he understood her numbers. She was also able to add two fried pork buns—she did thankfully know how to say that, as she had been enjoying them nearly every Monday at the farmers market: *sheng jian bao*.

The waiter smiled and nodded at her, then cleared their menus, and Joanna noticed Jack standing just over at the host stand, chatting with an older Asian man. She understood none of what they were saying.

When Jack returned to their table and asked how it went, she answered, "Well, we're either getting wonton noodle soup or a cold jellyfish salad…"

"Either are fine! I'm not picky," Jack laughed.

"It's so incredible how you can switch back and forth between Chinese and English so easily," Joanna said. "Even with years of study, I don't think I'll ever get there. Was it completely effortless for you?"

Jack shook his head. "Effortless? Definitely not. But the way I learned English—being sent here to live with relatives and thrown into an American school at age twelve—was definitely a jump into cold water, not unlike the one we just did."

"I can't imagine starting over like that in a completely new country, without your parents. Were you scared?"

"It was terrifying," Jack said. "But I also didn't have much of a choice—and it was seen as a huge opportunity, to get sent abroad to live with relatives. What about what you've just done, a whole new career change? To me, *that's* brave."

Joanna agreed, saying, "I admit, it was a big decision. But I had to. I was miserable at my old job." She stopped there, not wanting to elaborate on what had happened with her love life at the law firm.

The food arrived, two steaming bowls of thin noodles in a mouthwatering broth topped with delicate shrimp wontons and a plate of warm fried pork buns to share between them. *Alright, I did it!* Joanna cheered herself.

"Well done, Miss Joanna! No jellyfish salads here," Jack said, giving Joanna a little round of applause before picking up his chopsticks. "And you ordered *sheng jian bao*, too? Bravo!"

Joanna felt silly being applauded for such a small feat, but she did find comfort knowing that if she found herself wandering the streets of Taipei alone, at least she wouldn't starve. She picked up her large spoon and took a sip of the hot soup. "Mmm," she breathed. "Delicious."

"Hao chi," Jack said, translating her words into Mandarin, and Joanna repeated them.

"Does that translate into *good eat*?" she asked.

"Yes, that's the literal translation of the two words."

"And how would I say *really delicious*?"

"You'd say *hen hao chi. Hen* means *very*," Jack explained.

"Okay, so *very good eat*?" Joanna confirmed.

"That's right in Mandarin. English, maybe less so," Jack said, a twinkle in one eye.

"Ha ha," Joanna said, picking up a wonton with her chopsticks and bringing it to her lips to gently blow on it.

"So, am I forgiven for making you do the lake jump?" Jack asked, grabbing a pork bun and breaking it in half.

"I'm still suspicious of your teaching techniques," she answered, waving her chopsticks at him. "But I'll admit this soup is pretty darn good."

As they both continued savoring the food, Danny Chen emerged from the back of the restaurant and walked up to their table. "Mr. Sun, Ms. Lin, so wonderful to see you both!"

"Nice to see you again, Danny!" Joanna greeted him.

"Maja talks about her two favorite teachers all the time!" he said. "I'll go tell her you're here. She's just with my son, Gabriel, in the back."

A few seconds later, Danny came back out, this time trailed by Maja and a young boy with an adorable spiky haircut and a T-shirt with a picture of a plump cartoon dumpling on it.

"Hi, Maja, Gabriel!" Joanna greeted the children. "What have you two been up to?"

"We just made some dumplings. Well, actually

I made some. Gabriel mostly just ate the dough," Maja said.

Danny laughed, adding, "Maja's supposed to be just watching Gabriel while I work, but she's also a huge help in the kitchen. She made an entire batch of these buns yesterday while Gabriel was napping! I really should be paying her as a chef." He turned and smiled at Maja, saying some words to her in Mandarin. She answered in a modest tone.

"Really, you made the buns we just had?" Jack asked, adding something in Mandarin that ended in *hen hao chi*.

Joanna was thrilled that she understood what he had just said and repeated it as well. "I was just about to get another order to go." She pointed at the plate on their table, which was empty, save for a few black sesame seeds.

"It's not so different from making the bread at our bakery," Maja said, shrugging. She looked at her watch. "Actually, Mr. Chen, I need to leave. I told my mom I'd be back by now."

"Sure," Danny answered. "But wait, my father wanted to give you another book. It's full of interesting stories he thought you might enjoy." He walked over to the back counter and retrieved a paper bag, and passed it over to Maja.

She accepted it eagerly, and immediately pulled out the book and began flipping through it. "Oh!" she exclaimed, then asked him something in Mandarin.

Danny responded, then said something to Jack, and a lively conversation between the three started. After a few more exchanges, Maja left and Danny took his son back to the kitchen, thanking Jack and Joanna for dining and wishing them a pleasant day.

"It really would be a great loss if she couldn't continue studying Chinese," Jack said, nodding toward the front door where Maja had just exited. He told Joanna about Maja's parent-teacher conference, and how he had even asked Miss Wei-Wei for help in gathering resources for Maja. "I sent home a folder of materials for her parents to look over but I haven't heard anything back yet."

Oh, is that what Jack and Wei-Wei were talking about the other day? Although I distinctly recall Wei-Wei asking Jack if he wanted children. That's more than a discussion about Maja...

Refocusing on the conversation, Joanna observed, "I didn't understand what she said, but the way Maja chattered on with Mr. Chen about the book he gave her, she really seemed animated."

"That was rude of us. I should have translated for you," Jack said. She quickly waved him off and he continued, "Maja asked him if it was a book that explained the backstory behind the idioms, as she said she really enjoys those stories."

"It certainly does seem like she has a passion for Chinese."

Jack nodded sadly. "But there isn't any more I can do… I don't want to overstep with her parents."

"Do you think it's what Maja wants?" Joanna asked. "To continue studying Chinese?"

"I think so, yes," Jack answered.

"And she's told her parents?"

"I assume so. You know Maja—she's not one to hold back on what she thinks."

Joanna recalled the many times Maja had expressed her opinion on someone else's artwork in her classroom, rather bluntly. "Yes, that's for sure. But is it possible she hasn't told them? Maybe they don't really know how important it is to her. Maybe she doesn't even know herself."

"You could be right," Jack said, appearing to be thinking this over as he stared out the window to the street. "Sometimes it can be hard to tell parents how one really feels," he said, a faraway look in his eyes.

Joanna gazed at Jack, suddenly feeling like he was a world away, and wishing he would tell her what he was thinking.

CHAPTER ELEVEN

THE NEXT DAY at school, Jack found a break when the rest of his students were working in small groups to call Maja over to his desk.

"Hi, Mei-Ya," he said in Mandarin. "Do you mind if I ask you something?"

Maja shrugged in a detached manner. "Sure."

"I wanted to ask you if you were interested in continuing to study Chinese after you leave elementary school."

Maja looked back at Jack, her eyes focused squarely on his. "Is this about the packet you asked me to give to my parents?"

Jack nodded. "Do you know if they've had a chance to review it yet?"

Maja maintained her gaze. "Yes. I heard them discussing it. They're worried there won't be enough time outside of regular school and helping at the store." Her tone was flat, and it was hard for Jack to tell how she felt about all of this.

"And what do you think?" Jack asked. He didn't want to suggest that he disagreed with her parents, so he held back adding any more commentary.

"Well, they are my parents…" Maja said in English, then trailed off.

"Right," Jack said. "They certainly are your parents." He sent Maja back to her desk.

A few hours later, Jack walked into the teachers' lounge for lunch, where he found Wei-Wei and Alex already sitting together at a table near the door.

"Hi, Wei-Wei, Alex. May I join you?" he asked.

"Of course," they both answered. After he retrieved his bag lunch from the refrigerator, Jack sat down, first briefly catching up Alex on the Maja situation, then relaying to both women his interaction with Maja earlier that morning.

"So her parents haven't responded to you about the materials we compiled?" Wei-Wei asked. She shook her head. "That's a shame. She really is quite special."

"And it's not just her," Alex said, shaking her head as well, but more vigorously. "It's a shame for all our students! After these kids leave here, it's going to be so hard for them to retain their Mandarin knowledge if they don't continue their exposure. So many of my friends growing up—the ones who were only in China for a few years—after they left, they completely forgot all the Chinese they had learned. I don't want to see that happen to any of our students."

Jack agreed, and told them about his conversation with Principal Malik, how the school board still had not agreed to add Chinese classes in the middle school, despite the success of Lakeland Elementary.

"That's so disappointing." Alex wrinkled her brow. "He has to keep on trying."

"It sounds like he is," Jack said. "But it's been a slow process. In the meantime, I think Wei-Wei and I have done all we can to try to convince Maja's parents."

Wei-Wei pursed her lips. "I'm afraid that sometimes, there's only so much we can do. At some point it has to be up to the student. But your efforts are commendable."

"I think Maja does want to keep learning," Jack said. "It's her parents that have to be willing to commit time and resources, which unfortunately they don't have a lot of, given their family business. And it seems like maybe Maja doesn't know, or is afraid to express to them what she really wants."

Something I can definitely sympathize with.

Just then, Joanna entered the lounge, wearing an artist's apron. Jack waved at her, but after a glance at their table, she quickly strode over to the fridge, grabbed her insulated lunch bag, then turned straight back around to leave.

As she was almost at the door, she said, "Oh hi, Wei-Wei, Alex, Jack. How's everyone doing today?"

"Good, how are you doing?" Jack asked, feeling like something was off. "Is everything okay?"

"Yes, everything is fine. I just, um, need to get back to my classroom," Joanna answered, clutching her lunch bag against her apron. "I need to, er, finish something before my next class."

"You're welcome to join us for lunch," Alex invited her, pointing to the empty chair at their table.

"But also, don't feel like you have to," Wei-Wei added, "if you're in the middle of something. We all know how that goes."

"Thanks," Joanna said. "I'll catch up with you all later." Just as she was walking out the door, however, she stopped, as if remembering something. Her face brightened and she looked right at Jack. "Jack!" she exclaimed.

Jack's ears perked up. "Yes?"

"I just thought about something for Maja Andresson. Did you find out if she's spoken to her parents?"

"She has, but not like I had hoped," Jack answered, and told her about his conversation with Maja this morning.

"I think I can work on something with her during art class this week," Joanna offered.

"That would be amazing. What are you thinking?"

"The fifth graders are still completing their projects from last week, but I'm pretty sure Maja already finished hers. I was planning on giving those who were already done some free creative time. Let me see what I can do," Joanna said. "Maybe something will come out of it that can help!"

THE NEXT MORNING, Joanna announced to the fifth grade class, "For those students who are already done with their landscapes, feel free to grab a large sheet of paper and use any materials in the classroom—pastels, color pencils, paint, paper cuttings, anything—to make a piece of work expressing this theme. Happiness."

The room stirred as students started brainstorming ideas. "We can use anything?" one student asked, raising his hand. "Like, literally, anything?"

"If you can find it in the cabinets, you can use it," Joanna said. "But let's keep things neat and orderly, okay? Just take what you need and clean up after yourself. I know you can be responsible."

Another student asked, "What if I want to put a photo of my dog on mine?"

"Sure, that's fine," she answered. "You can bring in photos or anything from home that you want to include next week. But be careful about what you put on the page—every item should have meaning and purpose." She gave some more guidelines about contrast and space, and then let the kids loose.

Joanna watched Maja carefully as she planned out her collage.

She's deliberate, Joanna noticed, as Maja went

over to the cabinet and pulled out only a few items compared to her classmates, many of whom looked to be trying to use every single art supply available. Joanna continued to observe Maja, who, once seated with her supplies, did not get up again to get more materials. In fact, Joanna didn't see Maja look up at all during the entire period.

Joanna wanted to go over and take a peek at what Maja was working on, but she decided to give her room to create without a teacher looming over her.

At the end of the period, Joanna instructed everyone to leave their work on a side counter to dry. Maja set her poster down, and Joanna walked over to look at it.

Wow.

When Jack came back to get his class, Joanna asked him if he could send the students back to his classroom on their own. "I want to show you something," she told him.

As the class filed off by themselves—led by Maja, who Jack had put in charge—Joanna directed Jack over to where the day's projects were laid out.

"I told them to create a page with the theme of happiness. Look what Maja created." She knew she wouldn't have to point out which one was Maja's.

Placed neatly in the corner, Maja's collage was full of Chinese characters and designs. In the middle of the page, she had drawn herself in charcoal from behind, two yellow braids hanging down her back. The figure sat at a desk and was reading a book filled with tiny, neat Chinese characters that Maja had written using a fine ink pen. Down the sides of the poster, Maja had drawn two scrolls, the left one with the words *I love learning Chinese* in English, and the right one with several Chinese characters written vertically on it.

"I assume that means the same thing as the English words?" Joanna asked Jack, pointing to the scroll on the right.

"Yes," Jack said. "Soon you'll be able to read all of those characters."

"But not these!" Joanna pointed to the book page Maja had written. "They look very advanced."

Jack squinted. "You're right, it might take a little longer for you to understand those. This is incredible. Did she copy that from somewhere?"

"I'm not sure. I didn't see her take any books out. What does it say?"

"It's from a very famous classic Chinese novel. I've taught it to my older students, but an abridged version, as the original text is quite difficult. It's astounding Maja has even heard of it, much less can quote it."

"Maybe Danny Chen or his parents gave her a copy, or read it to her?"

"Yes, could be," Jack said, his face still showing awe.

Joanna admired the poster. "I'd say it's pretty definitive what Maja wants. It's right here in front of us."

"Thank you so much for this, Joanna," Jack said, smiling broadly at her. "Let's see what happens when she shows this to her parents."

"YOUR EASTER LILY'S finally budding!" Mindy exclaimed as she walked into Joanna's classroom later that week.

Joanna glanced over at her window. "Darn it! I've been so busy I've totally forgotten to water it. Luckily it seems to have done fine despite my neglect." She looked closer and saw the plant's stem was now full of thick, spiky leaves, like the top of a pineapple, and three tight, light green buds had finally formed.

"See, I told you to just have a little patience," Mindy said.

"You're right, you did," Joanna replied as she went over to the sink to fill a cup with water. "Thank you again for giving it to me."

"Of course. I'm so happy to see it thriving."

"How's your week been? I feel like I've barely seen you," Joanna said to her friend as she emptied the cup into the lily's pot.

"Yes, it's been really hectic with state testing happening next week—lots of stressed-out teachers and students," Mindy explained.

"I know how that feels," Joanna said, thinking about her upcoming Chinese test.

"How's the tutoring going?" Mindy asked. "You and Jack looked really chummy getting out of the lake the other day, huh? Alex mentioned she thought she saw sparks, too."

Joanna's face flushed as she thought about Jack putting a towel around her.

Oh no. There's already gossip about Jack and me?

"I was glad to just be out of that freezing water," she said, trying to change the subject quickly. "I still can't believe I actually did it. Next year, you'll have to join."

"Not a chance," Mindy said, her tone definitive.

"Anyways, the tutoring is going fine. I'm actually really enjoying writing characters," Joanna said.

Mindy made a frowny face. "Ugh, writing is the worst part for me! I can recognize them, but then when it comes to actually recalling each stroke, it's so hard. Maybe because you're an artist, it's easier for you?"

Joanna nodded. "Could be. I find it so beautiful. Each character is like a tiny work of art."

"That's true," Mindy agreed. "Miss Wei-Wei runs an after-school calligraphy class and every time I watch her write, I'm mesmerized."

"Oh, yes," Joanna said. "Jack said he'd ask her to do an individual lesson for me."

"It certainly sounds like he's going above and beyond," Mindy said, her eyebrows starting to dance. "Has there been a connection, beyond the material?"

"Aw now, stop it," Joanna said.

Mindy headed for the door. "In all seriousness, I'm so glad to hear it's going well. Jack sounds like a fantastic teacher."

"Yes, it's so nice of him to do all of this for me," Joanna agreed, "seeing as how Principal Malik kind of just sprang it on him last minute."

"Maybe you should offer to do something for him, too," Mindy suggested.

"Not a bad idea," Joanna said. "But I don't mean in the way you're thinking, Mindy."

Mindy smirked and waved as she left Joanna's classroom.

Joanna thought about earlier that week, when Wei-Wei and Alex had given her weird looks when she walked into the teachers' lounge.

Alex mentioned something to Mindy about Jack and me at the lake jump! And Wei-Wei basically tried to shoo me away.

Ugh, I shouldn't have stayed to talk to Jack about Maja in front of everyone.

She hadn't planned on doing so, but the idea for Maja just popped up in her head and she couldn't stop herself.

Or is everything perfectly normal and I'm just

imagining all of this, because of what happened back at the law firm?

Joanna shuddered as she recalled letting it slip to another paralegal that she and Tim were dating. Joanna had been excited to tell someone, but her coworker's icy look made it clear that she shouldn't have. Soon after that, everyone started treating her differently—more deferential at times, but also taking her less seriously, because she was dating a partner.

It would have saved me so much heartache and wasted time if I had just kept things professional with Tim.

Still, Joanna did agree with Mindy that it would be nice to do something for Jack, given how much time and effort he was putting into tutoring her.

But it would have to be outside of school. The last thing I need right now is to have all the staff thinking we're a couple.

Joanna wandered back to her Easter lily to admire its growth for a few more minutes before her next class arrived. As she was appreciating the fine lines in the plant's leaves, her eyes flicked up to one of the sunset paintings from her first day of school.

She remembered something Jack had told her when they had first met.

I think I've got something he might like!

CHAPTER TWELVE

Jack arrived at the waterfront on Saturday evening, unsure what to expect. He'd been wondering what Joanna had planned for him ever since she'd messaged him last night to see if he was free to meet at Lakeland's lighthouse.

"Surprise!" Joanna waved at him from the big lawn in front of the catwalk that led to the historic structure. Her hair was loose tonight, and she wore an oversize button-down shirt that was covered, notably, by a painter's apron.

"Hi! What's all this?" Jack asked, taking in the items Joanna had set up on the grass: two easels and two stools, paints and brushes laid out on a small table, and a second white apron hanging off one of the easels. "I have a feeling I may be in over my head."

Joanna held her arms out wide toward the arrangement. "I promise that your head will stay above water today. You were so nice to set up the lake jump for me last weekend, I thought I'd return the favor and get you to face *your* fear of not being 'good at art.'"

Jack chuckled. "I definitely did not expect this! Are you sure you want to take me on as a student?"

"Yes," Joanna said. "We're going to paint the sunset, and it looks like we're going to get another beautiful one tonight!"

Jack looked to the horizon and saw that Joanna was, of course, correct—the sun was on its descent, just peeking out from behind a cloud, and the sky was a vibrant mix of yellows and reds. Behind her, the lighthouse cut a silhouette against the sky, and the lake shimmered all around.

"I still can't get over how gorgeous the sunsets are here," he said. "And I can't believe you set all this up for me. But just so you know, the last formal art class I took, back when I was just a kid, ended in tears."

"No!" Joanna reacted with a mini frown. "That bad, huh? Was the teacher really strict?"

"I don't think so," he replied. "But to clarify, it wasn't me doing the crying." His mouth curled up on one side.

Joanna's eyebrows shot up. "Wait, did *you* make the *teacher* cry?"

Jack laughed. "No, it was my mother! When she came to pick me up, she looked at my drawing and was so embarrassed at my lack of talent—

or maybe it was just my inability to follow basic instructions?—that she wept."

"Come on, really?" Joanna asked, shaking her head in disbelief.

"For real! I told her that I wanted to drop out of the class, and she agreed, enrolling my brother in my place."

"Aw, how sad!" Joanna grabbed the apron from the easel and passed it to him.

"It's alright. My brother's a very talented graphic designer now. He really owes his entire career to me," Jack joked as he put the apron over his head but struggled to tie the strings behind his back. "And to his credit, his idea for printed fabrics has really transformed our textile business. So they tell me, at least."

"But that was it for you, huh? The end of your art education?" Joanna asked, following up with, "Do you need some help with that?"

"Yes, thank you." He gratefully let go of the apron strings as Joanna darted behind his back. A tingle shot through Jack's upper body as he felt her tie the apron firmly around his waist.

Whoa, he thought. He was suddenly acutely aware of how physically close the two of them were, and not sitting in a classroom hunched over a Chinese workbook.

Trying to stay cool, Jack said, "Anyways, I never took another art class after that."

"Until now," Joanna said, pointing at one of the

stools. "Come on, we better get started before the sun leaves us."

"Right," he said, gingerly sitting down. "What do I do first?"

"Just follow me," Joanna said, taking her seat and selecting one of the larger paintbrushes from the table between the easels.

"Okay, here goes nothing," Jack said, choosing a similarly sized paintbrush himself. He watched Joanna dip the brush into the red paint on her palette.

"What colors do you see in the sky?" Joanna asked, as she expertly started to blend yellow into the red.

"Um, yellow and red? Maybe some purple?" Jack said, feeling silly. "Sorry, is that too simple? I'm sure there are more descriptive colors to describe it."

Joanna smiled. "Simple is good! It looks red, yellow and purple to me. And I'm guessing I don't need to tell you that when red and yellow are mixed, they make…"

Jack chuckled and finished her sentence. "…orange!"

"Bingo! Are you sure you haven't taken a painting class recently?" Joanna teased. Apparently satisfied with the color she had created, she started painting the top half of the scene, using long, smooth strokes across her canvas. "Feel free to start whenever you're ready. Start with the lighter yellow paint first, and then gradually go darker."

Jack immediately started peppering her with questions before starting. "Is this paintbrush okay? How much pressure? Should I use the fat part of the brush or the tip? Does this color look right to you? What if I mess up?"

"Wow, so many questions!" Joanna laughed. "You're overthinking this. A wise teacher once told me 'Just jump in!'"

"Ha ha," Jack said. He refrained from asking anything else as he tried to mimic what she was doing on her palette, blending the reds, yellows and oranges together to match the real sky in front of them as best as he could.

He tentatively pressed his brush against the blank canvas to start his first stroke, with Joanna bobbing her head in encouragement. "Yup, there you go!"

Jack laughed, saying, "If my mother could see me now!"

"She must miss you a lot, being so far away."

"She does, but we do message or talk quite often. Well, until recently," he admitted.

"Oh, why is that?"

With anyone else, Jack would have given a generic answer, but being there, painting on the shore at sunset—suddenly he wanted to tell Joanna everything: that he had been poised to move back to Taiwan, then took the Lakeland job at the last minute to help an old friend, but truthfully was just stalling as he felt conflicted about giving up his life here in the US.

And yet, he held himself back, saying only, "It's not easy. Dealing with family relationships, especially from so far away."

Somehow, he couldn't say the words "I really don't want to quit teaching to run my family's company."

It feels disrespectful to even think it.

"I can't imagine," Joanna said, stopping her brush movements to look at him. "I've been happy living out here on my own, but I know my mom is just a few hours' drive away. Although I do worry about her, now that she's alone."

"Were you and your father close?" Jack asked.

"Yes…very. And it was my dad, basically at his deathbed, who really made me take the big step to start a new career. He knew I had been working as a paralegal long enough to know I didn't love it, and that there was something else out there that would bring me real joy. He told me to follow my heart." Her voice broke, and she had to use the edge of her apron to dab her eyes.

"He sounds wonderful," Jack said, wanting to give her a hug but thinking that might be inappropriate. Instead, he continued following her lead by moving on to paint the bottom half of the scene, the lake. *And how brave that you actually took the steps to live the life you wanted*, he thought.

"Yes, he was pretty wonderful."

After a few minutes of quiet painting, Joanna paused to lean back, saying, "I think we're ready to add a few things in the foreground. What do you think?"

"Um, sure," Jack said.

He watched as Joanna selected a thinner brush and dipped it into the black paint, then skillfully drew the silhouette of the lighthouse, the catwalk, and a few birds onto her painting.

Jack stared at her, mesmerized by her movements. "You make it look so easy," he said.

"You can do it, too," Joanna encouraged. "Just give it a try. Be careful with the black paint, though. Any mistakes now will be hard to fix!"

Jack made an expression of mock horror as he attempted a small bird near the top corner of his painting. "I'm so impressed with how comfortable you are at instruction, given you just started teaching. I really can't believe you haven't taught before."

As the sun slowly set, they continued painting, with Jack in awe of how intense Joanna was, how much focus she put into giving him instructions.

"You're amazing, Joanna. It's no wonder my students clamor to get in line to go to art class every Tuesday morning."

"Thank you, that's so nice of you to say," Joanna said, and her eyes lit up. "I feel very lucky for sure that I got this job. There were a few stumbles in the beginning, and I wouldn't say it's been all smooth sailing, but I just love seeing the kids find their own expression through art. It does feel pretty awesome. Now I just have to pass that Chinese test."

"Don't worry, we'll get you there," Jack said confidently.

As the horizon was cutting the sun in a near perfect semicircle, Joanna set down her paintbrush. "Alright, let's take a look," she said.

Jack set his brush down as well, saying, "Okay. How did I do? Not too bad? Give it to me straight, Miss Joanna."

Joanna stood up and walked over to Jack's easel, saying, "I'd say it's a lot better than 'not too bad!' It's fantastic, Jack!"

Jack felt silly, but he had to admit he was proud of his work. It was nothing compared to Joanna's, of course, but it did actually resemble a lighthouse at sunset. "It's only because I had a great teacher," he said, thanking her.

As they sat admiring their paintings and watching the sun disappear, Joanna suggested a selfie. "I can take it," Jack offered, and she handed him her phone. "Let's move the stools a bit closer to the easels."

Just as he was taking the photo, a strong wind blew in from the shore, knocking over his easel, painting and all.

"Oh gosh!" Joanna cried out before falling

right into Jack's open arms, knocking him off his stool.

They both tumbled to the grass in a heap. As Jack scrambled to get his bearings, his eyes locked on Joanna's, and for a moment, Jack felt the world stop.

The scent of Joanna's perfume filled the air and all Jack could see was her lovely face, eclipsing the sunset behind her.

Is this really happening? Joanna in my arms?

"Is your painting okay?" Joanna broke the silence, leaning over to check on the front side of the painting that she had miraculously managed to catch before it hit the ground. "Did it smear?"

Jack lifted Joanna up, set her gently on her feet and checked it himself. "Not a single smudge. What a catch, Joanna! Everything's just perfect."

And indeed, the moment *was* perfect, the violet sky above them, the tiny smear of yellow paint on Joanna's collarbone, the intoxicating fresh scent of her hair.

Looking into her eyes again, Jack started to lean in toward Joanna.

But, as much as he wanted to kiss her, he stopped himself.

I'm about to leave this country forever. I can't start something right now. It wouldn't be fair to her.

So, instead, he gently wiped the paint off the side of her collarbone with his thumb and said,

"Now *that* was some serious dedication to saving your student's artwork!"

BACK AT HOME later that night, Joanna replayed the evening over and over in her mind. It had been such a fun time. But, when Jack was talking about his mother, he seemed to be holding back from telling her something, but what, exactly, she didn't know.

I can't push him, she thought. *He'll tell me in his own time, if he wants to.*

Still, the evening with Jack had felt unreal, almost magical: the sunset, painting together, the wind blowing his easel over, the crash landing into his arms.

And she had felt such a *sizzle* when his arms circled her after she fell. Closing her eyes, Joanna imagined it happening again. Then she remembered they had been trying to take a selfie, and she reached for her phone to pull it up.

Oh my!

Joanna laughed out loud. Jack had captured the exact instant when Joanna dove to catch the painting, her eyes and mouth wide open and arms completely outstretched. Meanwhile, Jack was just sitting there, posing like a media personality, a beat slower in realizing what was happening.

Joanna zoomed in on Jack's face, admiring his cheekbones and dimples. Zooming back out, she couldn't help but think they made a cute couple. Heat filled her chest and rose up to her face.

Then she caught herself.

Stop, Joanna. You cannot let this happen again.

I promised Dad. I'm not going to let a work crush get in the way of achieving my goal.

She remembered Wei-Wei trying to get her away from Jack the other day at lunch.

She's clearly interested in him. I definitely don't want to make an enemy at work. Principal Malik already thinks I'm not engaging enough with others.

Jack is just a nice colleague. That's all.

But as she picked up her phone to look once again at the photo they had taken together, she thought, *Oh, Handsome Jack, what have you done to me?*

CHAPTER THIRTEEN

JACK WOKE UP to the sound of birds chirping and a giddy feeling in his chest. It was official: he was in serious trouble. If he'd thought he was in deep before, now he had sunk to the bottom of the ocean.

Painting at the lighthouse with Joanna had been an incredible experience. Before that, he had been attracted to her, yes, but last night, seeing her in action, hearing her speak so passionately about her career change and learning about how determined she had been to start her life over—all Jack wanted to do was see her again as soon as possible.

She's an excellent student, too. Based on her current progress, he didn't see any issues with her passing the level one CPT next month.

Joanna was the only thing he could think about all morning, and he wondered if she had felt something, too.

It couldn't have been just me, he thought, reliving the moment when she fell into his arms after catching his painting.

Then he felt self-conscious so, wanting to impress her, he sat down at his desk and started reworking the lessons he'd planned for the remaining few weeks over and over until it felt exactly right. He began researching nearby outings that could fit with each lesson.

She'll love this, Jack thought, as he confirmed the opening hours of the botanical gardens. *Hopefully, she didn't already go there on her own. Maybe we can do another painting session, too.*

He reached for his phone and started typing a message to Joanna. As he imagined them sitting side by side, brushes in hand, looking at each other like they did last night, a message from his brother came in.

Jonathan: Free for a video call? Just wanted to catch up!

Jack initiated the call, and his brother's face appeared on the screen, with a backdrop of his living room and Taipei's nightscape showing through his floor-to-ceiling windows.

"Hey, big brother," Jonathan said in Mandarin. "It's been a while!"

"Yes, how are you?" Jack answered, feeling bad when he realized that he hadn't actually spoken to his brother since moving to Lakeland. "Sorry I've been out of touch. This move to Michigan was very last minute, and it's been nonstop since I arrived."

"No worries," his brother responded. "You look good. Seems like it suits you! Meeting some nice people out there?"

Jack couldn't hide a broad smile as he thought about Joanna. "Er, yes, everyone at the school is really great. And it's beautiful here, although, I gotta admit, that's quite a view you got there from your living room."

Jonathan turned the camera so the entire cityscape filled the screen. "Speaking of my living room, Ma was asking me if you wanted to move into your old room at home or with me here? Of course, happy to have you stay."

Jack couldn't imagine living in either place, but he answered, "Staying with you sounds great, thanks! I'll start looking for a place of my own as soon as I get there, though."

"No rush at all."

"Cool, thanks a lot. Looking forward to seeing you."

"Likewise, but you really do look happy. Are you sure you're ready to leave there?" Jonathan asked.

Jack shrugged off his brother, saying, "Can't wait for Ma's cooking, that's for sure!"

The two chatted for a few minutes more, catching up on this and that, then Jack thanked Jonathan again for letting him crash at his place, and disconnected the call.

He returned to the message he had started to Joanna, but stopped himself. The call from his brother was a stark reminder that his life was about to change very soon.

"IT'S BEEN HARD to connect with you these last couple weeks," Joanna's mother said. "How are the Mandarin tutoring sessions going?"

"They're going well!" Joanna answered. "We just finished lesson six and I'm feeling pretty good so far." She couldn't hold back from gushing about the previous night, although she did withhold some details about Jack. *If Mom finds out I'm spending three nights a week with a handsome, single man, I'll never hear the end of it.* "I was also out painting on the coast last night, near Lakeland's historic lighthouse. It was just so beautiful out there," she said. She caught a glimpse of her reflection in the front entryway mirror, and couldn't refrain from smiling at herself.

Carol picked up on Joanna's energy, despite the fact that they were speaking by phone. "That's so wonderful, Joanna. I'm so happy for you, too. See, everything's working out splendidly for you, just like I told you it all would."

"Well, let's not get ahead of ourselves," she told her mother. "I still need to pass the Chinese test and, of course, keep up with my students."

"Yes, of course," Carol responded. "But I have full confidence that you can do this. And it sounds like you're getting out to see the sights, which is great, too, now that it's really reaching the peak of spring! Were you out painting last night by yourself, or were you with someone?"

"Oh, I was just with a friend," Joanna answered, quickly transitioning to describing how beautiful the flowers and trees were all around town. "It's seriously gorgeous here, Mom. Did you see all the photos I sent of the flowers lining my street? And just this morning, I saw a bird's nest on a tree branch outside my front window. There were three tiny eggs in it!" Joanna said. "I'll send you another photo!"

"There really isn't anything like spring in Michigan," Carol said.

"You got that right," Joanna agreed.

"Seems like maybe it's the right time to meet someone? What do you think?"

All that springtime talk wasn't enough to distract her!

"Sorry, Mom, can I take another rain check? I've just got a lot going on right now."

"Sure, honey, I understand," her mother said, but Joanna could hear the discontent in her voice.

After she hung up, Joanna pulled up the selfie from the night before.

She admitted to herself that now the reason she

didn't want her mom to set her up wasn't because she wanted to focus on her job.

It was because she was falling for Jack.

This is bad. I need to do something, and soon.

She started a message to Jack.

Joanna: Hey, are you free right now?

Jack: Sure, everything okay?

Joanna: Yes, just wanted to chat if you're available.

Jack: Was just going to go for a run. I could stop by your place in about fifteen minutes?

Fifteen minutes! Joanna rushed to change out of her pajamas and apply a bit of makeup before Jack arrived at her doorstep.

When he did arrive, he appeared to be just out of the shower, hair still wet and smelling like aftershave. He grinned broadly when Joanna opened her front door to greet him. "Good morning," he said.

"Morning!" she replied. "Thanks for coming on such short notice. Want to walk to the Swiss Bakery and then on down to the waterfront?"

"Sounds great," Jack responded.

It was a beautiful morning, and Main Street was in full bloom, flowers of all types and colors lining the sidewalk. Joanna soaked in the scenery, though she knew that Jack was waiting for her to initiate a conversation.

They entered the Swiss Bakery, where the delightful smells of coffee and butter filled the air. After greeting Maja's father, Luca, who was behind the counter, they both placed their orders.

SITTING ON A bench outside as they waited for their food to be ready, Jack looked expectantly at Joanna. He had enjoyed their walk over but was curious why she had asked to meet. "So, what's on your mind?" he asked.

Joanna turned to face him. Taking a deep breath, she said, "Maybe this is all presumptuous but…"

Jack wanted to reach out and touch her hand or cheek but held back.

"…I had such a great time last night, being on the shore at sunset, getting to know you more and painting together. And actually, not just last night, the past few weeks have been amazing. I've learned so much from you. You really are a wonderful teacher, Jack."

"And you as well," he said, thinking there had to be a *but* coming.

"I've felt a connection with you, but… I wanted you to know more about my past."

Ah, there it is.

"At my old job, a law firm, I started dating an older attorney," she said. "Right from the beginning, it created resentment among my colleagues. I probably didn't handle it the best, and I thought I was in love with him, but then as time went on, I realized I wasn't in love with either him or the job." Joanna explained that the relationship made her stay at the law firm much longer than she should have. "By the end, I didn't know who I was or what I wanted. After that, I promised myself to never let it happen again—let a relationship dictate my career," she said.

So she did feel something too, Jack thought. It was a small consolation given what she'd said after that, but at least he hadn't imagined it all.

"Thank you for telling me all this, Joanna," he said. "I understand, completely. I've felt a connection with you, too. And the past few weeks have been amazing for me as well. But I shouldn't be starting a relationship with anyone right now, since, as you know, I'll be leaving Lakeland in just a few weeks."

Joanna nodded slowly, her eyes filled with sadness. "I know. You're already planning to return home to Taiwan…" she said, sounding like she was asking a question.

Jack opened his mouth, nearly saying *It doesn't feel like home anymore*, but he bit his tongue yet again. "Yes, I am. So it seems like we're on the same page," he said instead.

It's over before it even started, Jack thought. *But this is how it has to be.*

Professionalism took over. "I'm really glad we talked. We both know that whatever we have between us can't go anywhere. But don't worry, I'm still taking my teaching duties very seriously. I'll get you to pass that Chinese test if it's the last thing I do. I know how important it is to you."

"Thank you for that," she responded. "I really appreciate it. And of course I'm happy to continue teaching you how to paint and even basic drawing, if you want."

"I do, definitely," he said. "And if you're worried about other teachers gossiping about us, we can keep our lessons out of school and away from prying eyes. Not that there will be anything to gossip about."

Joanna nodded, looking crestfallen. "Yes, that sounds like the right thing to do."

CHAPTER FOURTEEN

THE NEXT SUNDAY MORNING, a week later, saw the first official practice of this year's Lakeland Elementary dragon boat racing team. Joanna once again found herself standing on the shore of Lake Michigan, facing Coach Clay. He looked much more serious today, not joking around or doing silly dances to rev up the crowd like he had at the lake jump a couple of weeks ago.

He cast his eyes around the group slowly, as if inspecting them all.

Stopping at Alex, he pointed at her shirt and asked, "Is that dry-fit?"

"Um, I'm not sure?" she responded. She looked down at her torso, her normally cool appearance shaken by Coach's unusually harsh tone.

Coach pointed at her feet. "What about those shoes, are they waterproof?"

"I doubt it," Alex answered, frowning. "They're just, like, regular running shoes."

"Then take them off," he said. Projecting his voice to everyone, he announced, "You all should be wearing waterproof shoes or nothing at all! No flip-flops, either!" He turned to Mindy. "Ms. Perez, did you bring the gloves?"

"Yes, Coach!" She hurried to pull out a glove from the canvas bag she was holding to show him, and he immediately instructed her to distribute the gray-and-black half-finger gloves to everyone.

"Whoa, this is serious business," Joanna said to Mindy, thankful that she'd had the foresight to ask Mindy what she should wear today, and thus avoided being scolded.

"No kidding," Mindy responded, as she handed Joanna the last pair of gloves.

After confirming that everyone was clear on the correct clothing and footwear for dragon boat racing, Coach Clay started pairing people up.

"Could Mindy and I sit together?" Joanna dared to ask, not wanting to be paired up with Jack. Since their conversation a week ago, they had been having her tutoring sessions at the Lakeland Library, managing to avoid catching the attention of anyone from school, and she wanted to keep it that way.

Thankfully, Coach concurred. "Yep, I got you two in the front. You'll be our pacers. Wei-Wei's on the drum, Jack and Alex will take the back row by me," Coach said, and then continued giving out the rest of the seating assignments.

"Is it safe to talk?" Joanna whispered to Mindy. "And is he like this every year?"

"I'm sorry I didn't warn you," Mindy whispered back. "He does a whole Mr. Hyde thing every year as the festival approaches. He really wants to crush Beverly Harbor—it irks him to no end that they always beat us."

"Fingers crossed we give him a win this year. Maybe then he'll be nicer to Alex." Joanna peeked over at the other teacher, who, to her surprise, seemed totally fine after being scolded. Alex was standing at the front of the boat, reaching around Wei-Wei to try to tap on the large, wooden drum, while Wei-Wei swatted her hand away.

"I'm really surprised at Alex. She should have known better. It's not like it's her first race," Mindy chastised. "Also, I assume you're okay that Coach paired Jack with her and not you?"

Joanna gave Mindy a look. "Of course!"

"Right, uh-huh." Mindy gave her a look back.

Not really thinking, perhaps to put Mindy off the hunt, Joanna blurted out, "You know, I'm actually thinking of finally letting my mom set me up."

"No, really?" Mindy was all ears. "I can't believe it! Good for you! Come on, Mrs. Lin, make us a match!" she whisper-cheered.

"Joanna, your mother is a matchmaker?" Wei-Wei asked, as she took her seat across from them behind the drum.

"Yes, but, well, not professionally," Joanna said. "Although she certainly acts like it's her

job sometimes. Why, do you want to get set up?"
She was joking, but Wei-Wei apparently wasn't.

"I might, yes," Wei-Wei answered.

"Okay, um, what kind of person are you looking for?" Joanna asked, suddenly seeing Wei-Wei
in a whole different light.

So she's not after Jack?

"Let's talk more after practice." Wei-Wei shot
a wary glance over to Coach, who appeared to
be inspecting yet another team member's T-shirt
material.

"Sure," Joanna said, quite intrigued with her
petite colleague now.

*Mom would LOVE to set her up. Maybe with
that guy she wants to push on me!*

Hearing that Wei-Wei wasn't interested in Jack
put Joanna instantly in a better mood. Though
Jack had continued her sessions all week, it had
been a bit awkward, with both of them unsure
how to act after agreeing to put the brakes on any
potential relationship.

As if reading her mind, Mindy piped up. "Hey,
do you know where Jack is? I'm surprised Coach
hasn't thrown a fit over him missing the first
practice."

"I'm not sure," Joanna answered, glancing
around. "I assumed he'd be here. Should I text
him?" She started to reach into her back pocket
for her phone.

Mindy stopped her, saying, "Yes, but maybe

don't do it right this second, because it looks like Coach is about to bark another order."

JACK HAD MISSED the first dragon boat practice because he had been up all night on a Sun Textiles board of directors meeting. His brother, Jonathan, ran the meeting, but their mother kept asking Jack for his input, stopping on almost every slide of the presentation to see what he thought. He wondered if Jonathan was annoyed by this, but it was impossible to tell over video conference, so Jack sent him a surreptitious message on the side.

Jack: Hey, sorry that Ma keeps interrupting the meeting for me.

Jonathan: All good. I do want to get you as involved as possible—I need all the help I can get!

It seemed to Jack that the company was doing fine, but what did he know? The CFO, a gray-haired bespectacled man who had worked for the company for years, spent twenty minutes going through the last fiscal year's financial results. Considering it was already way past his bedtime, Jack quickly found himself glazing over looking at all the numbers.

It was 1:00 a.m. in Michigan by the time the meeting was over, and then Jack received a message from his brother.

Jonathan: I did want to talk to you about something, though. Are you still up?

Hmm? Jack thought. *Could he be offering me a way out?* Feeling guilty for even thinking that, he quickly sent his brother a message saying he was available.

"Hi, Jonathan," Jack said, when the video call connected.

"Hi, big brother! Sorry, I know we just had a marathon meeting and it's already late there."

"No worries, what's up?" Jack asked.

His brother hesitated. "Ma wanted to wait to tell you in person when you got here…but I figured I'd give you a little heads-up so it doesn't totally take you by surprise."

"Oh no, is she sick?" Jack's chest tightened. *I really am a terrible son.*

"No, no," Jonathan said, shaking his head. "Sorry to scare you. Her health is great. Better than ever, in fact."

"Thank goodness," Jack said, exhaling in relief. "So, what is it, then?"

"Well…she says she's ready to retire."

Jack felt the tightness return. "Ah, really?"

"Yes, and I think she's quite serious. She's planning on giving the company formal notice at the next board meeting, when you're here."

"She definitely deserves it," Jack said. "She's put in enough years."

"Yes, she has," his brother agreed. "Looks like it's all working out—you coming back and Ma retiring."

There's really no turning back, then. "Yeah, it's all working out," Jack echoed.

After saying goodbye, despite the painfully late hour, Jack couldn't fall asleep. He kept thinking about the company and what he was going to do when he got back to Taiwan.

I don't have the skills to be CEO or CFO. Do I even qualify to be my brother's assistant?

Then he thought about Joanna, about her clear passion for teaching art, and it reminded him of why he, too, became a teacher. Helping Joanna learn Mandarin the past few weeks had reinforced his desire to continue his career in education. And Joanna's insistence on living her own life for herself—and not anyone else—was making him reexamine if he really wanted to work at Sun Textiles at all.

But that is what a dutiful son must do. I would disappoint and dishonor my family by declining.

When he groggily woke up with a bright sunbeam shining right into his eyes, Jack realized it was past noon and he had slept straight through dragon boat practice. Reaching for his phone to text Coach Clay and apologize, he saw Joanna had sent him a message.

Joanna: Missed you at practice this morning! Everything ok?

His mood brightening immediately, Jack quickly typed back a response.

Jack: Yeah, unfortunately had a company meeting until really late and I completely overslept.

Joanna: Want to meet at the library? I owe you a drawing lesson!

Jack: Sounds great, let's do it!

LATER THAT AFTERNOON, Joanna met Jack at the library, and they settled into one of the small group study rooms.

"Ah, I see the tables have turned," Jack said when she handed him a sketchbook and a pencil. "The student has become the teacher."

"That's right," she responded, smiling. "We'll start with the basics—of sketching, that is."

She opened the sketchbook and showed him what she had started. "Just like Chinese, we're going to start with basic shapes—lines, circles, rectangles, triangles—then progressing to 3D shapes—spheres, cubes, cones and cylinders."

Seeing the doubtful look on his face, she had to laugh. "Come on, you can do it!"

Jack slowly picked up the pencil, saying, "Alright, let's give it a go. I literally just start by drawing straight lines?"

"Yes, just tell me when you're ready to move on." Joanna chuckled seeing the timid look on his face as he put pencil to paper.

A few minutes later, after Jack had filled half the page with lines, he told Joanna he was ready to move on to shapes. "But first, let me see what *you're* working on," he said, checking her workbook, where she was reviewing characters from their past lessons.

"Do these all look good to you?" she asked him. She had definitely reached a new level with characters, no longer having to ask Jack what order the strokes should be in. Now, it was just a matter of practice, which she enjoyed quite a bit. After Jack approved of her work, she looked back to his sketchbook and instructed him to go on to drawing the basic shapes she had outlined for him.

They continued on like this for a few more rounds, alternating teacher and student roles with each other's respective material.

After Joanna saw that Jack felt comfortable with lines, rectangles and squares, she said, "Alright, moving on to circles. There are several ways to do it, but here's the one I started with." She showed him how to draw a cross, then diagonal lines, then connecting the ends of the lines with arcs to make a circle. "Don't feel like you need to do it all in one stroke. Light lines are fine until you feel more confident."

His first few circles seemed very shaky.

"Don't think, just feel," she reminded him. "Eventually, you'll get to the point where you can draw a perfect circle at any time. It just takes repetition and practice."

"Just like learning Chinese characters, huh?"

"Exactly!" The tension between them seemed to have lifted, now that Joanna was in teaching mode, too.

As they were both at work, they settled back into easy conversation.

"So, about missing dragon boat practice this morning? How did Coach Clay let you get away with that?" Joanna asked, as she continued filling in her workbook.

"I feel really bad about that. I definitely owe him one now." Jack explained he'd had a late-night board meeting. "It didn't finish until well past midnight."

"A board meeting on a Saturday night? That seems unusual, no?"

Jack nodded. "My mother scheduled it specifically for my benefit, as she didn't want me to lose any sleep on a school night."

"That was considerate of her."

"I guess, although I'm sure the rest of the board wasn't thrilled to have to call in on a Sunday morning…" Jack trailed off, appearing to be lost in a large circle on his page. "Ack," he said. "Can I erase?"

"Sure," Joanna said, reaching into her supply box and tossing him an eraser. "Nothing's set in stone." She watched as he carefully erased the shape he had drawn and started over. "Did your brother also come here to study?" she asked.

"He actually went to Australia," Jack answered. "But not until he was a little older, for the last two years of high school, and then he stayed for college."

"Where he studied graphic design?"

"Yes," Jack said. "But also business. He went back to Taiwan right after getting his degree." He looked up at her. "He was the more dutiful son, clearly."

I don't know about that, Joanna thought. *After all, you're going back, too.*

"Do you ever wish you weren't sent here as a kid?" she asked. It might have been an inappropriate question, but Joanna felt like there was something Jack wanted to say but just couldn't get out. "I'm sorry if that came out wrong," she said hedgingly.

"Oh, don't worry," Jack answered. "It's not that uncommon in Taiwan, so I guess I didn't think much of it. I know my parents sent me because they wanted the best for me."

That's usually what parents want, Joanna thought, and then she couldn't help but push just a little. "And what's best for you now? Are you happy here?"

"Well, that's a great question. I'd say I'm happy how these circles came out, huh?" He held up the sketchbook proudly.

And though it seemed that Jack was dodging her questions, she had to agree with him. "Yes, those are pretty great circles."

Whatever it is, he's still not ready to let it out.

BACK AT HOME later that evening, as exhausted as she was from a full day of activity, Joanna felt inspired and decided to pull out some larger sheets of paper and her paints. Earlier in the week, Wei-Wei had given her a basic calligraphy lesson, but Joanna hadn't had a chance to try it on her own yet.

Writing the character for *love* in sweeping script using a paintbrush and black ink, Joanna stepped back and admired her own handiwork.

How cool is this?

Going back through her workbook, she wrote all the characters she had learned so far, and even a few she hadn't, using paint.

How beautiful all these words are!

Pulling out her phone, she started looking up more complicated characters and tried those out. It took a few more sheets of paper, but eventually she drew some that looked pretty good to her.

Joanna snapped some photos of her Chinese brushstrokes and sent them to her mother.

Joanna: What do you think? Wei-Wei, the teacher who I gave your number to, has started teaching me calligraphy

Mom: Oh yes, we just spoke! She seems lovely.

Mom: And your calligraphy looks beautiful! Actually, come to think of it, your grandfather, Dad's dad, was quite an accomplished calligrapher back in Taiwan.

Joanna: Wow, really? You and Dad never mentioned it.

Unfortunately, both sets of grandparents had passed away when Joanna was very young, and she didn't remember any of them.

Mom: It's a shame you didn't get much time with them. I guess it all seemed like ancient history to me, but now that you're learning calligraphy, I should try to see if I have anything of his up in the attic.

Joanna: Okay!

Mom: It's better than I could do, for sure! Your grandfather would be so proud.

Joanna: Thanks, Mom. So, have you got Wei-Wei engaged already?

Mom: I'm working on it! She did have some unique criteria, though.

Joanna: Really, like what?

Mom: I've already said too much! I should respect her privacy.

Joanna: Alright, alright. Good luck!

Joanna waited for the inevitable "Are you sure *you* don't want to meet anyone right now?" but to her surprise, it never came. It seemed putting her mother in touch with Wei-Wei had finally gotten Carol the matchmaker off her back, at least for now.

Thank goodness for that.

CHAPTER FIFTEEN

AT THEIR NEXT Mandarin-slash-sketching class at the library, Jack showed Joanna all the 2D shapes he had practiced at home, and Joanna declared he was ready to move on to 3D shapes. "Spheres are just circles with shading," she said, showing him how to imagine a light source, cast a shadow and shade in the rest.

"You make it sound so simple," Jack said as he picked up a pencil. He was thrilled to spend time with Joanna outside of school, as she seemed to be deliberately avoiding him at school. This wasn't surprising, given she didn't want anyone gossiping about them, but still, it stung a little when she turned the other direction every time she saw him coming toward her in the hallway.

And the other day, he'd thought he overheard her talking to Wei-Wei about one of them going out on a date. He really hoped it was Wei-Wei, not Joanna, and wished he could ask her about it, but he knew he had no right to have an opinion on any of it.

Instead, he asked, "What should I do next, Miss Joanna? I imagine your students must ask you this all day long."

"How about color?" Joanna suggested. "I can bring my color pencils next time."

"Whoa, easy now, I don't know," Jack said. "Are you sure I'm ready for that?"

"I have an idea." Joanna clapped her hands. "How about a field trip this weekend?"

"I'm game. What did you have in mind?"

"Let's go to Holland. I hear the tulips are in peak form!" Joanna said.

"Holland?" Jack asked. "An international field trip?"

Of course, he quickly found out that Joanna wasn't referring to the Netherlands, but the city of Holland in Michigan, just a few towns over from Lakeland, which held an annual tulip festival.

On Saturday, Jack met Joanna in downtown Holland—driving separately, on her request—where she was waiting for him, sketchbook in hand. As she passed the book to him, he, in turn, passed her a notebook.

"What's this?" she asked.

"A worksheet. You can work on it while I sketch," he said with a grin.

"Alright, that's fair," Joanna said playfully. "Always in teaching mode, aren't you, Mr. Sun?"

As they arrived at the main gardens, Jack had to stop to admire the sight of tulips everywhere.

Lining the streets in neat rows, bunched in boxes perched on the windows of restaurants and shops, growing in the distant fields—*now this is a lot of tulips to draw!*

"I'm in heaven," Joanna said as they made their way down the main thoroughfare. "Look at all this!"

"I agree, it's spectacular!" Jack responded.

They walked the grounds, admiring the foliage; everything was in bloom, not just the tulips but many other flowers and trees as well, aromatic scents all mixing together.

"My parents have mentioned coming to Holland before, but this is the first time I've been," Joanna said. "I'm so glad I did."

"Me too. So, Miss Joanna, how do we choose what to draw?" Jack asked.

"Let's walk around, maybe take some photos, see what moves you?" Joanna suggested. "Since you've been working on shapes and shading, you could draw the big windmill over there, or find one single flower to focus on? Then just take a seat and draw it." Her face was afire with excitement as she looked all around. "I just can't believe how many tulips there are. And in every shade of the rainbow, it seems."

"Except blue," a nearby gardener, who was tending to one of the flower beds, commented.

Jack and Joanna turned to him. "Is that right?" Jack asked. "No blue?"

"Yep." The worker nodded. "Tulips come in all violet shades, but no real true blue."

"Interesting," Joanna said. "I've lived in Michigan my whole life and never knew that fact about tulips! We'll definitely keep that in mind when we're using our color pencils."

"You two picked the perfect time to come. It's the last of the full bloom," the worker said. "In just a few days, all these flowers will reach peak opening, and then their petals will start to shrivel and fall."

"Then I better get to drawing them now," Jack said, taking a seat on a stone wall and bringing out the sketchbook.

"Good luck," Joanna said. "I've got work to do, too." She held up her own worksheet and walked off toward the fields. "I'll come back in a bit!"

Following Joanna's advice, Jack identified a distinct blossom, a stately red tulip over two feet tall. He started making marks on his page, lightly outlining the shape of the flower. It didn't look quite right, but he kept on, remembering Joanna's advice of feeling, not thinking. He quickly lost himself in the sketch, and after about a half an hour, he stopped to look at his work.

Not bad for a guy who couldn't draw a straight line just a week ago!

It wasn't anything to write home about, but still, he couldn't believe he had drawn something that actually looked like a tulip.

I assumed I just wasn't good at drawing. But like Joanna said, I just needed the right teacher.

As he continued to draw, Jack's mind started to wander. He recalled when Joanna had told him that nothing was set in stone. *I know she was just talking about my shapes, but still...could there be another path for me, here in the US?*

"Nice work," Joanna said from behind him.

"It's all due to you!" Jack exclaimed. "Between this and the painting of the sunset, my art skills have increased exponentially since meeting you."

"To be honest, the acrylic sunset painting was basically paint-by-numbers," Joanna said. "This one, however, was all you. It's really very well done. Five stars!"

"What about you?" Jack asked, switching to Chinese. "Did you finish your assignment?"

"I did," Joanna answered proudly, holding up her completed worksheet. "The view is very beautiful," she said in Chinese.

"It is indeed," Jack replied in English, unable to resist looking straight at her.

Walking through the fields, they took in the sweeping sight of tulips everywhere, with Joanna taking dozens of photos and remarking that her head was brimming with art ideas. After stopping at a shop on the corner for an afternoon coffee and biscotti, Jack looked at his watch.

"We should probably head out now. If we don't

leave soon, we're going to be late for dragon boat practice."

Joanna agreed, asking, "Did you get the message I sent you about wearing a dry-fit shirt and waterproof shoes?"

"Yes," he said. "I've got it all in my car. I better get going. Given I missed last practice, Coach Clay will probably kick me off the team if I'm late for this one." But as he said the words, he looked at Joanna's gorgeous smile, felt the warmth of the sun blanketing the gardens and wished he could stay there, in that moment with her, for just a little while longer.

ON THE LAST Sunday of May, Jack woke with a start, feeling the impending doom of leaving Lakeland in less than two weeks. His mother was messaging him several times a day now, asking what food he wanted, did he need her to buy him new bedding for his brother's guest room, or even some new clothes? He tried to respond as politely as possible that he could take care of his own personal effects, but then his mother simply shifted gears to telling him about company-related issues.

Jack checked his phone and saw that, sure enough, several messages from his mother had come in overnight telling him about a decision they had just made on a key supplier relationship, but also, was he okay taking a cab from the airport, or did he want to be picked up?

Setting down his phone, Jack looked out his window to see the flowering tree outside his apartment in full bloom. He didn't know what kind it was, but it was beautiful, and he immediately thought of Joanna. Snapping a picture and sending it to her, his mood brightened as he remembered that, at long last, they were planning to visit the botanical gardens later that day.

Good morning, he wrote to her. Pick you up at eleven? I'll pack a picnic?

When she wrote back in Chinese, the characters for "Very good!" he had to smile. They had completed the fifteen lessons on his syllabus right on schedule, finishing the last chapter on Friday, which left a little over a week to review before her test. It would be a hectic week, though, full of preparations for the Dragon Boat Festival, which was taking place in just a week as well.

He was confident that Joanna would do well— she knew the material, she just had to focus and trust herself. Just then Jack remembered that he had wanted to send Joanna a few practice tests, and went over to his desk to open his laptop.

He was searching through his files when his phone started vibrating. The call was from a number not in his contacts but, distracted by what he was doing, he answered anyways.

"Hello?"

"Hello, is this Jack Sun?" An unfamiliar voice of a woman rang through. "I hope it's okay that

I called you. My name is Carol. I know your old roommate Joe's aunt, Tracy?"

Jack detected a slight Chinese accent and automatically switched into speaking Chinese, also adding the customary pleasantries. "Hello, Auntie, how are you? Yes, I remember Joe's aunt Tracy. How is she? I haven't seen her in a long time, since our graduation."

The woman on the other end responded enthusiastically, but in English. "Ah, you speak Chinese! That's right, Tracy did mention that you were born in Taiwan. But no need, we're in America, after all, right? Anyways, she passed me your number. She heard from Joe that you just moved to western Michigan, running a company, right?"

Jack was about to correct her that he was a teacher and not running a company (*not yet, at least*), but the woman kept on talking without a pause for him to cut in. "I was wondering if you would be interested in meeting someone? I know you're probably very busy, but maybe just a coffee or a drink—"

Interrupting as nicely as he could, Jack said, "I'm very sorry, Auntie, but I'm moving back to Taiwan in two weeks."

There was silence on the line as the woman abruptly stopped speaking. "Oh! Tracy didn't mention that!"

"She probably didn't know."

"But didn't you just arrive in Michigan not that long ago? Was this a planned move?"

"Yes and no, I guess," he answered. But his usual diplomatic response got stuck in his throat. And suddenly, all the thoughts Jack had been holding inside released themselves, and he found himself revealing to this stranger the massive conflict that he was facing. "Yes, in that the long-term plan was for me to move back to Taiwan at some point. But no, in that I really don't want to leave. I have a job that I love here, and the US is home to me now, but my family expects me back."

Jack paused, a bizarre sense of relief washing over him as he finally said everything out loud, albeit to a stranger.

"That's tough," the woman said, sounding genuinely concerned for him. "It seems like a very difficult situation you're in."

"It is," he agreed. "I've thought about it over and over, and I'm not sure what to do. Do you have any advice for me? Where are you originally from, if I may ask? How long have you lived here? And would you want to move back?"

The woman chuckled. "Usually, I am annoyed when people ask me where I'm from because it implies that the US is not my home, but this time, I'll allow it. I'm originally from Taiwan, too. My journey sounds very different than yours, though. When my husband and I left Taiwan, it was with the intention of making the US our home. And that's what we did. We actually haven't been back since we left."

"Really? You've never felt a pull to return?" Jack had been back and forth to Asia so many times, he could not imagine never returning. "My family in Taiwan constantly reminds me that my homeland, my roots, are there."

Then he heard what sounded like the woman blowing a raspberry. "Well, I just say phooey to that. Everyone's story is different, and everyone's feelings toward their *homeland*, if you even want to call it that, are different. What might be true for one person, may not be necessarily true for someone else. So for your family, they may feel their roots are in Taiwan, but that doesn't mean yours are. You might have had roots there originally, but then you replanted them over here. Or you may not even have roots at all! There is such a thing as air plants, you know!"

Listening intently and thinking about what she was saying, Jack responded, "But I do feel a sense of obligation, that I have a duty to return to help my family. I feel like I'm being selfish for wanting to stay." Jack couldn't believe that he'd laid bare his deepest feelings to this random auntie.

"You sound like a smart young man. I'm sure you'll figure out the right decision," she said.

Though Jack wasn't so sure, he appreciated her

listening, and thanked her for her time. "You've given me some things to think about, that's for sure. It was very nice talking to you."

"And you as well, Jack! So, when do you want to meet my daughter?"

"Ahem," he responded, surprised. "You still want her to meet me? After all I've told you?" He was about to tell her that even if he wasn't about to leave the country, there was someone else he would want to pursue, but she continued before he could get the words out.

"Yes," the woman said in a firm tone. "I was actually calling you for another young woman, but now that I've spoken to you, I have a feeling you'd make a great match for my daughter, who's also in the area! You're clearly very thoughtful, and I think that would balance really well with my daughter's—"

"I'm very sorry, Auntie," Jack said, "but unfortunately I'm late for an appointment and have to go now. I do appreciate your call. Please tell Aunt Tracy I said hello as well if you speak to her."

The woman's voice rang cheerily through the speaker. "Okay, I'll let you go now. I'm not giving up, though. Like I said, I have a feeling about you!"

CHAPTER SIXTEEN

WELL, THAT WAS a bit odd, Jack thought as he ended the call. He turned his attention back to emailing Joanna the sample tests. After he sent the email, however, he returned to the conversation with the woman.

He was thoughtful, she was right about that. He always tried to look at things logically, considered the pros and cons of different paths he could take, and the consequences of taking each one. When he'd made the decision to get his master's degree in education instead of an MBA, his father had said he respected his decision but hadn't offered to pay for it. Jack had had to think hard about whether he wanted to take out loans and forge a path of his own as a teacher. At that time, of course, his father was still healthy and running Sun Textiles.

When he had won Teacher of the Year, Jack felt vindicated; it was solid proof he could show to his father that he had made a good decision. His parents didn't brag to their friends about it or anything, but one time, Jack had overheard someone ask his father if he was grooming Jack to take over the company, and his father had said, "No, Jack has a more noble calling than us capitalists."

This was his father's way of saying that he was proud of him. But then his father had passed away and Jack knew he had reached the end of the line of his American adventure.

Turning back to his laptop, though he felt guilty for doing so, Jack opened a blank document to write out a list of pros and cons of moving back to Taiwan or staying in the US.

Go back to Taiwan.
Pros: make Ma happy, help Jonathan
Cons: be miserable trying to run Sun Textiles...without Joanna

Stay in the US.
Pros: be happy as a teacher...with Joanna.
Cons: break Ma's heart, leave Jonathan running everything all alone

How does Joanna fit into all of this?
Though they had both ostensibly cut off any possibility of a romantic relationship a few weeks ago, they had continued her tutoring, and then she had offered to teach him how to draw, and well, now he couldn't deny how he felt about her.

Joanna...smart, beautiful, creative, capable, conscientious, empathetic Joanna.

Jack could name a dozen more words, in English and Chinese, that described her, but really the one word was…*perfect*.

What would Joanna do if she were in my situation?

She wouldn't make a list. She would follow her heart.

His pulse quickening, Jack was certain what his heart wanted.

Then, an idea came to him.

I'm just going to go for it.

I'll ask her today at the gardens.

"GOOD MORNING!" Hanna Andresson welcomed Jack as he walked through the doorway to the Swiss Bakery. "So great to see you!"

Taken aback by such a strong welcome, Jack looked around to see if he had been mistaken for someone else, or if someone had just come in behind him. After confirming that the warm welcome was, in fact, for him, he approached the counter where Hanna was standing. "Good to see you, too, Hanna. Thanks for putting together a picnic on such short notice."

"It was our pleasure," Hanna said, then turned to call to the kitchen. "Luca! Mr. Sun is here."

Now very confused why she would be calling her husband out, Jack wondered what was going on.

Does everyone who orders a picnic get the star treatment?

"Mr. Sun!" Luca Andresson called out as he walked into the front room, wearing an apron with a light dusting of flour on the front and carrying a large basket. He stuck out his hand for Jack to shake. "I'm so glad you came in today. Hanna and I wanted to let you know that we so appreciate all the effort you put into gathering those resources to help Maja continue her Chinese studies. We finally got a chance to review it all."

"That's great," Jack said. He hadn't forgotten about Maja, and had planned to call her parents this week to check in. "Miss Wei-Wei also helped come up with those resources. She's a big fan of Maja, too."

"Ah, that was very nice of her. We'll have to tell her thank-you as well. Maja recently showed us how happy it made her to study Chinese," Hanna said.

Then Jack remembered the artwork that Maja had made in Joanna's class.

Ah, so that's what this is all about!

"Yes," he said. "Miss Joanna showed me Maja's poster. It was really striking. Even as much as I knew of her interest in Chinese already, seeing it in art form really moved me."

Hanna nodded. "After I saw it, I realized that we were being very unfair to Maja by deciding her future for her. Although she had told us she was fine working at the store and giving up studying Chinese, she showed us in that art piece what is truly in her heart. Maja should continue learning Chinese—"

"Not just should, but she must!" Luca cut in.

"Yes, she must," Hanna agreed. "We will definitely make time in her schedule next year, using some of the resources you listed, as well as have her continue to babysit for Danny Chen."

Jack's heart leapt. "That's the best news I've heard all day," he said. "I can't tell you how happy I am."

"Not as happy as Maja was when we told her," Hanna said. "I certainly don't want to hold her back from what makes her happy. Anyways, we don't want to keep you—I'm sure you don't want to keep the person you're having a picnic with waiting, eh?" She passed Jack the picnic basket that Luca had set down on the counter.

Jack glanced at his watch. "You're right. I'll catch up with the two of you later, but thanks so much for the update on Maja, and for this." He held up the picnic basket.

"Enjoy!" Luca called out as Jack rushed out the door.

IN HER BEDROOM getting ready to visit the botanical gardens with Jack, Joanna decided to wear the dress she had worn on the first day of school—

the patterned belted one that had put her in such a great mood that morning.

I'm not sure why, but it feels like another day full of promise, she thought as she sat at her makeup table and applied a dusting of blush across her cheeks.

She had completed her final Chinese chapter on Friday. Jack's stamp of approval had given her confidence that she was ready for the test, even if she wasn't able to find much time to review in the coming week.

Today, however, she just wanted to enjoy her time with Jack. When he had suggested going to the botanical gardens, there was no mention of practice tests or sketching lessons. He had simply wrote that he would pack a picnic and pick her up at eleven.

Something felt very different about today.

It feels like a date, that's what it is, she thought, but didn't want to let herself go there.

She was waiting at her door and came out to the car as Jack arrived to pick her up.

"Sorry I'm a little late. Just had to pick up the picnic from the Swiss Bakery," he apologized.

"You're not late at all, and I was just reading online that there's a shade garden that's perfect for a picnic," Joanna said.

They arrived at the botanical gardens and picked up a brochure and map at the entrance. Joanna saw that the gardens had expansive indoor and outdoor grounds across more than a hundred acres, including a tropical conservatory, a sculpture garden, nature trails and the shade garden she had read about.

The apple tree–lined path that led from the entrance to the shade garden was so breathtaking that Joanna actually gasped out loud. The apple blossoms, clustered in groups, white and pale pink with dark pink undersides, were in full bloom, their branches hanging over the path from both sides like a canopy. The scent of the blossoms—hints of wild rose, jasmine and honey—engulfed them as Jack and Joanna walked down the path.

Joanna couldn't help but picture wedding photos being taken here.

I can't imagine a more beautiful setting anywhere on earth.

Voices to her left made her turn her head, and sure enough, a wedding party was spread out, five on each side, dressed to the nines, surrounding a lovely bride and groom. The bride wore a gorgeous layered gown with a high collar and looked the picture of perfection, while the groom, looking pretty spiffy himself, stared lovingly at his bride.

A photographer called out instructions, and Joanna felt her heart about to burst seeing the couple nestled together in each other's arms beneath the ceiling of apple blossoms.

Joanna and Jack reached the shade garden, which was full of red and sugar maples, flowers and flowering shrubs. On the lush lawn, which was dotted by fallen blossoms, Jack set out a blanket and started spreading out the food—warm pastries, freshly cut fruit, finger sandwiches and sparkling lemonade in sturdy drinking jars.

"This looks so delicious. Thank you for setting it all up," Joanna said.

"It's my pleasure," Jack responded. "And really, you can thank Luca and Hanna Andresson. All I did was pick it up from them."

As they started to enjoy the food, an apple blossom fell from the tree above and landed in Jack's hair. Laughing, Joanna plucked it from his head.

"Thanks," Jack said, smiling at her.

She gathered a small pile of flowers and twigs from all around them. "Just wait," she said. Expertly weaving the flower stems around the twigs to make a delicate ring, she placed the floral crown on top of Jack's head.

"Here I thought you were clearing flowers from my hair, not adding more," Jack said good-naturedly as he let her take a photo of him.

"I wonder how much longer it'll stay like this," Joanna mused, looking all around. "It really is a feast for the eyes."

"Hopefully at least a couple more weeks," Jack said.

They started eating, and again it seemed to Joanna that there was something hanging in the air between them, something important Jack wanted to say, but still, he didn't, instead just making light conversation.

After eating, they went to explore the gardens, venturing into the conservatory, a multistory facility featuring a waterfall and a variety of exotic plants from around the world.

As Joanna admired the display of exquisite orchids, she said, "Hey, did I tell you I found out my dad's dad was a calligraphist? I showed my mom some of the characters I drew and she told me. Isn't that cool?"

"Very cool," Jack responded. "I'm so glad you found a connection to something. The older students who I've seen really excel in learning Chinese usually find a personal connection or incentive to learning the language—wanting to work there, really liking the culture or having a romantic interest..."

Joanna blushed, changing the subject. "What about Maja? Have you heard from her parents?"

"Oh yes! I wanted to tell you but got distracted." Jack relayed what had happened earlier at the bakery with the Andressons. "Your art project did it, Joanna. Thank you so much."

She brushed off his gratitude. "No need to thank me—Maja expressed it all on her own. That's wonderful."

"And the fifth grade class will also be heading

to Taiwan after school lets out, which I'm sure Maja will enjoy."

At the mention of Taiwan, Joanna paused a beat before answering, "That'll be nice, that you'll get to see your class again."

"Yes, it will be…"

"Are there things you're looking forward to once you're back?" she asked, trying to stay positive.

"The food, for sure," Jack said. "Don't get me wrong, I love The Dumpling Spot, but in Taipei, the selections are endless. The night markets are incredible. I'll actually be meeting the fifth grade class at one of my favorites, in Shilin. It's one of the largest night markets in all of Taiwan."

"That sounds so fun," Joanna said.

"Maybe you could come visit sometime," Jack said. "Do a summer residency, study art and calligraphy? You'd love the calligraphy there. It's in traditional script, so a lot more strokes, and it's just beautiful when you see it."

"I'd love to do that, someday."

AFTER STROLLING THROUGH the sculpture garden, Joanna saw the sun hanging low in the sky and realized they'd been at the gardens the entire afternoon and into the evening. Back in the shade garden, Jack stretched out on a blanket, basking in the setting sun as she idly sketched him on the back of the garden map. She thought about reaching over and intertwining her fingers into his.

Be careful, she told herself. *You're in dangerous territory again.*

Just as she was chastising herself, Jack suddenly sat up and looked directly into her eyes.

"Joanna, I wanted to talk to you about something."

Joanna snapped her head up. *Is he finally going to say what I think he's been holding back these past couple of weeks?*

"Yes…?" she asked.

Jack cleared his throat. "As I've gotten to know you over the past two months, my admiration for you has grown more and more every day, for following your dreams and starting over in a new career, for being such a wonderful teacher—to not only your students, but to me, too.

"For how you've found so many effective ways to communicate, and not using words at all. What you did with Maja—how you got her to show her parents what I hadn't been able to tell them—I'm so grateful to you. And not to mention how dedicated you've been to learning Mandarin. You're simply amazing, Joanna."

As he was saying all this, Joanna's face started turning red, hotter than she'd ever felt before. "You're really making me blush, Jack," she said. *What's happening? What is he trying to tell me?*

He took a deep breath. "What I'm trying to say

is, despite my best efforts at trying to avoid it, even as I've tried to stay as professional as possible, I couldn't stop it. I've really started to care for you, Joanna Lin, and I can't imagine my life without you."

Joanna's heart was fluttering so fast she felt like it was going to fly away, taking her whole body with it.

And he still wasn't finished.

"I wanted to ask you something—" He took a deep breath, as if summoning up the courage to say the next sentence.

"Joanna, will you move back to Taiwan with me?"

JACK SEARCHED JOANNA'S wide eyes, waiting for a response. When she didn't say anything, he feared the worst.

Oh no, what have I done? I should have thought more about this!

"Joanna?" he asked tentatively.

"S-s-sorry," she stammered back, covering her face with her hands. "I just wasn't expecting that at all! I'm not sure, um, well, there's been a lot happening, and yes, I've loved spending time with you and getting to know you…"

Jack's heart sank. *But I don't feel the same way about you*, he assumed she was going to say.

Thankfully, however, she asked, "Could you give me some time to think about it?"

At least it's not a flat-out no.

Jack nodded. "Of course, I understand. Please, take as much time as you need." But as they looked at each other again, Jack's heart started beating intensely, like the countdown of a ticking timer, and he sensed Joanna could feel it, too.

CHAPTER SEVENTEEN

THE FINAL WEEK before the school's big Dragon Boat Festival arrived, distracting Joanna from—or perhaps allowing her to put off answering—Jack's Big Ask. Preparations were in full swing; by Monday morning, even the teachers' lounge had been taken over by Alex and several tables full of PTA volunteers making *zongzi*, sticky rice dumplings that were a huge part of the festival's tradition.

"Hey, morning," Alex said to Joanna from one of the round tables.

"Good morning," Joanna said. "This looks like quite an operation."

"Yeah, it's a lot of fun! Have you eaten or made *zongzi* before?"

"Eaten, yes," Joanna answered. "We've gotten them from my parents' friends from time to time. But made them, no." She watched as people hustled around the room, down a line at the counter, to the tables and back again. "I'm not sure I can keep up!"

"It's easy once you've done it a few times," Alex said, showing Joanna the steps. "First, we prepare the bamboo leaves to wrap the rice dumplings, then we make the rice filling." She pointed at a table where volunteers had large mixing bowls in front of them. "Then, we wrap them." She demonstrated on the table in front of her, saying, "Using two leaves, form a cone, fill the leaves, fold and wrap, then tie with twine." She held up the cute pyramid she had just folded.

"So neat," Joanna complimented. "How'd you learn to do all this?"

"It was my favorite food when we lived in China," Alex said. "And I figured out the easiest way to get to eat them was to make them myself, so I quickly learned how to do it!"

"I'd love to learn," Joanna said. "And eat them, too!" She rubbed her stomach.

Alex laughed. "Well, they're not quite ready to eat yet. We have to boil them for six hours first. And since we don't need them right away, we'll store them in a fridge, and then on Sunday morning, we'll have to steam them to rewarm for serving."

"Got it," Joanna said. "Can I come back at lunch to help?"

"Sounds great," Alex said. "I'll be back then, too. We have to make several hundred by Sunday. I was tempted to call in a sub for my class today but looks like the parents have things under control."

One volunteer gave Alex a thumbs-up just as the bell rang and Joanna and Alex departed the lounge for their respective classrooms.

Joanna's classroom was bustling, too, as she had taken charge of decorations and leading art activities for the festival, and was having her students help her during their classes throughout the week. Her morning classes were busy with students making piles of precut craft packets for the festival—dragon boats, paper-folded *zongzi*, cloth sachets and satin Chinese knots.

When the lunch bell rang, Mindy walked into Joanna's classroom unlike her usual self. Instead of hips and earrings swinging, she was on crutches.

"Oh no, Mindy! Are you alright? What happened?" Joanna asked, running up to help walk her in.

"Taiko drumming accident," Mindy groaned.

"You were drumming?" Joanna asked, surprised.

"Not me, my sons! I was picking them up from rehearsal over the weekend when I tried to get by all the drums and fell off the stage."

"Oh no, was anything damaged?" Joanna asked. "Here, take a load off." She pulled out her desk chair for Mindy to sit down and brought over another student chair for her to prop up her braced ankle.

"Luckily, the drums were all fine…just sprained my ankle, unfortunately." Mindy looked forlornly at her foot.

Joanna shot her a sympathetic look. "Can you still paddle in the dragon boat race?"

"Unfortunately, no," Mindy said, shaking her head.

"Um…have you told Coach?"

"Not yet." Mindy grimaced. "I was thinking about how I might soften the blow."

"I definitely don't want to be there when he sees you on crutches," Joanna said. "This is *way* worse than wearing the wrong shoes."

"I know. I have an idea to make it up to him and actually, was hoping to get your help."

Joanna raised an eyebrow. "*My* help? I can't paddle for two!"

Mindy chuckled. "Ha ha, I know that. Can I ask a huge favor and have you whip up a quick shirt design that we can make for all the dragon boat team members? I can get them made by Sunday."

Joanna looked around at the piles of artwork she had all around her room. "When do you need it by?"

Mindy winced. "Tomorrow?"

Joanna gave her a look, but took out a notepad to take down the specs Mindy wanted. "You're lucky I love you," she said to her friend. "And don't forget, the shirts better be dry-fit!"

"I won't forget! Thank you," Mindy said. "By the way, that lily is looking *fabulous*!"

Joanna looked over to her window. Mindy was right—her Easter lily was finally in full bloom. Five gorgeous trumpet-shaped flowers were completely open, their creamy white petals curled back elegantly. "It certainly took its time to get there," she commented.

"The wait was worth it, though, wasn't it?" Mindy said.

"Yes," Joanna agreed, walking over to admire it. "But," she sighed, "like all the flowers outside everywhere, it's not going to last."

Of course, she was thinking of Jack's departure. She had kept his ask to herself, not wanting Mindy or her other colleagues to find out she was considering leaving Lakeland and her job so soon after arriving.

"But that's what makes them so wonderful," Mindy said. "Because their beauty is fleeting. We have to treasure it while we can."

"I suppose you're right, Mindy…and I guess it's futile to try to make it last longer," Joanna said sadly.

THE SCHOOL WAS abuzz with energy, not just the staff and parent volunteers, but all the students as well, who were busy rehearsing individual and group performances for the big year-end celebration at the Dragon Boat Festival.

But every time Joanna saw the event posters—which were everywhere, all around the school and even along Main Street—she felt a sadness in her heart, as just a week after the festival, Jack would be leaving for Taiwan.

If I decide to go with him, would I feel less sad?

Ever since Jack's Big Ask, Joanna had been playing out the scenarios in her head: if she said no, she'd be losing him. But if she said yes, she would be losing her dream job.

It's a lose-lose situation.

On top of all this deliberation, Joanna still had her Chinese test, which she would take on Monday, the day after the festival. The test was administered online and results provided directly to the school, so Principal Malik would find out in short order if she had passed. Joanna tried not to think about what she would do if she didn't pass—or if she did but then told her boss she was leaving—and instead focused on the colorful cloths she was laying out all over her classroom tables.

"Hey, need some help?" Jack asked, coming into her classroom. "I mean, only if you want me around."

Despite her conflicted feelings, Joanna brightened up as soon as she laid eyes on him. "Of course. But Alex hasn't roped you into *zongzi* wrapping?"

"She saw my first one and took pity on me, releasing me for other, less complex, tasks."

"Ha." She handed him a box of materials. "Here, you can help me assemble these sachet-making kits."

"Glad to," Jack said. "You've become a calligraphy master," he added, nodding toward the giant banners that she and Wei-Wei had made, which were now spread out on her classroom floor.

"Thanks," Joanna replied, pleased with her work in writing the large Chinese script of the characters for *Dragon Boat Festival*. "It's been my favorite part of learning Chinese—the characters are just so beautiful to write. I owe it all to you, Jack."

"No, I only taught you a hundred and fifty characters and enough Chinese to pass the level one CPT," Jack responded. "This—I had nothing to do with! Didn't you say you found out that your grandfather was a calligraphist? Maybe it's in your blood?"

"Maybe," Joanna said. "But seriously, one of the reasons I left my old legal job was that I thought I wasn't great with words, always thought art was more my medium of communication. But after discovering Chinese, I see so much beauty and meaning in the written language. It's really made me want to continue learning. Maybe this is a language I could really express myself in."

"Looks like we've both learned a lot about ourselves from each other," Jack said. He looked expectantly at her. Joanna knew she owed him an answer, but unfortunately, she still didn't know what it was.

ON SATURDAY MORNING, Jack, along with the Lakeland Elementary dragon boat racing team, gathered in front of Coach Clay for their final practice before facing off against their rivals at tomorrow's race.

"For those of you who may not have heard, unfortunately our team faced a crushing blow when Mindy sprained her ankle," Coach said.

Gasps erupted from some of the team members who didn't already know about Mindy's mishap. Wei-Wei, up front with her drum, called out to Mindy, who was sitting nearby with her crutches underneath the picnic table, "I had no idea! Are you okay, Mindy?"

"I'm fine," Mindy answered. "But I'm so sorry to let the team down. I'll be cheering the loudest from the shore! And I tried to make it up to everyone by getting these shirts made." She held up a red T-shirt, printed with the school's name, and Dragon Boat Team written across the back in English and Chinese. "With the help of Joanna."

Everyone cheered and clapped as Mindy hobbled around and passed out the shirts, a few team members even putting them on right away. "Don't worry, they're dry-fit," she assured Coach.

Coach Clay appeared to be partially consoled. "After some last minute scrambling, I was able to recruit a substitute, our esteemed principal, who will join us at the event tomorrow. But I did have to do some reconfiguration to balance the boat out, so Alex, you're going to move up a row, and Jack, you're now paired with Joanna in the back."

Jack smiled at Joanna as he took the empty seat next to her. She looked ready to race, wearing sunglasses, paddling gloves and a well-fitted T-shirt.

"Alright, now, I'm not much of a speech giver, as you know, not like our Mr. Sun here, who was born to be on television."

"You're doing a great job," Jack called out.

Coach Clay gave him a nod, then pulled out a sheet of paper and started reading. "Dragon boat racing originated in China thousands of years ago, when it was believed that a heavenly river dragon controlled the rain. Around the summer solstice, villagers would race to rouse the hibernating dragon and encourage it to send rainfall for the upcoming growing season. Sometimes, even human sacrifices were offered to the mythical dragon."

"Whoa," someone said. "That got dark."

Coach Clay continued, "For hundreds of years,

dragon boat racing was quite violent. Racers and spectators threw stones and used sticks to strike opposing villagers' boats. The event was considered inauspicious if no one drowned."

"If *no one* drowned?" someone else asked. "I don't think I've heard this version of the Dragon Boat Festival before."

"Yeah, alright, that doesn't seem to be the same story I read last year…" Coach said, looking confused. He crumpled up the piece of paper and tucked it away in a pocket. "This is what I want to say. I'm feeling great about our team, our times in practice in both the 250 meter and 500 meter have been strong, and besides the major setback—"

"Hey!" Mindy called out. "I got you shirts!"

"Besides the small setback—" Coach Clay cleared his throat and continued "—we're well-positioned to kick those Beverly Harbor butts tomorrow!"

"And if we don't win, Mindy'll be there on the side to throw stones at them?" Alex asked. "Like they did in ancient times?"

"Er, right, sure." Coach wrapped up his pep talk, ending with *"Jia you!"*

"What does that mean?" Joanna whispered to Jack.

"Literally, it translates to *add oil*, but it means *step on it* or *go for it*," he explained.

"Got it," Joanna said. *"Jia you!"* she yelled out. The rest of the boat joined her in cheering.

"Beverly Harbor will never know what hit 'em!" Alex yelled.

JOANNA SPENT SATURDAY night reviewing her test materials one last time, as she suspected she wouldn't have much time—or energy—after Sunday's festival. As she reviewed all the characters she had memorized, she thought about the day she first walked into Lakeland Elementary, how unintelligible the Chinese characters she saw all around were—just a combination of lines and strokes.

But now, as she wrote the word for *love*, finishing the last stroke with a longer, stylized flourish, she marveled at how she recognized every character on the school's banner, knew not only their meaning, but their components and stroke order, too.

Like all good teachers, Jack had also extended her learning, introducing her to combinations of characters that created more advanced words, and she admired the elegance and simplicity of many of them.

Many combinations in Chinese were much simpler than their English counterparts. *Compassion*, for example, in Chinese was represented by the character *ai*, meaning *love*, and *xin*, meaning *heart*; similarly, *empathy* was made up by *gong*, meaning *public*, and *qing*, meaning *feeling*.

She had to credit Jack for being such an amazing teacher, and opening up a world to her—both outside and inside of herself—that she never even knew existed. The added connection to her grandfather was a fun bonus. Even though she didn't remember him, knowing that she shared an interest and ability with her dad's father gave her a warm feeling inside.

Joanna listened to one last practice comprehension test, then shut her laptop, confident that she knew the material and was prepared for any question that might be asked of her.

On the level one Chinese Proficiency Test, that is.

Now, on to the other question—the much more difficult one.

And then she finally made her mind go there.

I do like Jack. A lot. But can I give up everything I've worked so hard for to move across the world with him? Don't I owe it to Dad—and myself—to succeed in my new career? Jack has so much devotion to his family, but what about mine? I can't move even farther away from Mom.

And I've barely mastered basic Mandarin. How will I even get around in Taiwan, much less get an art teacher position? I'd be starting over from an even worse position.

But then Joanna thought back to that perfect afternoon in the botanical gardens. For a moment, she let herself imagine a future with Jack—the sights they would visit together, students they would share, the Chinese and art they would teach each other, even the wedding photos they might take in that very garden.

I'm way beyond liking him, Joanna realized. *I've totally fallen for him.*

But he's leaving. There's no future for us here.

And there was something else that didn't feel quite right about the whole situation. Joanna definitely felt like Jack had been wanting to tell her something, but she didn't think it was asking her to move to Taiwan.

The more she thought about it, the more she felt like crying.

This is impossible.

Taking a deep breath and letting it out, she picked up her phone and messaged Jack, asking him to meet her early the next morning at the festival, before all the activities started.

CHAPTER EIGHTEEN

ARRIVING AT THE site even earlier than when Joanna had asked to meet, Jack paced back and forth at the waterfront. Lake Michigan was in full splendor this morning; there was not a cloud in the sky as the sun shone off the lake, covering the surroundings in a brilliant glow. Large tents and tall banners at the entrance had already gone up, and a crew was currently setting up the stage just in front of the water, where Jack would be emceeing the full day of performances.

Down the shore a few hundred feet, teams were bringing in their dragon boats, paddlers working together to unload the heavy boats into the water and attach the heads and tails of the regal-looking vessels. The sight of dragon boats reminded Jack what a busy day it was going to be—after emceeing the day's program, he would have to paddle in the dragon boat race, too.

Taking shade under a large oak tree where a picnic table was conveniently situated, Jack sent a message to Joanna that he had arrived.

Well, this is it. Whatever her answer is, at least I tried.

Just then Jack's phone buzzed.

Joanna: I'm so sorry, Alex and the zongzi team needed an extra car to bring them over. I'll help unload everything and meet you down by the water in about ten minutes.

Jack: No problem, do you need help unloading? Why don't I meet you?

Joanna: That'd be great, thank you!

Putting his heart on hold, Jack headed over to the parking lot, where activity was beginning to really pick up. Teachers, parents and students were milling about everywhere.

Shoot. We might not get time alone now that the festival's getting started.

Joanna's car pulled up to the curb and he walked over to meet it.

"I'm so sorry to be late!" Joanna called through the passenger-side window.

"No worries! That's a huge amount of *zongzi*!" Jack commented as he looked through the windows of Joanna's car. Several open boxes containing dozens of the triangular rice dumplings covered the back seat and footwell.

"There's more in the trunk, too," Joanna said,

putting the car in Park. "And three other carloads full!"

"Wow, how long did it take to make all these?" Jack walked around to the back of the car and opened the trunk.

"The food committee's been working on them all week, but my guess is that Alex made at least half of them." Joanna pulled out two boxes from the back seat and started stacking them on the grass next to the curb. Together they quickly unloaded the rest of the *zongzi* from her car.

"Why don't I bring these to the food tents and you go park." Jack didn't want to have to wait out the whole day to hear Joanna's decision.

"Yes, thank you. I'll meet you down by the big oak tree in a sec," she responded, getting back into her car.

Planning to make a few trips, Jack carried a couple of boxes over to the food area, which was filled with people prepping for the day. In addition to the Lakeland food committee, other food vendors, including Danny Chen, and Luca and Hanna Andresson, were also setting up their own tents.

"Jack, you can set them down over here!" Alex shouted, waving him over from the other end of one tent.

As he walked by Danny, Jack said to the restaurant owner, "Danny Chen! I'm definitely coming over to your tent later to get a few of your famous *sheng jian bao*."

Danny patted Jack's back heartily. "Ah, Jack, it's great to see you. But soon you'll be headed to Taiwan to have your hometown kind, right?" he laughed.

Jack smiled but Danny's words sunk to the pit of his stomach.

I need to hear Joanna's answer.

After quickly depositing the rest of the *zongzi* boxes with Alex, Jack excused himself and hurried back out to the big oak tree.

Seeing that Joanna hadn't arrived yet, his hands shaking a little, Jack checked his phone to see if she had texted. She hadn't, so he put the phone down on the picnic table and started pacing around the shaded area.

"Hey," Joanna said.

Jack looked up to see her approaching him. She wore the red dragon boat team shirt, and her hair was tied up, but with a few strands loose around her face. The bright morning sun was lighting her up like the star of the show.

All he wanted to do was sweep her up in his arms.

"Hey," Jack said, stopping his pacing. "Good morning, again."

"Good morning to you, too. So sorry again for

being late." Her tone was sweet as usual, but her face revealed nothing. "I know I owe you a response."

LOOKING AT JACK'S handsome face, Joanna wanted to melt into him, but then, out of the corner of her eye, she saw a familiar figure walking down from the tents toward the waterfront.

Wait, is that—

"Joanna, honey! I found you! You weren't kidding—this event looks like it's going to be *extremely* well attended!"

"Mom?" Though she was happy to see her mother, who seemed to be wearing the world's biggest straw hat, Joanna had to blink several times, as she had totally forgotten she had invited Carol to the festival.

Joanna walked over to her mom, trying to decide if she wanted her mother to meet Jack under these circumstances.

"Traffic was very light and I got here in record time! I even found parking." Carol gave Joanna a big hug. "Was that your handiwork at the entrance? The calligraphy looked fabulous! How did you write them so large?"

"Miss Wei-Wei and I spread out the banners down the school hallway," Joanna answered, her mind in a bit of a muddle. She glanced at Jack, who was still standing over by the tree and looking quite surprised as well.

Should I introduce the two of them? Joanna

wondered. Suddenly, she felt bad for hiding such a big part of the past few weeks from her mother. *But we're kind of in the middle of something.*

"Looks like it's going to be a great event!" Carol took her hat off and fanned her face with it. "But it does feel like it's gonna be a hot one!"

"You're right, it does," Joanna answered, deciding that it would be better to send her mother off—in a nice way, of course—and finish her conversation with Jack rather than introducing them.

Before she could distract her mother, though, Carol said, "Listen, Joanna, since I've got you before everything kicks into gear, remember Tracy's nephew's friend, the man I told you about who lives around here?"

"Um, yeah, what about him?"

"I thought we could call and invite him here today." Carol took out her phone, squinting as she tapped on the screen.

"Listen, Mom, it's really not a good time," Joanna said, then mouthed *I'm so sorry* to Jack.

"Come now, Joanna, don't look at it like a setup."

"No, it's not that, it's just—"

"Isn't this your school's big event for the whole community? He *is* part of the community, isn't he?" Carol looked at Joanna, eyebrows raised.

"Sure, but you can't just call him up completely out of the blue for an event that's happening right now," Joanna said, trying to reason with her.

Carol swiped at her screen. "Well, it wouldn't be *completely* out of the blue. I actually spoke to him last weekend."

Joanna frowned, her eyes flicking to her mother's phone. "Wait, you called him already? Didn't we agree that you wouldn't?"

"Before you jump all over me, dear, I called him for your friend, Wei-Wei…"

"Okay…?"

"…but I came away from the conversation thinking he'd be a better match for you!"

So much for getting her off my back! Needing to get back to Jack, Joanna said firmly, "Mom, please, today's going to be busy enough as it is." *Not to mention Jack poured his heart out to me a week ago and he's waiting for my response.* She couldn't imagine what must be going through his mind right now as he stood by.

But instead of listening to her, Carol shushed Joanna, having already initiated the phone call. "Shhh, it's ringing."

Ugh, Mom! Joanna rubbed her temples. *Hopefully, he doesn't answer. No one answers calls from unknown numbers, right?*

A second later, a phone that was lying faceup on the picnic table lit up and started vibrating noisily against the wood surface.

Bzzzt! Bzzzt!

All three of them—Joanna, Joanna's mother

and even Jack himself—looked over to the buzzing phone in surprise.

Isn't that Jack's phone?

Joanna's eyes fixed on the screen, where a number was displayed without a contact name. She recognized her mother's cell number.

"Jack, why is my mom calling you?" she asked. Jack had walked toward the phone and was now standing at the picnic table, his hand hovering over it. When he responded with a bewildered shrug, she turned back to her mother. "Mom, why are you calling *Jack*?"

"You know Jack Sun?" Carol frowned and brought her phone back down from her ear. "And that's his phone? Is he here already?"

"Yes, I am," Jack said, stepping forward, his face showing an expression that Joanna couldn't read. "Hi, Mrs. Lin, I'm Jack Sun. It's nice to meet you in person. It appears I already know your daughter."

Joanna was stunned. "What is going on? You two know each other? I don't understand."

"Jack Sun is Tracy's nephew's old roommate!" Carol said dramatically. "The one I wanted to set you up with."

"What?" Joanna asked. "*Jack* is the guy you've been wanting to set me up with? And you've already spoken with each other?" She looked between Jack and her mother.

"Yes, I called him the other day, for your friend, Wei-Wei! But how did you meet him already?"

"Jack is a teacher at my school! And my Chinese tutor!" Joanna said, shaking her head in disbelief.

Carol seemed equally surprised. "The tutor, the one you've been spending all this time with? He's a man? And Jack works at your school? He's not running a company?"

"Well, this is a very strange coincidence," Jack said.

"You already met my daughter?" Carol asked Jack. "Why didn't you mention it on the phone?"

"I didn't know she was your daughter until just now!"

Joanna put her hands on her head. "Everyone, please. Just stop for a second." She turned to Jack. "How long have you been talking to my mom? Wait, was this a setup *this whole time*?"

Jack shook his head. "No, no, not at all. I did talk with her, but I didn't know she was your mom. She called me last weekend and we talked for a bit—"

"Yes, Joanna, we actually had a lovely conversation," Carol interjected. "So, Jack, since you're here now, how are you feeling about your dilemma? Any more clarity?"

"*Dilemma?* What dilemma?" Joanna felt blood

rushing to her head, and not in a good way, as it sounded like Jack and her mother had been talking about *her*.

JACK DIDN'T KNOW how to answer Joanna's question. Just a few minutes ago, he thought that maybe Joanna was about to reciprocate his feelings. But then her mother appeared, and not only did he not get to hear Joanna's answer, but her mother turned out to be the same woman who had called him the other day. And Joanna was the daughter she'd wanted him to meet?

What were the chances? And how did she get my phone number? He'd have to have a talk with his former roommate, Joe. Jack would never have imagined that his old friend would be responsible for getting him in the middle of the strangest mother-daughter squabble he'd ever seen.

"Jack?" Joanna addressed him directly. "What dilemma is she talking about? Were you and my mother discussing *me*?"

"No," he said, stepping closer to her and lowering his voice. "I told her that I couldn't meet anyone because I was leaving the country very soon."

"Oh, *that's* why you said you couldn't meet a random stranger's daughter? Because you were leaving? Not because there's someone else in your life?" Joanna asked, her voice shaky. Jack felt the bright sun heating up the back of his head uncomfortably.

"Wait, are the two of you dating?" Carol's face lit up. "Joanna, you didn't tell me this!"

Jack waited for Joanna to answer her mother's question.

"No, we're not dating," Joanna answered, and Jack's heart sank. *I was wrong. She wasn't about to tell me she likes me, too.* "Er, not really," she clarified. "Because of, well, you know, his *dilemma.*"

"I see," Carol said, her face darkening almost as quickly as it had lit up. "And, Jack, are you still planning on going back to Taiwan? What about your career here? You spoke so passionately about it."

"Wait, you talked about your job with her, too?" Joanna frowned. "You know, Jack, the past few weeks, I thought that you were holding something back from me, something you wanted to say but couldn't. But then you go and confess all of your issues to my mother?"

"I'm so sorry," he admitted. "But I really didn't know who she was."

Oh man, I really messed this up.

"Don't blame Jack, darling," Carol said. "He was quite distressed, and it really seemed like he needed to talk to someone about it. It definitely did not seem like an easy decision," Carol added. "But wait, did I interrupt something important between the two of you?"

Joanna turned to her mother. "Oh stop it, Mom.

I can't believe you! I told you I didn't want to get set up. You promised you'd leave my love life alone!"

Carol held both hands, palms up, in front of her chest. "Joanna, I promise you, I called him for Wei-Wei! If he seemed good for her, I wasn't going to say anything about you. But he did not seem like a great match for what Wei-Wei is looking for, and, given what I'm hearing now, *clearly* a good match for you!"

"Mom! That's not the point at all. I told you I wanted to make sure I was successful at my new job first, and that I didn't want anyone to get in the way of that."

Jack stepped closer to her. "Joanna, please, can I just speak to you alone?" he asked.

"Yes," she agreed, thankfully. "Mom, maybe you can go walk around or something." Her tone was the strongest he'd ever heard coming from her.

Her mother nodded. "Right, I'll just head over to the festival, then! It seems like you two need to talk this out."

"You and I are going to have a talk about this, too," Joanna said, shooting her mother a stern look.

"Of course, honey. I'll see you both later!" Carol waved cheerily at them, even as Joanna was fuming at her.

Jack watched Joanna's mother walk away, and

he turned back to Joanna. "I'm really sorry for talking about my issues to, who I thought was, a random stranger," he started. "And she *is* right, I did not mention that I was dating anyone."

Joanna stiffened.

"Honestly, I didn't know how you felt about me. But then, at the botanical gardens…" He trailed off. "I didn't imagine that between us, did I?" He leaned into her, hopeful.

She opened her mouth, and Jack waited to hear the words he'd been dreaming about all morning—that she had feelings for him, too.

But, just then, the sound of drumbeats thundered through the air. The event gates opened and the entire student population of Lakeland Elementary, all of their friends and family, and dozens of other members of the community were now streaming into the waterfront area.

Lakeland Elementary School's annual Dragon Boat Festival was officially underway.

CHAPTER NINETEEN

"I'M SO SORRY, Jack, but the festival is starting! I have to get to my table! I'll talk to you later." Worried about all the kids arriving at the art tent and finding it unmanned, Joanna hurried away, cursing her mother for meddling at a very inopportune time.

As she approached the tent, a crowd of students had already gathered around the tables. Thankfully, Maja and her mother were there, too, and they had started handing out the paper-cutting activity to the first set of students.

"Sorry to be late," Joanna apologized as she caught her breath.

"No problem," Hanna Andresson said. "The materials were already organized so we figured we'd just get everyone going."

"Yes, thank you so much," Joanna said. "Looks like you have everything under control here, Maja."

"Yes, Miss Joanna," Maja said as she was helping a younger student with a pair of scissors. "The paper cutting is quite simple."

Joanna quickly became absorbed in helping all the kids make crafts, forgetting about the disruptive events of the morning, at least for the time being. A constant stream of students filled her tent, and many parents came by to say hello to her, as well. The mood became quite festive; a lively lion dance started off the performances, and music and singing could be heard up and down the waterfront. Joanna didn't see her mother all morning and assumed she was off exploring the festival.

Or maybe Mom's having another private conversation with Jack, she thought cynically. But, deep down inside, she knew she was overreacting—Carol couldn't possibly have known Joanna had already met the man she wanted to set Wei-Wei up with.

But why was Jack able to tell her what he wasn't able to tell me?

And I really do owe him an answer.

But was his question—will I move with him—even the right one for his life right now?

UNDER AN UNCHARACTERISTICALLY blazing June sun, the twenty-two members of the Lakeland Elementary dragon boat racing team sat in position, paddlers two by two, facing the front of the boat where Miss Wei-Wei was positioned as the drummer.

Wei-Wei had changed out of the traditional Chinese-style dress she had been wearing earlier at the calligraphy table. She was now wearing the red Lakeland team T-shirt with the sleeves rolled up to her shoulders and water-resistant shorts, her hair tied back in a tight ponytail. Sitting on a small chair with her knees gripping the wide drum, eyes hidden behind mirrored sunglasses and gripping her wooden drumstick with both hands, Wei-Wei looked like she was ready for battle.

Coach Clay also stood up front, but he would soon move into position in the back of the boat as the steersperson. He, too, was dressed differently than usual, trading his baseball cap for a red bandana tied around his forehead. "Alright, 500-meter team! Are you all ready? Only two races stand between us and victory!"

Everyone cheered enthusiastically, including Joanna, although she kept her head straight and her attention on Coach Clay, not wanting to be distracted by looking at Jack next to her. Coach continued, "The top two boats of each heat advance to the finals and we drew a lucky first heat in that Beverly Harbor isn't in it. So let's work hard but save a little for the final race, okay?"

Another cheer erupted from the boat as Coach Clay gave a fist pump of encouragement, then started making his way to the back of the boat.

"All right, then." Coach leaned down to pick up the long steering oar. Positioning his stance with one foot in front of the other, he called out, "Take it away!"

The team put their paddles in the water, following the motion of the paddlers in the front row. As they maneuvered their boat to the start line, Jack asked Joanna, "So, how has your day been going so far?"

"Very busy, but good. And yours?"

"Same…and, Joanna, I really am sorry for baring my soul to your mother. I swear I didn't know who she was."

Joanna tried to keep her voice even. She wanted to have a serious talk with him, but was worried about their colleagues overhearing. "I know, it's okay. How could you have known it was my mother? I overreacted back there. It's just not how I imagined the morning going." Joanna jerked her paddle through the water unsteadily.

"Joanna, stay in sync," Coach warned from behind her.

"Sorry, Coach!" Joanna sat up straighter and adjusted her position closer to the edge of the boat, farther away from Jack. "But why were you able to talk to a stranger about your problems and not me?"

Jack's wraparound sunglasses masked what his eyes might have shown her. "I don't know. It's been so hard these past few weeks. It was already difficult enough to leave my career, but I never imagined that I'd meet someone as amazing as you two months before I had to leave this country for good."

Joanna couldn't help but dive in deeper. "I'm sorry, but I have to ask. The dilemma you talked with my mom about—you said it wasn't about me. So even if I move back to Taiwan with you, would that solve your problems?"

"It would certainly help," Jack said. She kept her eyes on her paddle but felt him looking at her. "Because we'd be together..." he continued.

Skeptical, she asked, "But the other issues? Would you be happy? Why is it so hard for you to tell your family that you don't want to go back to work at the company?"

"Not everyone is as strong as you," Jack answered.

"What about everything you did to help Maja? Helping her parents see what makes her happy? Isn't this the same thing?" Joanna asked.

Jack didn't respond right away, perhaps thinking about what she had just said. "You're right," he said finally. "It's similar."

Just then Coach Clay shushed everyone as he prepared the team for the start of the race. "Paddles ready!" he commanded as Wei-Wei held her drumstick, elbow bent, above her head. Everyone placed their paddles in the water, blades fully submerged, top hands high above their heads and bottom hands just grazing the surface of the water.

HONK! The starting horn went off. Wei-Wei

yelled, "Take it away!" and started drumming, her pace quickening with each beat. Coach Clay yelled encouragement from the back and Wei-Wei yelled out the counts matching her drumbeats. "One, two, one, two, one, two!"

Joanna listened to the drumbeat as she paddled, feeling the rhythm and trying to release the tension in her mind. As her mother had guessed, the temperature was scorching, and sweat started beading up on her hairline.

Wei-Wei's drumbeats accelerated, and Coach called out, "More power, come on! Bring it home!"

Joanna paddled faster and faster, leaning forward and pulling back, in coordination with the rest of the team. Water splashed everywhere, entering the boat and soaking her feet. She looked over to her left, and saw Jack's face filled with intensity.

"Woo-hoo! Let it ride, team!" Coach Clay cheered. The Lakeland team crossed the finish line first, winning their heat. Everyone stopped paddling to let off a collective congratulations for each other.

"Well done, everyone! Now that's some Lakeland teamwork!" Coach yelled.

Both Joanna and Jack cheered exuberantly, high-fiving the rest of their teammates. From the shoreline, Mindy was hopping on her good foot, waving a crutch in the air and screaming, "GO, LAKELAND!"

"What a rush!" Alex said, wiping her brow. "That was awesome!"

"You all did amazing!" Wei-Wei said from up front, shaking out her drumming hand.

The Lakeland team pulled up onto shore, and disembarked from the boat to get some relief from the sun. Jack and Joanna found some shade under a tree, a little away from the rest of the team, both looking on as Beverly Harbor's boat, a black-lacquered vessel with an impressive, fierce dragon head, paddled past them. Their team looked imposing, dressed all in matching black tank tops and headbands.

"They must be boiling," Jack commented.

"Hopefully that slows them down a little," Joanna said. Though her mind was on Jack, she did want the Lakeland team to win.

When the starting horn of the next race went off, however, the Beverly Harbor team showed no signs of the day's high temperature affecting them. They handily came in first in their heat, beating the next closest team by at least a boat length.

Coach was standing at the water, and verified the times of all the qualifying boats. "Beverly Harbor beat our time by a nose. But I know we were all holding back a little. Let's leave it all on the water on this last race, alright? *Jia you!*"

As they were waiting for the boats from the last heat to clear, Jack turned to Joanna. "To answer your earlier question, will I be happy back in Taiwan? I've been thinking about this a lot. Do you know the legend of the Dragon Boat Festival?"

Joanna nodded uncertainly. "You mean the one that Coach told us at the last practice? About the human sacrifices and drownings and all that?"

"Yes, that's one of the traditional stories," Jack said. "There are several. The one I learned growing up is this one. There once was a famed poet in ancient China named Qu Yuan, who served the emperor faithfully until he was accused of treason and forced into exile. While in exile, he continued to write poetry, expressing his undying loyalty to his emperor and country. Knowing he could never return, he grew depressed, and threw himself into the Miluo River on the fifth day of the fifth lunar month, the date on which the Dragon Boat Festival is still celebrated today."

"And people threw *zongzi* in the river for him?" Joanna asked. She remembered reading about that when she was researching craft activities.

"Yes, to keep the fish from eating him, so the legend says."

"Oh," Joanna said, cringing a little. "I suppose that's better than the human sacrifices that Coach described."

"Right. My point," Jack continued, "is that these are the kind of stories I grew up hearing. They're each a little different, of course, but the theme is always the same—we must be devoted to our country, ancestry and family. Qu Yuan is heralded as a hero for his loyalty and sacrifice. This is what I am up against—not just my mother, but thousands of years of history."

Joanna listened intently, and tried to absorb Jack's words. "I see," she said. "It's hard for me to truly understand, but I'm trying."

"From what I've seen living and teaching here in the US, your legends have slightly different themes," Jack said.

Joanna thought about the folk heroes she had grown up learning about. Christopher Columbus, an explorer and risk-taker who wanted to circumnavigate the globe, and ended up "discovering" the Americas; Johnny Appleseed, a dreamy wanderer who planted apple seeds while traveling across the United States on foot; and Paul Bunyan, a brawny frontier lumberjack and symbol of American strength and vitality.

"Yes, now that I'm thinking about it, you're absolutely right." Though she hadn't thought of these stories as particularly influential, Joanna wondered how differently she might have lived her life if all the stories she had heard growing up were about honor, duty and loyalty to her country and family, like Jack was describing.

"Back in Taiwan," Jack said, "in January or February, we celebrate Lunar New Year, and then in April, Tomb-Sweeping Day. These are two of our most important holidays, and both involve being with family. Because of the school calendar in the US, I haven't been able to make it back for either in ten years. I get grief for it every single year from my mother."

"I guess it's sort of like missing Thanksgiving and Christmas," she said.

Jack nodded. "Yes. On Tomb-Sweeping Day, we visit our ancestors' gravesites, clean them, burn incense and lay out offerings to honor them. The tradition is meant as an expression of gratitude for one's parents or grandparents. It's considered one of the most important acts of a truly filial son or daughter. Every year that I miss it, I feel like I'm letting my parents down."

Joanna didn't even know if her grandparents had gravesites, and felt ashamed. She realized Jack's upbringing was very different from her own. She tried to imagine what it had been like for him, to go against his parents' wishes and study education instead of business.

I wouldn't be here if Dad hadn't pushed me, or if Mom hadn't given me her full support on starting a new career and moving away from home.

"I can see now why you're having trouble telling your mother that you don't want to return to Taiwan," she said. "And how hard all of this must be for you. It really is a dilemma."

CHAPTER TWENTY

OVER THE LOUDSPEAKER, an announcement for the final race was made. "Competitors for the 500-meter final, please ready your boats."

Down at the water, Coach Clay waved his bandana and called out, "Alright. Let's go, Lakeland. Load her up! Jack, Joanna!" Coach bellowed at them. "Come on, let's get moving!"

The rest of the team had already loaded onto the boat, all the rows filled except for the last one—her and Jack's row. She stepped out from under the shade. "I've thought about this every spare second for the past week," she said to Jack as she started hurrying down toward the water. "I'm sorry it's taken me so long to give you an answer. You know how hard I've worked for this job."

"Yes, and I definitely know how hard you've continued to work at it every day," Jack said, running up next to her, "but I was thinking, well, you've done so well studying Chinese, that maybe moving to Taiwan would be the ultimate way to really be immersed and get in touch with your heritage. You said you might be interested in going to Taiwan to study calligraphy—"

"To *visit*, not live permanently," Joanna cut in gently. "Yes, I've learned and discovered a lot about Taiwanese culture and my parents' heritage, but, Jack, my home is here." She had to keep the volume of her voice from rising and attracting the attention of the entire team as she and Jack stepped onto the boat.

"O-of course," Jack said. "I didn't mean to suggest that this wasn't your home. I just thought, well, you've been learning more about your Taiwanese identity, by learning Mandarin—"

"My Taiwanese identity? Jack, I'm learning Mandarin because I have to, to keep my dream job, which is here, as an art teacher, in the US." One of Joanna's hands flailed out as she took her seat, grazing the back of Alex's neck. "Oops, sorry, Alex!"

Alex spun her head around, uttered a short "No worries!" then quickly turned away, clearly not wanting to be pulled into their lovers' quarrel.

Behind them, Coach Clay was starting another pep talk as he directed the team to paddle into position for the final race, but Joanna was too distracted with what Jack had just said to hear what Coach was saying exactly.

"Let's talk about this after the race, okay?"

Jack asked. "I'm sorry I brought this up right now."

Overwhelmed with everything that had already happened that day and tired from being out in the hot sun, Joanna didn't think before she said, more harshly than she intended, "I don't think you should be talking about my identity. I think maybe you need to examine your own identity. I can't give up everything and pick up my life because you don't have the courage to admit what you want. I hate to say it, but I think you're a coward, Jack."

As soon as the words were out, Joanna drew in a sharp breath and covered her mouth with one hand, the other still on her paddle.

Oh, shoot.

She'd gone too far. She knew it.

Even Alex turned around for a second, eyes and mouth wide, as if to say "Whoa, girl. You did *not* just call Jack a coward, did you?"

Crap. That is not what I wanted to say to him.

Joanna wanted to take it all back, tell him that she didn't mean it, but before she could, Coach yelled for everyone to place their paddles in the water, and then the blare of the starting horn went off.

THE HORN SOUNDED and the boat thrust forward. Right from the beginning, Jack's rhythm was all wrong. Coach yelled for him to get back with the rest of the team, but even after pausing for a beat, he couldn't get in sync.

I shouldn't have said those things about her identity.

I should never have asked her to move back with me.

I've made such a mess out of all of this.

Joanna's reply hit him like a punch in the gut, her words sending him reeling.

I think I'm being a good son by suppressing my wants, but am I really just a coward?

His paddling was still off-kilter and Coach again called out to him. "Find the rhythm, Jack, find it!"

But Jack couldn't get his mind off Joanna's accusations.

He thought back to when he'd arrived in the US—what a trial by fire that first year had been. How quiet his aunt's suburban house had been, and how homesick he had felt for the hustle and bustle of Taipei. But then he'd gotten used to it all, and after less than a year in the US, he couldn't sleep his first summer back in Taipei because of the city noises outside the window of his parents' home.

He reflected on how important it was to him to honor his parents—his father especially, now that he had passed on—which meant moving back to Taiwan and helping with the family's company.

But then he thought about how much he loved

teaching—really, truly loved it—and living here in the US.

Joanna's totally right.

I am a coward.

I think I'm a great communicator, but I can't even tell my own mother how I feel.

"Come on!" Another yell from Coach Clay jolted Jack out of his head. "One-two, one-two, one-two," Coach yelled in time with Wei-Wei's drumming.

Tasting the salt of his sweat, Jack looked over to the Beverly Harbor boat, which was already a half-boat length ahead of them. In addition to the team members' shirts and headbands, their paddles were also completely black. The Beverly Harbor drummer yelled out counts, and the paddlers matched in perfect harmony, their swift movements cutting through the water.

On the shoreline, the onlookers were all clapping and screaming, waving banners and signs. In the distance, Jack could see strings of lanterns and sachets, and the grand banners that Joanna had written.

Joanna was paddling hard, moving with the rest of the team, her eyes on fire. He felt terrible for asking her to give up her whole life here.

How could I ask her to do that for me?

Trying to match Joanna's intensity, Jack braced himself and focused on his own paddling, and finally found the cadence of the rest of the boat.

Unfortunately, by the time Jack found his rhythm, the race was already half over, and Beverly Harbor was nearly a boat length ahead of the Lakeland team.

"Come on! Let's go! Power up!" Coach Clay continued shouting.

Up front, Wei-Wei's drumming hit a frenzied pace, her ponytail flying as she struck the drum. The entire boat was sweating.

Breathing hard, Jack rocked his body forward and back, slicing his paddle deep into the water and pulling back with all of his might.

"Last push, COME ON!" Coach screamed.

But it was no use.

Jack watched helplessly as the sleek Beverly Harbor boat glided across the finish line in front of them, and even another boat, a blue one adorned with two dragon heads on both ends, managed to sneak in to finish a hair before Lakeland.

The Lakeland boat crossed the line third.

"Darn it!" Coach Clay shouted, pulling his bandana off and shaking his head.

Dropping his paddle onto his lap, Jack hung his head in defeat.

CHAPTER TWENTY-ONE

"WE'LL GET 'EM next year!" Coach Clay still tried to cheer the team on as they carried their boat off the water. "Good effort, everyone!"

"How did we lose that?" someone on the team lamented.

"I thought for sure we'd win," Principal Malik said.

"Well, we tried our best," Wei-Wei said, clearly disappointed.

Joanna dropped her paddle in the boat and pulled off her gloves, leaving Jack and the rest of the team to commiserate over their loss. Trudging back up to the arts tent, Joanna was completely drained, both physically and emotionally. She felt horrible for how she had acted toward Jack in the boat, and completely embarrassed that she and Jack had fought in front of their coworkers.

So much for keeping things professional at work. Now everyone knows that I was considering leaving my job before I even got a permanent offer! What a joke I must look like to them.

Despite Joanna's rough day, however, the festival was a huge success. Scores of teachers, parents and students stopped by the arts tent on their way out to praise Joanna on how beautiful the decorations were. Children clutched their cloth satchels at their chests and waved their paper *zongzi* crafts as they left the event. When interviewed by a local news reporter at the closing of the festival, Principal Malik said it was the highest-attended and, in his opinion, the best Dragon Boat Festival the school had ever put on.

But for Joanna, it had been a day that started with confusion and ended with despair.

"Tough loss," Carol said as Joanna was cleaning up. "Looked like you and Jack lost some of your rhythm back there on the water."

"Yeah," Joanna said, starting to sort a pile of fabric that had gotten mixed up. "He has a lot on his mind. You probably know all about it."

"Alright, dear, there is no need to be rude. How many times do I have to explain myself?" her mother asked. "I didn't know who he was when I called him! And I'm sorry he told me so much. Can I help you with that?" She reached for a piece of fabric on the table.

"But did you know, Mom?" Joanna asked, yanking back the piece harder than she had perhaps intended. "Did you know Jack asked me to move to Taiwan with him? *Did you tell him to?*"

Carol recoiled, face frozen in obvious shock.

"He asked you to move to Taiwan with him? When?" Her voice dropped two octaves. "I *did not* know about this, Joanna, and I *most certainly* did not tell him to! Why would I tell a man I only just met on the phone to take my only child across the world with him?"

"Because you had some kind of *feeling* about him?" Too tired to sort it all, Joanna grabbed the whole pile of fabric and shoved it into a bag.

"Joanna," Carol said firmly, "I did not tell Jack to ask you to move to Taiwan with him. In fact, I thought for sure he was going to decide *not* to go back, given everything he told me."

Joanna sighed. She knew she shouldn't stay mad at her mother, and Carol did seem genuinely surprised to hear about Jack's request. "Alright, alright, I'm sorry. It's been a long day."

"Yes, why don't we all just take a breath," Carol suggested. "Should we go get some dinner? What's the place you've been telling me about? The Dumpling Place or something?"

Taking her mother's advice, Joanna stopped loading the supplies, took a deep breath and let it out slowly. "You're right, Mom, I do need a break. But alone, I think. Can I meet you back at my place in a bit? I'm just going to help with cleanup and try to clear my head."

Carol nodded. "Sure, honey, of course. I'm sorry the day was so intense but I'm so proud of you. It was a spectacular event." She gave Joanna a hug, then kissed her on the forehead. "I love you. I'll get dinner started at home."

"Thanks, Mom," Joanna said. "I love you, too. Oh, if you stop by the food tent, Alex said she had some extra *zongzi* she deemed unacceptable to serve."

"Will do, honey," Carol said. "You'll work this out, I know you will."

As Carol departed, her figure was replaced by Mindy, on crutches and her arms laden with festival items.

"Hey girl, how are you?"

Joanna could tell from the expression on her friend's face that Mindy had heard all about the fight she and Jack had had on the dragon boat. "I guess word got around about Jack and me?"

Mindy nodded. "Why didn't you tell me Jack had asked you to move to Taiwan? What a huge decision you must have been dealing with, on top of everything else you've got going on."

Joanna was surprised to realize her friend wasn't thinking critically of her at all. "Oh, Mindy, I really should have told you. I was so worried that everyone would think less of me as a teacher if I got involved in a relationship with Jack."

"Why would we think that? One thing has nothing to do with the other!"

In a fit of relief, Joanna gave Mindy the abridged version of everything that had happened with Jack.

"I'm so sorry to hear what you've been going through," Mindy said, putting down her items and one of her crutches so she could give Joanna a half hug. "And I'm sorry I can't give you a proper hug! You really didn't need to worry at all about the staff thinking any less of you. We're all rooting for you! Me, especially. You're a fantastic teacher and everyone loves you at Lakeland! But I know you'll make the right decision for yourself, whatever that might be."

"Thanks, Mindy," Joanna said. "You are a true friend."

Mindy gave her another squeeze just as Jack appeared at the entryway to the arts tent behind Mindy.

"I'll let you two talk," Mindy said, loading her items into her arms again and shuffling away.

"Hi," Jack said gingerly.

"Hi," Joanna said, in the same manner.

"I'm not trying to start another discussion about Taipei… I just wanted to make sure you felt okay for your test tomorrow."

Oh my god, the test! Joanna hadn't thought about it the entire day. *It's tomorrow!*

"I could do some last minute review tomorrow morning, or at lunch, if you like," Jack offered.

She considered it, given how important passing the test was to her, but in the end, she said, "Thank you for the offer, but I think I'm okay on my own."

AFTER THE FESTIVAL, Jack sat on his balcony, letting dusk fall all around him. *This definitely isn't how I thought today would end.*

The more he thought about it, the more he realized how thoughtless and inconsiderate he had been.

Why did I assume Joanna would give everything up for me? What was I thinking?

Completely broken up, he wished he could talk to someone. He found himself tempted to call that random auntie. *It's not a random auntie*, he reminded himself. *It's Joanna's mother!*

But he knew he couldn't do that. *Joanna would never forgive me if she found out I talked to her mother, knowing it was her mother this time.*

He kept replaying in his mind the appalling fight in the dragon boat, in front of all their co-workers, no less.

Where do I go from here?

He checked his watch and saw it was already past 9:00 p.m.; the sun had long gone down, yet he was still sitting on his balcony, staring out into nothingness. Realizing he hadn't even eaten dinner yet, he went into his kitchen and was about to root through his fridge to see if he could scrounge up a meal, when his phone buzzed with an incoming video call from his brother.

"Hi, how are you?" Jack greeted Jonathan as he turned on some lights and adjusted his phone so his face wasn't in the darkness.

Jonathan's face was sunny and bright, it being morning in Taipei, and from the background, Jack could see he was at the office. "Hi, big brother, how are you?" Jonathan said. "Just wanted to check in before the big move next weekend. Looking forward to seeing you, man!"

"Me too. It's been a busy few weeks," Jack said, trying to feign some pep in his voice.

"Sure, I understand. Hey, why the long face? Everything okay?"

Jack wanted to tell him everything that had happened with Joanna, but where to begin? It was too much to get into in one conversation. Instead, he simply answered, "All good here, just wrapping everything up at school. We just had our big Dragon Boat Festival today."

"No way, Americans celebrate that, too?" Jonathan asked. "That's wild!"

"You're right, it's pretty wild that it's made it this far west," Jack agreed. He thought back to the festival. For almost everyone, it had been a day of joy and celebration; no matter the origin, it had evolved to a wonderful event that this little elementary school in western Michigan got to share with the entire community. The food vendors and performers came from all different ethnicities and backgrounds, not just Chinese. Most of the community came to spend time together, to enjoy the songs and dances, arts and crafts, food and treats—not just to honor the tradition of Qu Yuan. Clearly, the festival had evolved from its traditional roots in ancient China.

So why am I not strong enough to break with tradition?

"Ma's so excited," his brother said. "It's like all her dreams are coming true, both of us back home."

"Yeah, I bet she is."

"Any arrival requests? Special shampoo? We haven't lived together since I was, what, still in diapers?"

"Ha, I'm easy, bro. It'll be nice to be back. And I definitely don't want to step on your toes at the company."

Jonathan laughed. "No worries at all—plenty of work to go around! You sure you're good with moving back?" his brother asked, leaning into his camera a little.

Jack paused for a beat, wondering what to say to this. Before he could answer, though, a phone rang in Jonathan's office. "Ah, sorry, but I have to take this call," his brother said, apparently forgetting the question he'd just asked. "I'll see you in a week, yeah?"

"Great, yes, good talking to you," Jack responded. Disconnecting the video, he left his kitchen and headed to the bathroom to take a shower, realizing he had no appetite at all.

AFTER AVOIDING JOANNA the entire day to let her concentrate on her test, Jack finally messaged her on Monday evening to see if she was free to meet him down on Main Street.

When she responded with a singular "Okay" and nothing else, he hoped that she had performed well on the test, despite all the weekend turmoil.

Dusk was settling downtown, the automatic streetlamps switching on as Jack walked toward the Swiss Bakery. Being a Monday, the bakery had closed early, and the rest of the street was quiet as well; the restaurant crowd was light, with just a couple of tables still lingering on the French bistro's front patio at the corner of Fourth and Main.

Joanna was already there, sitting on the same bench where they had agreed to keep things professional.

Well that certainly didn't happen, he thought, recalling the argument they had had in front of the entire dragon boat team.

"Hey," he said, arms hanging awkwardly at his sides. He didn't know if he should hug her.

How do I get back to the way things were at the botanical gardens?

"Hey," Joanna responded. She wore a lavender dress and looked as beautiful as ever.

"Shall we take a walk?" he asked.

She stood up from the bench and nodded. "Sure."

They headed toward the waterfront, passing

clothing boutiques, candy and toy stores that were all closed, the soft lights from the streetlamps reflecting on their dark windows. Crickets chirped in the distance, and the scent of flowers growing somewhere in the darkness permeated the street.

"The gardenia smells so nice," Joanna said, inhaling deeply.

"It does," Jack agreed. Now that the silence had been broken, he ventured to ask, "How did your test go?"

"It was fine," she answered. "I think I did okay. More than okay, actually."

"That's great," he said. "You were definitely ready."

"Yes, thank you for that."

"It was all you. I just gave you the material."

"You know that's not true."

"When do you get the results?" he asked.

"The school should get them in a few days. I've got a sit-down scheduled with Principal Malik on Thursday."

"Right," Jack said, "when he'll extend you a permanent offer for next year."

"Hopefully," Joanna said. "I don't want to jinx it."

"Right," Jack said again.

They walked for another half a block, reaching the path where the farmers market had been set up earlier that day. A few stray lettuce leaves and paper napkins lay on the path, and Joanna bent down to pick up the litter.

"It's really different here at night, isn't it," Jack commented. It was a moonless night, and he could see fireflies flickering in the distance.

"Yeah, it's so dark," Joanna said. "I can't even see the lake from here."

They reached the water and stopped at another bench. Jack motioned for Joanna to sit and she did so, at the far end of the bench from where he was.

"So, I just wanted to apologize," he started. "I shouldn't have said all the things I did. I really messed up the dragon boat race for you."

"You didn't mess it up for me," Joanna said. "Maybe for Coach Clay, though."

Jack hung his head like he had at the race. "I'm never going to live that down. I went by the gym this morning and he gave me the biggest stink eye I've ever seen."

"You're going to have to find a way to make it up to him," Joanna said, cracking a smile.

"I'm not sure there's anything I can do! Anyways, I'm also sorry for confessing all my issues to your mom on the phone. I think maybe I was scared to admit that I'm not as secure and in control of my life as you are. But I should have talked to you about it, not your mother."

"It's okay. You didn't know she was my mother. I shouldn't have gotten so angry about it. And it is true, my mom really is a good listener."

"And apparently a pretty good matchmaker too."

"Yeah," Joanna said, her mouth turning up on one side. "Eerily good, huh?"

"Almost supernatural," Jack said.

"What if my mom came away from your conversation thinking you'd be a good match for Wei-Wei instead?"

"Well, she wouldn't have because, you know, she had a *feeling* about us," he teased.

Joanna flashed a soft smile. "I should also apologize for calling you a coward and saying that you had identity issues. That wasn't right."

He shook his head—he was there to apologize to her, not the other way around. "You were absolutely justified to call me what you did. I shouldn't have asked you to move to Taiwan in the first place. It was not the solution to my dilemma."

"So what is the solution?"

Jack paused and thought of his mother. "I know what I have to do. This is where I am right now in my life."

"I get it," Joanna said. "And while I might have feelings for you, too, my new job—*my* life—is here. I have to honor my father, too. This is what he wanted for me, and what I want for myself."

"I understand," he said sadly. "I know you can't go with me."

"So you're still going?" Joanna asked.

"Yes, my family needs me."

"Then I wish you good luck, Jack."

He wanted to continue the conversation, but it seemed after that, there was nothing more that could be said.

CHAPTER TWENTY-TWO

JOANNA SAT IN front of Principal Malik's desk, her leg shaking once again. It felt a lot warmer in his office compared to the last time she had been here.

"Not nervous again, are you, Joanna?" he asked, looking over his reading glasses at her. He was in his usual Lakeland-T-shirt-over-a-button-down-shirt uniform, although he had the sleeves of his button-down rolled up, perhaps feeling the heat himself a little as well.

"Oh, I am definitely nervous," she answered. Though she had felt good about her test after completing it on Monday afternoon, three days had gone by since then—long enough for her to start feeling anxious about it again. "Is it just me, or is it really hot in here today?"

The principal laughed, apparently thinking she was joking. "I won't keep you in suspense. Joanna Lin, here are the results of your level one Chinese Proficiency Test." He rotated the sheet of paper on the desk in front of him so Joanna could see the results.

Her name and birth date were at the top of the page. Then, a table with a column on the left side listing Listening, Reading, Writing.

"As you know, the test was broken up into three sections—100 points each for a full score of 300 points. You need an 80 percent, or a score of 240 points, to pass."

Joanna's face broke into a huge smile as the numbers on the page registered in her mind and her boss read out the results. "You scored a 91 on Listening, 96 on Reading, and a whopping 100 on Writing," he said, "for a grand total of 287, or 96 percent! A pass with flying colors. Congratulations, Joanna!"

Joanna let the relief wash over her as she threw her head back and let out a big breath. "Thank you so much, Principal Malik!"

"Please, how many times do I need to tell you? Call me Omar," the principal said.

"Right, sorry! Thank you so much, Omar!"

He leaned forward in his chair, asking, "Now, Joanna, were you really surprised by these results? I've been hearing from Jack Sun all month how hard you were studying and that you were sure to pass."

Joanna's smile faded a touch at the mention of Jack's name. "Oh, that's, um, really nice of him to say." She looked down at her hands. "He was a really great teacher."

"One of the best I've ever had the pleasure of working with," Principal Malik said, shaking his head. "I'm still disappointed that I couldn't convince him to stay on."

"Me too," Joanna said, almost to herself.

The principal shot her a sympathetic look. "Speaking of staying on, I'll get right onto the next thing—not sure if you've been nervous about this as well?"

"Oh, yes!" She'd nearly forgotten the reason she needed to pass the Chinese test in the first place. Joanna looked to her boss in anxious anticipation.

"It's my very great pleasure to present to you this letter." He passed another sheet of paper to her. "A formal offer to join Lakeland Elementary School's faculty as our permanent art teacher for the next academic year. I hope this is good news."

Joanna nodded and clasped her hands in front of her mouth in gratitude. "Thank you, Omar. Yes, it's *really* good news."

I did it.

But it felt bittersweet, like she had to sacrifice something very large to achieve what she had been wanting for so long.

Why am I not more happy?

The principal wrapped up the meeting, rising and offering his hand for her to shake. "Congratulations again, Joanna. If I don't get a chance to say it tomorrow, have a great summer and I look forward to seeing you in the fall."

She shook his hand and thanked him again. As she turned to walk out of his office, the principal said gently, "Joanna, we're all going to miss him a lot, too."

"Thanks," she replied sadly.

"So…BIG SUMMER PLANS?" Mindy asked. On the last day of school, she was leaning on the side of Joanna's desk, crutches propped up next to her. "Sorry I can't help out more with packing up your room," she added, as Joanna finished putting all her personal items into a box to take home for the summer. "Let me know if I can do anything… without moving from this position."

Joanna managed a half smile as she emptied the last of her belongings from her desk drawers. "No worries, I'm about done here—my last class was really great in helping to clean up. And thanks for trying to distract me from, well, you know…"

Mindy gave a big, heaving sigh. "How did the year end like this? We should be celebrating! Instead, you're moping around like Coach Clay after losing to Beverly Harbor yet again, and I'm still shuffling around on my busted foot. Definitely not an acceptable start of the summer."

"Ha," Joanna said. She went over to the side cabinets to check that the materials inside were organized neatly. "I'll probably go back and stay with my mom for a bit, but other than that, I don't have any plans. What about you?"

Mindy shifted her weight to turn slightly, and she started absently rifling through the box on Joanna's desk. "We're heading up to our cottage in the UP in July if you're interested in meeting us there? It's on Lake Superior. If you thought Lake Michigan was cold, wait until you feel Superior—it's like a frozen mammoth! You could stay with us as long as you like."

Joanna couldn't imagine being on a lakefront without thinking about Jack. "Thanks, that's a really nice offer. Can I get back to you later?"

"Of course," Mindy said.

"Could you see if you can make some room in that box?" Joanna asked. Closing a cabinet door firmly, Joanna then went to the window to retrieve the last remaining personal item she had in the classroom: the Easter lily Mindy had given her on her first day of school. Although the flowers had bloomed and fallen off already, the remaining foliage was still green and vibrant. "Thank you for this, Mindy. It was really beautiful while it lasted."

"If you prune and plant that in a sunny place, it should bloom again in a year or two," Mindy said.

"Oh, really?" Joanna asked. "Maybe I'll try that."

I wonder what Jack will do with his.

She placed the pot inside the cardboard box on her desk.

He won't be able to bring it with him to Taiwan. He'll probably have to throw it away.

Just then Maja walked into the classroom, her blond hair tied up in a ponytail and cheeks rosy, likely from dashing about, Joanna assumed.

"Hi, Maja," both Mindy and Joanna greeted her.

"Hi, Ms. Perez, Miss Joanna," Maja replied. "I realized I forgot my Happiness art project and wanted to bring it home."

Joanna smiled and reached for the poster that was lying on her desk next to the box. "I have it saved right here. I was going to bring it by the bakery if I didn't see you today." She passed the sheet over to Maja. "It's really gorgeous. Thank you for bringing it back so I could display it these last few weeks."

"Thanks," Maja said, accepting it with both hands. "Actually, it was my mom who asked about it. She says she wants to frame it and hang it up in our house. I think that might be a little excessive." She shrugged.

"I don't think so!" Joanna said. "It's definitely frame worthy."

"I wholeheartedly agree," Mindy said.

"Thanks. Oh, and Miss Joanna? I really loved art class after you arrived at Lakeland."

Joanna felt her heart warm, especially as she knew Maja wasn't one to give insincere compliments—although she did feel a little bad for Ms. Rani, given Maja's implication that she didn't like art class before Joanna arrived. "I'm so glad I got to know you, Maja. Good luck in middle school!"

"Come back and visit us, okay?" Mindy said.

"I'll try," Maja said, turning to leave the room.

"Oh, and have a great trip to Taiwan!" Mindy called after her.

"Thanks. Bye." Maja's figure disappeared out the door, ponytail swishing.

Mindy and Joanna followed shortly after, walking slowly down the hallway, with Joanna noticing how bare the walls looked without any student work hanging up on them.

It's strange how different everything looks... empty and lonesome.

Heading out of the school's front entrance, Joanna opened one of the double doors with her box and held it there as Mindy hobbled through the entryway. The parking lot was empty, save Joanna's car.

"Wow, guess we're the last ones here?" Joanna asked as they walked toward her car, which was parked at the far end of the lot.

"Looks like it," Mindy said. "Thanks again for driving me home all week. I think everyone's over at happy hour already. It's Jack's going-away party, in case you didn't know..."

"Yes, I know," Joanna said as she helped Mindy get into the car.

"Coach Clay said he's finally forgiven Jack for his big fumble at the race."

"That's good to hear," Joanna said as she loaded her box into the trunk and got in the driver's side. "I guess I have to take some responsibility for that loss, too."

"Nah, I'm just kidding with you," Mindy said. "Coach doesn't blame anyone but himself. Just warning you, though, he's probably gonna start training even earlier for next year's race."

"I'll be ready this time," Joanna said, flexing a bicep and trying to stay upbeat even as she felt an ache in her chest picturing herself at school next year without Jack. She started the car engine and pulled out of the parking lot, driving the short distance to Patrick's.

As she pulled in front of the restaurant, however, she put her car in Park without turning off the engine.

"You alright?" Mindy asked. "The parking lot is in the back, remember?"

"I know, but..." The thought of seeing Jack surrounded by all their friends, knowing that he would be leaving tomorrow, was too much for Joanna. "I just think it'll be too hard. I don't want to distract him from getting to spend time with all of you. You all mean a lot to him, too, you know?"

"I know," Mindy said.

"Do you mind getting a ride home from Alex or Wei-Wei, or someone else?" Joanna asked. "I think I'm just going to go home."

"Of course. I'm not going to beg you this

time," Mindy said, reaching out to put a hand on Joanna's shoulder. "But are you sure you don't want to say goodbye?"

Joanna nodded, giving her friend a hug. "I'm sure. Tell everyone 'bye' from me, okay? And Jack, too."

"Yes, I will. I'll text you later, okay?"

"Sounds good." Joanna helped Mindy get out of the car, keeping a brave face as she walked to the front entrance of the restaurant and held the door open for Mindy, but quickly rushing back to her car hoping that no one, especially Jack, had seen her.

TEARS STARTED BLURRING her vision as Joanna drove away from Patrick's, down Main Street, past both the Swiss Bakery and The Dumpling Spot. She pulled up to her apartment building, the entrance of which was framed by lilac bushes all around, the flowers having already given way to thick, green leaves. Summer was nearly upon Lakeland, and while the foliage all around her was green and lush, Joanna mourned the dropping of tulip petals and wilting of daffodil heads, signifying the end of spring.

As she carried her box from the car up to the front door, she saw her Easter lily's twin, sitting right in the middle of her building's front porch. *What's this?*

A small envelope was propped on the pot's drip

tray. In Jack's neat handwriting was her name, *Joanna*.

She tore open the envelope.

Dear Joanna,
I have enjoyed every second with you and
miss you so much already. Maybe you can
plant this lily next to yours, and think fondly
of me when they bloom together, year after
year.
Love, Jack.

Blinking back tears, Joanna put the plant in the box and stared at the two identical pots.

Dreading the idea of being in her apartment alone when all her friends and colleagues were at the bar celebrating the end of the school year and bidding farewell to Jack, she went back out to her car.

She considered going back to Patrick's, but what would she do and say once she got there?

I'll probably just start crying and embarrass
myself in front of everyone.

She thought about walking down to the shore, or driving up to the lighthouse or the botanical gardens, where she could clear her mind.

But all those places will just make me think
of Jack.

Joanna realized the entire area of Lakeland and

its surrounding towns were filled with memories with Jack.

How am I going to spend the summer here, alone, without him?

Without another thought, she started her car, drove away from her apartment building and turned onto the highway going east. She didn't stop until three hours later, when she arrived at her mom's house on the other side of the state.

Carol, as if she knew Joanna was coming, was already on the doorstep of the red-brick home when Joanna pulled up the short driveway.

"Joanna, darling. Are you okay?" She ran down from the porch to Joanna's car.

"No, not really," Joanna said, getting out of the car and falling into her mother's arms.

"What happened? Did you speak to him?" Carol asked, walking Joanna into the house. "Is he still leaving?"

"Yes, I spoke to him," Joanna answered. "And yes, he's still leaving."

"Did you ask him to stay?" her mother asked.

"How could I?"

"So it's over?" Carol's eyebrows wrinkled with concern.

"Yes," Joanna said, "it's over."

"Oh, Joanna, I'm so sorry."

She laid her head on her mother's shoulder, silent tears running down both cheeks.

CHAPTER TWENTY-THREE

"I'M GOING ON a walk with Amita around the neighborhood later this morning. Do you want to join?" Carol called into Joanna's childhood bedroom, a clear ploy to get Joanna out of bed. "Some air might do you good. What do you say?"

Joanna rolled over so she could see her mother's face at her door. Feigning cheeriness, she answered, "Sure, Mom, that sounds good." She waited until the sounds of her mother's footsteps faded down the stairs before burying herself back under the covers.

A walk with Amita around the neighborhood? I don't think so...

After arriving home a week ago, Joanna had barely left her bedroom, much less the house. She'd spoken to no one other than her mother, answering the multiple texts a day from Mindy with one-word responses. Her mother had given her some space, but this morning's "invitation" to go for a walk indicated Carol's patience had worn thin.

Joanna felt like she had gone backward in time

three years, to when she and Tim had broken up and she had spent weeks moping around the house feeling sorry for herself. This time, however, she kept scrolling through all her photos with Jack, reliving and cherishing every moment with him, instead of deleting them in anger.

Starting from the first photo she had of him, a group photo from happy hour on that first week she had started school, Joanna recalled how she had actively avoided standing too close to him, fearing that he would feel her body temperature rising in his presence. She remembered, even then, that he was struggling with his relationship with his mother.

Maybe I could have been more understanding.

Scrolling forward to the selfie they took on the shore after painting, Joanna almost laughed again at seeing his perfect smile on the backdrop of the falling canvas.

The photos that followed were plentiful, as Joanna felt freer to take pictures of the two of them once they had established they weren't going to take the relationship any further than friendship.

She scrolled through many shots taken in Holland—the two of them in the main square, Jack holding his sketch up, Joanna in a field of tulips.

Then came photos from the day at the botanical gardens. Joanna almost couldn't bear to look at them, because it had been such a perfect day. Jack in the floral crown she had made him, a shot of the picnic spread, then a selfie of the two of them on the apple tree–lined path as they left the gardens.

After that, the photos of Jack stopped. She hadn't taken any pictures with him at the Dragon Boat Festival, nor in the week that followed leading up to his departure.

I'm a terrible person, she thought, remembering the half hug she had given him on the last day of school in the teachers' lounge, knowing she was planning on skipping his going-away party. She wished she had said a hundred different things, apologized again for getting so mad about him speaking to her mother, for saying the awful things she had said during the dragon boat race.

"Joanna? Are you coming down?" Carol's voice called up again.

Joanna reluctantly clicked off her phone and rolled out of bed. "Coming." When she arrived downstairs, she found her mother in the front sunroom, unpacking a dusty box.

"Change of plans," Carol said. "I pulled some of your old paint supplies out of the basement— hopefully you can still use them. I was thinking you may just want to paint, instead of listening to me and Amita gab away about Henry."

"Is that the mailman's cousin?"

"Yes. Amita thinks he's about to propose."

Carol gently patted Joanna's arm. "I figured you probably wouldn't want to hear all that."

Joanna nodded, crossing the room to the kitchen, to the coffee maker, and opening a cupboard to get a mug. "Yeah, thanks, Mom."

Going back into the sunroom after filling her mug, she looked out the front window to the big dogwood tree in the middle of the front lawn, the pink flowers already gone and replaced by dark green leaves. She imagined how different the tree must have looked just a few weeks ago.

I would have loved to bring Jack here.

A tiny spark of inspiration lit within Joanna. Setting down her coffee mug, Joanna looked into the box her mother had brought up from the basement. The paints were all fine, but when Joanna reached out and felt one of the brush tips, it was brittle and frayed. Peering closer, she saw the others in the box seemed in similar condition.

Well, this won't do.

She ran upstairs to change, then out the door to the art store. Forty minutes later, Joanna brought back a large, blank canvas and a set of new, soft paintbrushes. Tying on an apron, she sat down in front of her easel, feeling better than she had in over a week, since the day of the Dragon Boat Festival. As she made the first dip of her brush into a smear of crimson paint, Joanna released her mind, letting herself be consumed by painting. Moving her brush from the paint palette to the canvas, she was finally able to stop thinking about everything that had happened with Jack, and what they had said to each other in the dragon boat.

Engrossed in her work, Joanna didn't even notice when her mother came back from her walk, or that the sun had already passed from the front of the house to the back, or that she hadn't eaten anything all day.

When Carol came in to call her for dinner, she gasped audibly. "Joanna! It's breathtaking."

Joanna set her brush down and stood up, stepping back to look at her painting. She had drawn it completely from memory, the tree-lined path in the botanical gardens leading out to the shade garden where she had seen the wedding party. Gorgeous apple blossoms hung over the path, creating a natural canopy more beautiful than any manufactured one she could imagine.

"I think it turned out pretty nice," Joanna agreed.

"This isn't like Tim," Carol commented, putting an arm around her. "With him, everything you painted was dark and stormy."

"No," Joanna said, "it's not like with Tim at all." She felt tears welling up in her eyes and couldn't stop them from falling. Plump drops ran down her cheeks and she wiped them quickly away. "Oh, Mom, I miss him so much."

"Honey, this is so hard. Have you reached out

to him at all? I'm sure he'd be glad to hear from you." Carol grabbed a tissue box from a side table and passed it to Joanna.

Joanna shook her head and she pulled out a tissue. "No, I think it would be too hard for both of us."

Carol nodded, pulling Joanna in close. "It's okay, just let yourself grieve. Take your time. It'll pass, I promise."

Upon hearing this, Joanna's tears fell even harder. "But I don't want it to pass! I thought I needed time to work on me, to find myself, but then I found myself in love with Jack."

"Really?" Carol asked, leaning back to look at her daughter's face. "You're in love with him? Like, really, truly?"

Joanna nodded, sniffling. "Yes."

"Well then, obviously, you should go to him!" Carol said. She threw her hands out to the side, palms up.

Joanna looked up at her mother. "What do you mean?"

"What do you think I mean? You're not on house arrest! You can get on a plane!"

Joanna wiped both cheeks with the crumpled tissue. "Are you serious, Mom?"

"Yes, of course I'm serious! Buy a ticket to Taipei and go to him!"

"That's ridiculous! I can't just show up on his doorstep!"

"Why not?" Carol asked, hands on her hips. "What's the worst that can happen? He says 'Thank you, but I don't love you'? So, you spend a week touring Taiwan and come back, no worse off than you are right now."

"But what do I say to him? I still don't want to move there."

"Just be yourself! Tell him how you feel, and see what happens. That's all you have to do. You don't have to decide right this minute what you will do when you get there. Or do you want me to call him for you?"

Could I really do that? Just fly to Taipei?

She recalled that the fifth grade class was starting their trip any day now, and wondered if they needed an extra chaperone.

Maybe I could use that as my guise.

Then she remembered when Jack made her jump into the freezing lake. *Just dive in!* Jack had said.

"No, don't call him!" she said to her mother. "I'm doing it. I'm going to Taiwan. I don't know what's going to happen when I get there, but I'm going."

THANKFULLY, JOANNA HAD a valid passport and no obligations keeping her in Michigan. She went online and saw that there was a flight leaving the following night connecting through San Francisco that would get her into Taoyuan International Airport at 5:00 p.m. local time two days later.

So I guess I'll show up on Jack's doorstep right around sunset.

There were some logistical issues, though. Although she knew Jack was planning on staying with his younger brother until he got settled, she didn't know his address. Sleuthing through the internet, she was able to find the address of his family's business, Sun Textiles, in Taipei county, in what looked to be an industrial zone.

But I'm guessing Jack and his brother aren't sleeping at the factory.

After searching a bit longer but not finding anything useful (*maybe if I could read more Chinese, I'd be able to find out more...*), Joanna wondered if Mindy or any of the other teachers might have asked for his forwarding address.

Biting her lip, she typed out a message to Mindy and sent it.

Joanna: Hey, sorry to be MIA the last few days. I've decided to go to Taipei.

Mindy: WHAT?! To win back Jack's heart?

Joanna: Something like that! There's just one problem.

Mindy: What??

Joanna: I don't have his address.

Mindy: Ooooh, that's a biggie.

Joanna: Did you happen to ask for it before you left?

Mindy: No, sorry, girl! Do you want me to message him to ask for it?

Joanna: I want it to be a surprise...

Mindy: I know the fifth grade group is planning on meeting him sometime during their trip. Do you know the parent organizers?

Joanna: Oh yes, Maja's mother! I'll reach out to her, thank you! I'll keep you updated.

Mindy: You better!

Joanna shot off a message to Hanna Andresson, hoping that the other woman would see it soon and reply.

As she waited for a response, Joanna looked around her room to start packing. Unfortunately, as she had left Lakeland in such a hurry, she had none of her recent clothing other than what she had worn on the last day of school.

Should I drive back to Lakeland to get clothes?
Or should I go shopping?

How long am I going to be in Taiwan?

What if Jack slams the door in my face and I have to turn around and come right back?

As she was mulling over the worst-case scenario, her phone buzzed with a reply from Hanna Andresson.

Hanna: Good morning, Miss Joanna! It's so nice to hear from you. We're literally at the airport about to board our plane!

Joanna: Ah, I'm so glad I caught you! Can I bother you with an odd question? I heard you'll be meeting up with Jack Sun, right?

Hanna: Yes, he's going to show us around one of the big night markets on Tuesday. Everything okay?

Joanna: Yes, everything's fine. I was just hoping to, well, maybe meet him, too.

Hanna: Great, do you have his contact info?

Joanna: Thanks, I do, but...

Hanna: Did he not respond?

Joanna: I haven't reached out yet. Can I tell you something a bit personal?

Joanna then confessed she had a romantic motive for surprising Jack in person at his brother's apartment, after which Hanna Andresson was an eager coconspirator, sending Joanna multiple messages in a row with possible ideas.

Hanna: Maybe I could tell him that the kids want to see where he lives?

Hanna: Or that they want to send him a postcard?

Hanna: I got it! We want to send him an Uber to pick him up?

Joanna: Wow, so many ideas!

Hanna: Don't worry about a thing. I will get his address and send it to you shortly. Just leave it to me!

Joanna: Huge thank you!

Sure enough—and Joanna didn't know what method she used—less than fifteen minutes later, Hanna Andresson sent through Jack's brother's address in Taipei. She also sent Joanna the group's full itinerary, including where and when they were going to meet Jack at the night market, and told Joanna she had pushed their meeting time with Jack back an hour, so that Joanna could have plenty of time alone with Jack at his apartment before he would have to leave to meet the fifth grade class.

Thanking Hanna again and wishing the whole group safe travels, Joanna went back to her laptop, which was still open on the airline website.

With determination, Joanna entered her credit card information for the flight leaving tomorrow, and an open-ended return date.

Here goes nothing.

Taking a huge breath, she hit the purchase button.

CHAPTER TWENTY-FOUR

JACK ARRIVED IN Taiwan exhausted. He hadn't slept well on the flight over, and his bags somehow got diverted to a different terminal, causing him to wait over an hour for them to be sent back to where they were supposed to have come out. By the time he finally got to his brother's high-rise apartment in central Taipei, rumpled and laden with luggage, all Jack wanted to do was collapse into bed.

Unfortunately, his mother had other plans for him, greeting him at Jonathan's apartment door with a huge, relieved smile on her face.

"Jack, welcome home," she said, embracing him. She looked the same yet different, her body thinner and frailer when he hugged her back compared to the last time he had seen her in person last summer.

"Hi, Ma, good to see you," he said. "It's been too long." She held the door open for him and he first took off his shoes, then walked in, dragging his luggage behind him.

The aroma of Taiwanese spices hit his nose, along with a blast of air-conditioning on his face, as Jack stepped into the apartment. Sleek and modern, the unit was decorated in monochrome colors, fitting his brother's contemporary aesthetic. The living room also had a floor-to-ceiling window that overlooked the sprawling and dense metropolis, the city lights sparkling like a layer of low stars as dusk fell on Taipei.

Quite a different sunset here, Jack thought, as he observed the skyscrapers wrapped in orange light.

"Hey, man!" Jonathan emerged from the hallway, giving Jack a hug as well. He, too, looked different from the last time Jack saw him in person—taller, filled out, more manly. "So happy you finally made it. Ma said I had to wait until you arrived to start eating. She's been cooking up a storm all afternoon." Jack saw every inch of the dining table was covered in dishes. "I even went all the way to your favorite boba place to get that taro kind you like."

Jack immediately thought of Joanna. *She would really get a kick out of this.*

"Ah, that's so great, thanks to you both." Jack tried to look excited, but his stomach was still on Michigan time—when he would be sleeping. "Let me just go wash up."

"Of course, take your time," his mother said. "We'll wait for you."

"Please start," Jack said, as he headed to the bathroom. "I insist. The food will get cold!"

"We'll wait!" his mother called back.

In the shiny, black-and-chrome bathroom, Jack looked at his reflection in the mirror. His eyes were sunken, ringed by dark circles.

Come on, Jack, you'll be okay. This isn't the end of the world.

He imagined what Joanna would do if she were in this situation.

She'd try to make the most of it, for sure.

She'd find joy in the angles and reflections of the apartment, scents and tastes of all the new foods, prospects and opportunities of a new place.

If Joanna were here, he thought, he'd take her to all his favorite places, where he was sure she would find inspiration for new art projects—the miles of stunning coastline of the island country, the mountains that cut through it, and the dozens upon dozens of night markets that offered so many delicious foods.

And we'd discover new places together, just like we did in Lakeland.

Then Jack turned on the tap and splashed cold water on his face, and it gave him a wake-up jolt.

Who am I kidding? Joanna's not coming here. She made that very clear.

"Son? Everything okay?" His mother's voice jarred him out of his thoughts.

His brother's booming voice quickly followed.

"Hurry it up, will you, big brother? I'm about to pass out from hunger!"

"Sorry, coming," Jack answered, wiping his face quickly and hurrying out of the bathroom.

Sitting down at the table, Jack felt his stomach growl, apparently having woken up and ready to eat now. He dug into the food, thanking his mother again for making all his favorites, and to his brother for going to the other side of town to get his favorite drink. "You went all the way up to Shilin?"

"Sure did, and let me tell you, that boba shop is as busy as ever. I waited in line almost thirty minutes," Jonathan answered. "But don't thank me—you know Ma made me." He threw an impish glance over to their mother.

"It's a special occasion," she responded, gently slapping her younger son's shoulder. "I knew it was what Jack would want."

"Thank you very much, Ma," Jack said.

"Come now, let's raise a glass," his mother said, lifting her teacup to the center of the table. "It's not every day I get to have dinner with both my sons. Cheers."

Jack and Jonathan both did the same, clinking the cups together, then all taking a sip of their drinks. When Jack set down his cup, though, he saw that his mother was looking at them both expectantly.

"I'd like to make a little announcement, if I

may," she said. Jack and Jonathan exchanged a knowing glance. "As you know, I'm getting on in years. I've worked at Sun Textiles, side by side with your father, since we got married over thirty-five years ago. Now that Jack is home, I've decided that it's time for me to pass on the torch to the next generation. I know now that the company is in good hands with both my sons steering the ship." She raised her teacup again.

"Hear, hear, Ma," Jonathan said. "You deserve this. I hope we can make you proud."

"Likewise," Jack said, relieved his brother had prepped him for this conversation, and that he had had time to fully internalize what it meant for him. "Time for you to finally put your feet up, Ma."

"I'm so proud of you both. If only your father could see you now, running the company that his grandfather founded."

Jack took a swallow of his drink, trying to keep a neutral expression on his face, even as he felt a sinking feeling in his stomach that wasn't from the food.

JACK SPENT THE next few days mostly trying to get over jet lag—he was unable to stay up past sunset until the fourth night—while also trying to shadow his younger brother at work.

I wonder if this was what Joanna felt like at school, he thought one morning as he walked into a sales meeting already in progress; the terms that were being thrown around were completely unfamiliar to him and he realized his understanding of both business Mandarin and the actual underlying concepts weren't even close to being fluent enough for him to participate.

I think I may need to take a class, just like Joanna.

But she was doing it for a job she loved, he thought again, as he entered one of the company's processing plants, trailing Jonathan, agitated by the noisy machines and smell of chemicals as they made their way through the factory floor.

Though he had been through the Sun Textiles plants many times over the years, on the prior visits he had been a mere observer; this time, he walked in realizing that he was supposed to know what was going on in every corner of the factory, on every machine, from the thickness of the fibers to the colors of the dyes in every vat.

And for sure, yellow *and* red *aren't the right answers this time*, Jack thought, remembering the evening he and Joanna had painted the sunset together.

"You alright?" Jonathan asked him, as they stopped in front of one of the bigger pieces of equipment. "You look like you're about to faint. Is it the odors? They're strong, but you'll get used to them." He raised his voice to be heard over the loud humming coming from the machinery.

"Yeah, yeah, I'm fine," Jack answered. "Remind me what this line does again?"

His brother said something, but Jack couldn't hear over the machines, and had to put a hand to his ear. Jonathan motioned to follow him down the aisle, away from the clamor, then said, "That's a finishing line—washing, bleaching and coating."

"Right, right," Jack said, trying to retain everything his brother was saying.

Apparently, Jack's bewilderment was showing on his face, as Jonathan patted him on the back. "Don't worry, I felt overwhelmed when I first started working here, too. You'll figure it out in no time."

I'm not so sure about that, Jack thought, but nodded back to his brother, saying, "Right, I'm sure I will."

"But maybe when we bring KC Industries for their plant tour on Tuesday before dinner, I'll take the lead?" Jonathan suggested.

It was only then that Jack remembered their biggest customer was coming for a visit the following week. "Of course. I'll hang in the back and try not to get in your way."

As Jack's first week back in Taiwan drew to a close, a part of him hoped that his mother was too devoted to the company to really retire, but to his dismay, she cleared out her side of the executive office that she and Jonathan shared. The large office overlooked a park, and Jack remembered his parents sitting side by side facing the window, but Jonathan had rearranged it, explaining to Jack he preferred to sit facing the center of the room, rather than out the window.

As Jack sat down directly across from his brother, he felt ill at ease. When Jonathan raised his head and looked at him, Jack feared he would be called out immediately as an imposter.

"Let me take a picture of the two of you," his mother said, seemingly unaware of her older son's discomfort. When Jack protested that she, too, should be in the photo, she shook her head, saying, "I want a photo of the future of Sun Textiles."

ON MONDAY, Jack was finally getting over his jet lag, managing to actually wake up at a normal hour for the first time since he had arrived, when he received a message from Maja Andresson's mother, Hanna.

Hanna: Hi, Jack, hope it's not too early to message you!

Jack: Not at all, nice to hear from you! Is the class all ready for the trip? When do you leave?

Hanna: About to board the plane any minute now! The kids are all very excited, Maja especially!

Jack: And the parents, too, I hope?

Hanna: Yes! Just wanted to confirm the details of our meeting on Tuesday.

Jack: Right, 7:00 p.m. at Shilin Night market! I'll meet you at the entrance to the market. I haven't had a chance to get there yet since I've been back so I'm really looking forward to taking you all!

Hanna: Do you mind if we make it 8:00? Just want to make sure we give ourselves enough time to get there from our hotel.

Jack: Of course, no problem.

Hanna: Can I get your address just in case we can't reach you?

Finding it a little odd that she was asking where he lived, Jack typed out his brother's address anyways, thinking, *That Hanna Andresson's one thorough travel planner.*

Jack pulled up his calendar to input the details of the meeting when he saw the KC Industries plant tour and dinner was scheduled for the same evening.

Oh no. Our biggest customer. I can't miss that.

Typing out a message to Hanna Andresson to see if they could move their night market visit to another day, Jack realized she had likely boarded the plane already and wouldn't see his message until they landed.

Disappointed, Jack spent the entire day in a funk when he should have been preparing for KC Industries' visit.

The class's itinerary is surely already set for the entire trip. It's doubtful they'll be able to change their schedule and I'll miss seeing them.

Clearly sensing something was wrong, Jonathan asked, "Hey, big brother, are you okay?"

Jack considered feigning illness to get out of tomorrow's customer visit so he could instead meet with his former fifth grade class.

What am I thinking? This is my life now. I have to accept it.

"Still shaking the jetlag, I guess," Jack fibbed. "Anyways, do you have KC's order history by product line for the last five years?"

"Yes, I've got that all here," his brother answered, passing him a folder.

"Great, thanks," Jack said, readying himself to spend the next few hours reviewing the data.

TUESDAY MORNING, Jack received a call from Hanna Andresson.

"How has the trip been so far?" Jack asked, after they exchanged hellos.

"We've only just arrived but everyone's having so much fun already. And, Jack, let me tell you, for Maja, it's just incredible. *Truly incredi-*

ble. She's having the time of her life." Hanna went on to describe how Maja had started chatting in Mandarin with the flight attendant the minute they had stepped on the plane, and hadn't stopped since. "I've never seen her like this!"

"Her Chinese is going to be even better than it already is by the end of this trip," Jack said.

"I think that's definitely true!" Hanna said, her voice rising in excitement. "This morning, our tour guide was pulled away for a short time, and Maja took over translating for all the parents. She's over the moon. And it's not just the language—it's everything, the culture, the people, the food. Luca and I really owe you a big thank-you, Jack."

"No need at all for thanks, Hanna," Jack responded. "So, about tonight—" He was about to ask her if the class was able to move their schedule but she continued, cutting him off.

"The class is so excited for tonight!"

"Right, but would it be possible—"

"Oh, and I also need to apologize for being so curt to you, Jack, when you first mentioned wanting Maja to continue to study Chinese. I really had no idea how important it was to her—she probably didn't even know herself. If it weren't for you—and Miss Joanna—we'd never have opened our eyes to it. You helped me realize what Maja is passionate about, and I'm so grateful for that," Hanna said. "As a parent, I just want her to be safe, happy and healthy. But you were the one to show me that I also have to let her choose her own path."

There was a pause, and Hanna's words really sunk in. It made Jack recall what he had said to Joanna on the dragon boat, about filial piety and needing to honor his parents.

Is it possible that all of that is just in my head, and that my mother doesn't really expect or need me to help run Sun Textiles?

Could my mother react the same way as Luca and Hanna Andresson if I told her how I really felt about my life back in the US?

Jack cleared his throat. "I should be the one thanking you, Hanna. There's no better gift to a teacher than to hear that one of his students is not only loving learning his native language and culture, but thriving while doing so."

"Well, you're very welcome, then! And are we still on for the night market at eight o'clock tonight?"

Jack's answer was unequivocal—after hearing Hanna talk about Maja, he was finally able to make his choice. "Yes, we're on. I'll see you and the class tonight at eight. I can't wait."

It was crystal clear to him now.

I want to go back and resume my teaching career, to inspire more students like Maja.

The first time he had said it aloud was to Joanna's mother, and the world hadn't collapsed.

Now he just had to say it to his own mother.

CHAPTER TWENTY-FIVE

JOANNA BOARDED HER plane in San Francisco in a fog, hoping to sleep on the long flight to Taiwan, as she didn't sleep a wink the night before.

After buying her airline ticket and concluding she didn't have time to go shopping and would have to make do with the few old outfits she had hanging in her closet at her parents' house, Joanna then sat down to think about what she was going to say to Jack when she arrived at his door.

Mr. Sun, what a coincidence, running into you here.

Hey, Jack, just seeing if you wanted another sketching lesson?

Jack, can you spare a minute to let me apologize for how I treated you?

Ugh.

Then she thought, *Maybe I should do a speech in Chinese?*

But as Joanna tried to actually compose a speech, she was embarrassed that she couldn't get very far at all. Turns out, passing the level one

CPT did not give her nearly enough vocabulary to express being in love with someone beyond "Hi, how are you? Isn't the weather nice today? I love you!"

She toiled for half an hour or so, then decided to go ask her mother for help. But after Carol spent another hour composing a Chinese speech, her mother couldn't stop correcting Joanna as she read it aloud, and then said it felt "strange and forced" for Joanna to pour her heart out to Jack in Chinese.

"I think maybe you should speak in a way that you are most comfortable," Carol finally said.

This prompted Joanna to consider falling back into her comfort zone—drawing or painting Jack something to express her love for him. Her mother suggested that she give him the apple blossom painting she had just made, but somehow that didn't feel quite right. "I painted that for myself, I think," Joanna said. "Not him."

"You could paint another one?" Carol offered. "You still have nearly a full day until you leave."

But as Joanna sat in front of a fresh canvas, all the colors of the rainbow laid out for her choosing, it didn't feel right, either.

Painting something for him seems like my way of communicating. I want to tell Jack how I feel using his way.

Setting her paintbrush down, Joanna went back to her bedroom, opened her laptop, and started a blank document.

"Dear Jack," she started typing. "I still remember the first moment I saw you." She went on to describe that first day in the teachers' lounge, how the crowd had parted and she had laid eyes on him. She continued writing, pouring the last two months onto the page, completely captivated in a way she had never been before with words. After she had filled an entire, single-spaced page, at the bottom, she signed it "Love, Joanna."

She re-read and edited the letter several times until she was satisfied, then printed it out and folded it twice, slipping the sheet of paper into her handbag.

Now, seated and all buckled up on the plane, about to take off for the long journey to present it to Jack, Joanna drew the page out, reading it again in her head and imagining his reaction.

What if he says "You came all this way to say that?"

Or "Uh, thanks, I guess?"

Well, if that's his reaction, so be it. The important thing is that I tell him how I feel.

As she reread the letter yet again, she began to have second thoughts about what she had written.

Maybe I should ditch this and just draw him something, like Mom suggested.

Yawning, and figuring she'd sleep a couple of hours and think about it some more when she woke up, Joanna leaned against the window and closed her eyes.

A little while later, Joanna woke to a flight attendant patting on her arm. "Miss, can you raise your seatback, please? We'll be landing in Taipei shortly," the woman said, her tone quiet but firm.

Joanna blinked groggily. *What did she just say? We're landing soon?*

Unwinding herself from the fetal position she found herself in, Joanna looked at her watch and realized that she had slept the entire thirteen-and-a-half-hour flight.

Oh no. I didn't have time to practice my speech at all.

Holding the piece of paper in one hand as she deplaned, Joanna tried to commit the words to memory, so she wouldn't be reading from it in front of Jack and appear insincere.

At immigration control, when the officer asked her purpose for visiting Taiwan, she almost answered "I really don't know!"

Seriously, what am I doing here?

After clearing customs, she stepped onto the MRT train that went into Taipei, still trying to work on her speech for Jack. Although all the signs and announcements on Taipei's public transit system were in both Mandarin and English, Joanna was distracted reciting the speech in her head while holding on to a hand strap, and missed her transfer stop at Taipei Main Station.

Crap.

Getting off at the next stop and crossing over

to catch the next train in the opposite direction, Joanna looked at the time and started panicking. By the time she managed to get on the right line, then finally get off at the MRT stop nearest to Jack's brother's apartment, Joanna was already over a half hour late.

Racing up the stairs from the underground station, Joanna reached the street level and had to stop to catch her breath. Looking all around, she widened her eyes in wonderment at the dense mix of high- and low-rise buildings, the cars and mopeds whizzing by, and the towering, resplendent Taipei 101 in the distance.

I'm definitely not in Michigan anymore.

Pulling up a map on her phone, Joanna navigated to Jack's brother's building, a shiny, high-rise building with an elevator in the lobby but no doorman. Grateful she didn't have to attempt to speak Mandarin to anyone, Joanna entered the elevator, pressing the button for the eleventh floor. When she got to the right unit, she knocked on the door, tapping her shoe until she heard faint footsteps approaching from the other side.

The door swung open inward, and Joanna almost launched into her not-quite-memorized speech before realizing that the handsome, black-haired man in the well-tailored business suit wasn't Jack.

"Oh!" she said, covering her mouth as she took in the baby-faced version of Jack standing in front of her. "You are Jack's younger brother," Joanna said in Mandarin, stuttering over the word for *younger brother.*

"Yeah, that's right," the man answered in English. He had a strong Australian accent and a charming disposition. "I'm Jonathan Sun."

"H-h-hi," Joanna said back, also in English, scrambling to compose herself. "Sorry, I was looking for Jack."

"Right," Jonathan answered, smiling, a dimple appearing on one cheek. "Unfortunately, he just left."

"Oh no, he did?" Joanna dropped her bag to the floor with a thud. She looked at her watch. "Darn it."

Jonathan looked at her, then the bag. "Are you alright? Do you want me to try giving him a call...?" He reached into his pocket and pulled out his phone.

"No!" Joanna reached out to stop him, almost knocking the phone out of his hand. "Oops, I'm so sorry! I didn't mean to actually touch you, or the phone!"

He eyed Joanna curiously. "I'm guessing he wasn't expecting you."

"No," she said morosely.

What now? So much for trying to memorize a speech. He's not even here!

"I think he said he was going to meet his students, who are on a class trip here?" Jonathan offered. "Are you part of that group?"

Joanna nodded. "Sort of, well, not really, but they're meeting at the Shilin Night Market. I was supposed to try to meet him here before he left. Unfortunately I missed my MRT stop, and now I'm late..."

"Do you want to leave a message or something? Or come in and wait for him? Unfortunately I have to leave for a dinner right now, but you're welcome to stay." Jonathan opened the door wider, and Joanna could see a bright living room behind him.

As he did so, a voice came from inside, speaking Mandarin. Joanna couldn't make out what the person was saying, but the voice sounded like a woman's.

Oh no! Is that Jack and Jonathan's mother? What am I going to say to her?

Sweeping up her bag and slinging it onto her shoulder, Joanna quickly turned her back to the door. "I'm good, thank you! I'll just go and figure out something else. Sorry to bother you." She ran down the stairs, afraid to look back and see Jack's mother standing at the door. "Bye!" she yelled out.

"Alright then, bye!" Jonathan called out. "I hope you find him, *Joanna*!"

Wait. He knows who I am?

LEAVING THE BUILDING, Joanna hurried to the MRT station, messaging Hanna Andresson on the way.

Joanna: I arrived at Jack's brother's place too late! He said Jack already left!

Hanna: Was just about to write you. Yes, Jack messaged me that he's already at the meeting place outside the MRT station. We're just heading there now. Should I try to hold back our group?

Joanna: I hate to ask you to do that…but yes, please!!

Hanna: Let me see what I can do!

Joanna: Thank you SO much!!

Arriving at the MRT stop, Joanna got off and ran up to street level, praying that it was the right exit. Once outside, she looked up and saw two soaring concrete pylons at each end of the station and a long string of great big metallic lanterns strung between the pylons.

The station's shaped like a dragon boat?!

Remembering the disaster that had occurred between her and Jack at the school's Dragon Boat Festival, Joanna couldn't help but think, *Please don't let this be an ominous sign.*

The sun was setting, and it blinded Joanna temporarily as she crossed the street to the entrance of the night market, where masses of people were moving in every direction. In front of her, a line for a food stall seemed to extend out a mile long. Joanna peeled her eyes for Jack's figure.

"Miss Joanna!" Turning around so she was facing the MRT station again, Joanna saw the big group of Lakeland students and chaperones, all wearing red Lakeland T-shirts and some the matching red baseball caps. In the front, leading the pack, her blond hair in her signature plaits, stood Maja Andresson. "What are you doing here?" Maja called out.

"I'm so sorry!" Hanna Andresson stepped in front of her daughter and ran up to Joanna. "I tried to lead everyone out a different entrance but Maja stopped me."

"You were doing that on purpose?" Maja asked her mother. "Why would you take us out the wrong entrance?"

"I'll explain later," Hanna told her daughter.

"Thank you so much for trying. It's my fault, I was distracted and missed a stop on the way from the airport," Joanna answered.

"Was it at Taipei Main Station?" Maja asked.

"Um, yes, I think so," Joanna responded.

"Or Bei Men? Both are transfer stations from the airport line."

"Stop distracting her, Maja," Hanna shushed her daughter. "She's here looking for Jack."

"You're here to meet Sun *Laoshi*, too?" Maja asked. "Why?"

Joanna nodded, saying, "I need to tell him something."

"Did you fly from Michigan? Just to tell Sun *Laoshi* something?" Maja asked. "What do you need to tell him so badly that you had to fly here? Why didn't you just send him a message?"

"Maja, just hold on for a sec," Hanna said. "Darling, can you please go stand over there with the rest of the group?" She turned to Joanna. "Sorry, Joanna, we haven't seen him yet."

Joanna scanned to her left, then to her right. "I wonder where he—"

Before she could finish her sentence, she saw him.

There he was, with the backdrop of the magnificent dragon boat station behind him: Jack Sun, hair a little longer but still perfectly unstyled, wearing a bright white T-shirt, well-fitted jeans and a shocked look on his face.

The shiver Joanna had felt the first time she laid eyes on him ran up her spine again, a hundred times stronger than on that first day of spring.

This time, it felt like a lightning bolt.

Oh, Handsome Jack, how I've missed you.

"Joanna?" he said. He placed one hand above his forehead like a visor to shield the glare of the sun coming from behind her. "What are you... how are you...here?"

"Jack," she said. The contents of the letter she had written replayed in her mind as he walked toward her: the moment she had met him in the teachers' lounge on her first day of school, how he had impressed her with his oratory and comedic skills and how devastated she had felt when he agreed they shouldn't start a relationship. Then she pictured him in the botanical gardens, the scene that she had painted, the moment that *she knew*.

But she was unable to pull the words inside her out of her mouth. The only thing that she could manage was "I'm sorry."

Stepping closer to her, into the shade of the neighboring buildings, Jack dropped his hand from his eyes. "For what? Not for what you said to me at the Dragon Boat Festival? I already forgave you for that," Jack said.

"No, not that," Joanna said. "I'm sorry for letting you leave before telling you this—"

She looked into his eyes. Everything—the people streaming out of the MRT station, the Lakeland group, the lights from the surrounding buildings—all became a blur as Jack's face came into focus. "I've been wanting to tell you since the afternoon we went to the botanical gardens. I should have said it back then. But I'm here and telling you now."

Joanna took a deep breath.

"Everything you said to me that afternoon, I feel, too. In fact, I think I'm in love with you, Jack. Do you still feel the same way about me?"

CHAPTER TWENTY-SIX

MANAGING TO SPURT out only a few barely intelligible words, Jack was in complete and utter shock. Right here in Taipei, in the middle of one of the busiest night markets in the city—sights, smells and sounds swirling all around—standing not ten feet in front of him, was Joanna Lin.

Surrounded in a halo of the rays of the setting sun shining through the neighboring buildings, she looked, quite simply, like an angel.

A slightly lost angel, but an angel nonetheless.

Then she said the words "I think I'm in love with you."

She's in love with me!

Suddenly, the cloud that Jack had felt surrounding him ever since he had arrived back in Taiwan lifted. Elated, he wanted to pick her up in his arms, spin her around and never let go. "You don't know how much it means to hear you say that," he said. "The answer is yes. I meant every word I said to you at the botanical gardens. And yes, Joanna, I'm utterly and completely in love with you."

Relief showed across her face as she heaved a giant sigh. "Oh, thank goodness!" she exclaimed. "I should have said it the morning of the Dragon Boat Festival before my mother arrived and everything spun out of control."

"I still can't believe you're here, in Taiwan," Jack said. "How did you get here? I mean, how did you know where to find me?"

"Well... I did go to your brother's apartment first," Joanna said, with a part mischievous, part sheepish gleam in her eye.

"You did? When?"

"Just before I came here," Joanna answered. "Apparently, you had already left to meet the fifth grade group."

"Ah," he said. "So that's why Hanna Andresson asked me to move the time back, and for my address. She wasn't just being a bizarrely thorough travel planner."

"Is that what you thought?" Joanna laughed. "It did take a bit of scheming. I hope you're not mad." She gestured over to her right, and Jack saw the big Lakeland group standing near the long line for the fried chicken chop stall.

"Oh my! How did I not notice them standing there before?" Jack waved to them as he exclaimed in Mandarin, "Welcome to Taiwan, Lakeland students!"

"Hi, Sun *Laoshi*!" Maja called out in Mandarin as she ran over to him, her mother, Hanna, close behind. "Can we start walking down the night market now? I'm starving."

"Maja, Hanna, everyone, hi!" Jack greeted all the students and parent chaperones. "You made it. Great to see you all! How was the flight over?"

"Long," Maja answered.

"*So* long," another student said, yawning, then asked, "Are we going to go to your house?"

"No, sorry," Jack answered. "We're going to tour this huge night market, but could you give me just one minute?"

Thankfully, Hanna Andresson spoke up. "Hi, Jack. We didn't mean to intrude on your, er, re-union with Joanna. Why don't we start walking down this street, and you catch up when you're done?"

"Why, Mom?" Maja asked. "I thought Mr. Sun was going to show us around?"

"He will, darling. Let's just give him and Miss Joanna a minute, okay?" She put a hand on her daughter's shoulder to turn her toward the entrance to the night market, where neon signs were lit up and glowing brightly now that the sun had set. "We can start off on our own, can't we? How about we get some of that fried chicken?"

Jack responded gratefully, "Yes, thank you, Hanna. We'll be right behind you."

"No problem," Hanna said, leading the students away, even as Jack could hear Maja protesting.

"Thank you!" Joanna called after them.

As the group filed off, Jack turned back to Joanna. "Where were we?"

"I was saying that I hope you weren't mad that I asked Hanna Andresson for help to find you," Joanna said, lights from the night market reflecting in her eyes.

"How could I be mad at you, Joanna? You're here." Jack rubbed his face with both hands. "I still can't believe my eyes."

"It was actually my mom's idea," Joanna admitted, grinning.

"Why doesn't that surprise me?" Jack asked, chuckling and shaking his head. "She really *is* dedicated to her craft. She wasn't kidding when she told me she wasn't giving up."

"She even offered to call you herself. Could you imagine? Another call from my mother? What would you have said if she had?"

"That I made a huge mistake back in that dragon boat." Jack gazed into Joanna's eyes. "Everything you said was true. I was afraid to tell my mother and brother how I really felt about moving back and quitting my job. I *was* a coward—"

"I'm sorry to have used that word," Joanna said, smacking her forehead. "It was incredibly rude."

Jack shook his head, placing a hand on hers and gently pulling it down from her face. "No, it was the right one. I wanted to stay in the US but still felt an obligation to my family. Instead of openly discussing it with them and dealing with my issues, I asked you to uproot your entire life to be with me here. That was wrong of me.

"Since I arrived back a week ago, I've been shadowing my brother. He really has everything at the company under control—design, manufacturing, sales, finance. I told him I felt totally useless. Then I spoke with Hanna Andresson—"

"You spoke with her, too?" Joanna cut in, clearly surprised. "When?"

Jack raised an eyebrow. "After she wrote me to ask for my address."

"Ah!"

"Anyways, she said something that gave me the courage to speak to my mother."

"So Hanna helped us both," Joanna said.

"Yes, she certainly did. She thanked me—and you, also—for helping her and her husband see something in Maja that they hadn't seen before. They realized that they had to let Maja choose her own path. It made *me* realize that perhaps the obligation I felt to my family was something I had put on myself, and if my mother really knew how I felt, she wouldn't want me to give up my career as a teacher in the US."

"Wow," Joanna said, shaking her head. "So did you talk to your mother and brother?"

"I did, indeed. After I hung up with Hanna, I sat down with both of them and told them that I want to keep teaching, not run the company. I also told my mother that I should have told her long ago, and not waited so long, and that I'd been scared."

Joanna's eyes lit up. "You really said all that to your mother? What did she say? When I was at your apartment, I heard a voice and wasn't sure if that was her. I scurried away before she appeared." Joanna grimaced. "Was she mad?"

Jack smiled. "That might have been her, but thankfully, no, she wasn't mad at all. Hanna was one hundred percent right. My mother said she understood and was sad that I hadn't brought any of this up before. She told me that because she wanted to retire, she didn't want to leave the burden all to my brother. And she, too, felt an obligation of sorts that her eldest son should carry on the family business. But after I spoke to them, she and Jonathan both agreed that my brother is completely fine running the business with the current management team in place. Then Jonathan admitted that he was only encouraging me to run the company with him because he, too, wanted to make my mother happy.

"Turns out my little brother isn't so little anymore," Jack finished.

"That's fantastic, Jack! Good for you!"

"One more thing… I also told them about you."

"Oh, so that's why your brother knew who I was," Joanna said. "What did you say about me?"

"Just how wonderful you were. And how I

made the biggest mistake of my life leaving you. And then my mother *really* understood why it was so hard for me to leave the US."

Joanna blushed. "I can't believe your mother really took it that well."

"Me too. But she also did say that she wished she could see me more."

"Of course," Joanna said. "She must miss you so much. You've been away a very long time."

"Yes. So, I told her if she retired, she could see me as much as she wanted…back in Michigan."

"YOU'VE DECIDED TO move back to Lakeland, already?" Joanna asked, wanting to make sure she had heard him right.

"Yes," Jack said, nodding emphatically. "I called Principal Malik right away—even though it was past nine p.m. in the US—and asked if his job offer was still available. Thankfully, he answered his cell, and wasn't even annoyed that I had called so late. He told me that yes, the job was still available."

"Oh, Jack!" Joanna covered her mouth in excitement. "When are you coming back?"

"I told my mother I'd spend the summer here and return to Michigan in time for the first day of school."

"I can't believe this," Joanna said, her heart overflowing with so much happiness she thought it was going to explode. "But does this mean I didn't have to scheme and scramble to make the long trip over here to find you?" she asked.

"Well, it's certainly nice to have you here right now with me. And it makes it much easier to do this," Jack said, leaning toward her and, at long last, under the bright lights of the Shilin Night Market, he circled his arms around Joanna, pulled her in close to him and kissed her.

CHAPTER TWENTY-SEVEN

JOANNA STEPPED INTO her classroom and spun around happily. The bulletin boards, which had looked barren and lonely on the last day of school, now appeared primed and eager to be filled. The only part of her classroom that still felt empty was the window sill; as she went over to raise the blinds, she made a mental note to pick up a new plant at the farmers market that afternoon.

Maybe a pot of chrysanthemums? And I'll get ones for Mindy and Jack, too.

She had noticed heaps of the attractive, jewel-like bushes on her walk into work that morning, a staff in-service day before the school would be filled with students again.

It's here again. The first day of school is tomorrow! And I finally did it. Officially. Miss Joanna, permanent art teacher for Lakeland Elementary!

Happy feelings for the first day of school danced through her body once again. She had her outfit already picked out, a hunter green linen jumpsuit she had bought in Taipei a month ago but hadn't worn yet, wanting to save it specifically for tomorrow.

Scanning the cabinets and shelves in her classroom, Joanna jotted down a list of additional supplies she wanted to get, as she had a notebook full of ideas from her summer in Taiwan.

Rice paper, sumi ink and brushes, felt pads she wrote, her head wagging side to side in delight. *The kids are going to love using all these materials for calligraphy and painting.*

"Helloooo, beautiful!" a familiar voice sang out from the door.

"Mindy!" Joanna spun on her heel to run over and give her friend a huge hug. "So wonderful to see you! How are the boys? How was your summer? You look amazing! And your hair!" Honey-blonde highlights streaked through the guidance counselor's—now much longer—locks.

"Thanks! I thought I'd lighten it up a bit." Mindy gave her head a little toss. "My summer was fabulous. My ankle healed, and we had a ton of fun at our cabin, and my husband and I even got a few days away to Mackinac Island while my mom watched the boys. We're sad you couldn't join us. But I'm sure my summer wasn't nearly as good as yours, huh?" Mindy shook a finger at Joanna. "Did I call it or what? Your mom might think *she* put you and Jack together, but we all know who the real matchmaker was, huh?" She turned the finger back to herself.

Joanna laughed. "You're absolutely right, you did call it, Mindy. And my summer was indeed quite memorable."

"I want to hear all about it. Don't you dare leave a single thing out. Your sporadic messages were extremely unsatisfying. And you didn't send nearly enough photos."

"For sure, we need a long catch-up. But first, Principal Malik wants us in for a staff meeting, right?" Joanna looked at the clock to check the time.

"Right, let's make the long trek over there," Mindy said as she led the way to the teachers' lounge next door.

As they arrived, Joanna heard the voices of a few teachers speaking Mandarin. To her delight, she understood almost everything they were saying.

"How was your summer?" Alex asked Yang *Laoshi*, one of the first grade teachers. "Did you go to China?"

"Yes," Ms. Yang answered. "It was very relaxing. And you, were you able to see your parents in Beijing?"

"I did," Alex replied. As she saw Joanna and Mindy approach, she switched to English. "It was only for a couple of weeks, but it was great."

"Oh, you can keep speaking Mandarin," Joanna said, in Mandarin herself.

Alex shot her a shocked look. "Miss Joanna,

listen to you! Did you spend the summer studying Chinese or something?"

"Yes," Joanna said, blushing, but with pride, not embarrassment. "I was in Taiwan the whole summer, so had a lot of practice."

Just then Miss Wei-Wei walked into the lounge. After exchanging hellos with everyone, she pulled Joanna off to the side. Lowering her voice, she said, "Joanna, it's great to see you. I wasn't sure if you had caught up with your mother on everything that's happened to me. I just wanted to explain a little if she had."

"No, she hasn't said anything, other than a few months ago, when she said that she must respect your privacy! What's going on?" Joanna asked, extremely curious. "Did she set you up with anyone?"

Wei-Wei leaned in closer and said, "I have a confession to make. I've actually been looking for a sperm donor for quite some time."

Ohhhhhhh. Suddenly everything Joanna had observed last school year made sense.

"Had you been thinking to ask Jack? Is that why you wanted to know about his family lineage, commented on his athleticism and asked if he wanted children?"

Wei-Wei covered her mouth. "Ha, yes, exactly. But after I saw you two getting close, I realized that it was a bad idea to consider him."

"Oops, I really was trying to hide it," Joanna said.

"It became pretty clear you two had chemistry together. We were all just waiting to see how it turned out. Anyways, so yes, I realized I couldn't ask him, and when you mentioned your mother was a matchmaker, I thought I'd see if she could help make a match. But I gave her some strange criteria, like telling her I wasn't interested in anything too serious."

"Ah, that probably didn't make any sense to her," Joanna commented. "She's all about getting to the wedding."

"Yes, then over the summer I admitted I was just looking for a donor, and she wished me good luck, but that she couldn't help me with that."

Joanna chuckled. "Yeah, that's not really what she does."

"She did try to convince me to keep looking for a real partner but I didn't want to wait any longer. So I decided to try my chances with a sperm bank."

"That's great, Wei-Wei. You'll be a great mother. Hopefully they had some qualified candidates for you?" Joanna asked.

"They did," Wei-Wei said, winking and rubbing her abdomen.

"Oh!" Joanna said. "Are you…?"

"I think so, but it's still early, so…" She put an index finger to her lips.

"Of course," Joanna said. "How exciting, Wei-Wei!"

Just then, Alex stepped over to them, asking, "What's exciting?"

Wei-Wei covered quickly, saying, "I heard we're adding an additional kindergarten class this year!"

"Oh, really?" Alex asked. "Did Principal Malik hire a new teacher?"

"I believe he did." Wei-Wei pointed her chin toward the door and the others followed her gaze.

Walking into the teachers' lounge, wearing a crisp blue button-down shirt, with not a hair out a place, was Lakeland Elementary School's newest kindergarten teacher: Mr. Jack Sun.

Joanna strolled through the crowd to him, feeling the shiver up her spine that she'd felt so many months ago in the very same room.

That's one good-looking man, she chuckled to herself, remembering Mindy's whispered words that day.

"*Zao an*, Sun *Laoshi*," Joanna said to Jack, courteously.

"Good morning, Miss Joanna," Jack said back, similarly professional.

Mindy snorted at both of them. "Are you two for real? Is this how you're going to be all the time, seriously? You know we don't have an antifraternization policy, right?"

Jack responded by smiling and leaning over to

give Joanna a kiss on the cheek, which resulted in Mindy whistling and hooting until Joanna shushed her. "Alright, alright, Mindy! Principal Malik's starting the meeting."

"Good morning, teachers!" the big man said, welcoming everyone back to a new school year. "Before we get into the nitty-gritty stuff, I want to first welcome Jessica Zhang back from maternity leave—we hope both she and her baby twins are doing well."

The room cooed over the mention of babies, with Mindy calling out for Ms. Zhang to please bring them in for a visit soon, and Joanna exchanging a look with Wei-Wei.

Principal Malik continued, "I'd also like to announce our two new permanent hires for the year, although their faces will be familiar to you, of course. Joanna Lin has accepted the position of Lakeland's permanent art teacher, and Jack Sun will be taking on our newest kindergarten class."

The teachers all started to clap, and although Alex called out "Speech! Speech!" both Joanna and Jack declined to give one this time.

"I already made my first impression in the spring," Jack said, with a wave to the room.

"Me too," Joanna said.

Attention went back to the principal. "You're going to want to really applaud this one. My last announcement—and this one's a biggie—is that Jack will also be teaching an after-school class at the middle school up the road, so that our graduating class from last year—and any other students who may want to join—can continue their Chinese studies. I was absolutely thrilled when Jack brought up the idea, and hopefully we can convince the school board and principal over there to offer Chinese classes during their regular schedule starting next fall."

Now the room really roared, and Joanna squeezed Jack's hand.

"I'm so proud of you," she whispered.

"I'm so proud of us," he responded, squeezing her hand back.

ON SATURDAY MORNING, the first one of September, Joanna heard both her doorbell ringing and cell phone buzzing at the same time. Unlike back in the spring, however, today she was already awake and fully dressed, sitting at her kitchen table and paging through her level two Chinese Proficiency Test textbook. Although Principal Malik hadn't mentioned anything about needing to pass another test, Joanna was eager to discover how much of the material she had already learned during her summer in Taiwan.

At the sound of the ringing and buzzing, Joanna jumped up from the table and rushed to throw open her front door.

"Hi!" She greeted her mother, who was once again standing on her building's front porch, laden with food and somehow ringing her doorbell and calling her at the same time. "It's so good to see you!"

"Joanna!" Carol said as she dropped the bags to give her a big hug. "I missed you so much!"

"I missed you so much, too," Joanna said as she embraced her mother. "Sorry again that I ended up coming straight back here from Taiwan without stopping at home first."

"No need for apologies," Carol said, coming into Joanna's kitchen, again rolling a cooler behind her. "Who wouldn't have jumped at the chance to stay in Taiwan the entire summer? I'm glad to hear your first week of school went well, too, and the jet lag not too bad."

"Yes, it was so great to be back in the classroom. Having a regular schedule definitely helped me adjust to this time zone," Joanna said, as she helped her mother haul in the rest of the bags. "You know you didn't have to bring any food! Jack's mother's been cooking nonstop since she arrived. Once she heard you hadn't been back to Taiwan in over thirty years, it seems she's preparing every single Taiwanese dish in existence for your arrival."

"Oh, that's so nice of her," Carol said, starting to unload containers into Joanna's fridge. "I've prepared a few things for her as well—she'll see that the food options aren't too shabby on this side of the ocean, either."

"Thanks, Mom. I'm sure she'll love everything," Joanna responded. "But for today's lunch, Jack and I thought we could bring you to our favorite restaurant in town, The Dumpling Spot. It's just downtown and owned by our friend Danny, who makes the best dumplings and buns this side of the Pacific."

"Yes, I remember you mentioning the place. It sounds delicious," Carol said. "And how has Jack's mother's stay been so far?"

"Great, really great." Joanna told her how Jack's mother had visited their school several times during the past week, and how astounded she had been. "She never imagined she'd find a handful of people here who could speak Chinese, much less a whole school."

Carol's head popped out from the fridge. "That's wonderful! And Jack's brother, when does he get in?"

"Any minute now. Let me confirm." Joanna typed out a quick message to Jack, who replied right away. "Looks like Jack just got back from picking Jonathan up at the airport. He said they're heading over to the restaurant now."

"Okay," Carol said, closing Joanna's freezer door. "What do you think? Am I dressed alright?"

"Of course, you always look great." Joanna nodded at her mom's silk top. "And I've never known you to fuss so much over your appearance, Mom."

Carol walked over to the hall mirror and glanced at her reflection, fixing a strand of hair. "Well, it's never been this important."

"What happened to what you told me when I left for Taiwan? *Just be yourself*?" Joanna reminded her mom.

"I know, I know, you're right. Okay, let's go meet Jack's family!"

They walked the short distance to downtown Lakeland, arriving at The Dumpling Spot to find Jack and his family already seated around a table in the middle of the restaurant. Jack, his mother, Jia-Yang, and his brother, Jonathan, all rose when Joanna and her mother entered. It had only been a couple of weeks since Joanna had seen Jonathan back in Taiwan, but he already looked more mature, as tall as Jack and even more self-assured.

Is it possible he grew a few inches? Joanna thought. *He's really looking like a CEO.*

A flurry of hugs and handshakes ensued, with everyone greeting each other enthusiastically and Jack's mother offering to pour the tea. Carol heartily welcomed Jia-Yang and Jonathan to Michigan.

"How long will you be staying?" Carol asked. "I hope long enough so you can witness the leaves changing color as it turns colder."

"I'm definitely looking forward to seeing that—this will be my first Michigan fall," Jack chimed in.

"I can't wait, too," Joanna said. "I foresee a lot of leaves in the upcoming art curriculum at Lakeland."

"I would love to take you on a tour around the state while Jack and Joanna are busy at school," Carol said. "The upper peninsula will start to see colder weather in a couple of weeks, and let me tell you, it's just magnificent."

"That sounds marvelous," Jack's mother answered. "I'm planning on being here in Michigan for at least a month, now that I'm retired." She paused and smiled at her sons. "Goodness, it's been three months and I'm *still* getting used to the sound of that."

"Sounds great to me," Jack said, and thanked Carol for the offer to take his mother around.

"Perfect, we'll set it all up for the last week of September," Carol said. "And you, Jonathan, will you be able to join us?"

"Unfortunately, Auntie, I can only stay a week this time. I have to get back to Taiwan, now that I have a company to run." He looked to his mother, who beamed back at him. "But I actually have some business in Chicago in mid-October, so maybe I can come a few days early and drop by here for another short visit."

Carol nodded. "That timing works just fine, too. There should still be some beautiful colors left on the trees down around these parts."

"I'll plan on that, then," Jonathan said. "If you don't mind playing tour guide again."

"Not at all," Carol answered. "And tell me, Jonathan, are you single?"

"Here it goes," Joanna whispered to Jack. "We should have warned him…"

Joanna and Jack looked on with interest as Jonathan answered, "Yes, actually, I am."

"Interesting. Single, huh?" Carol murmured, bringing out her phone from her handbag. "When did you say you'd be back again?" she asked. "I'm going to mark the dates in my calendar."

"Look out, little brother, looks like Carol's matchmaking reach is about to extend across international borders," Jack said, chuckling.

"I'll raise a glass to that." Carol winked and raised her teacup with one hand. "I've always wanted to go global. As long as it's okay with you, Jia-Yang."

"You have my blessing," Jack's mother said, raising her cup as well. "Now that Jack has found his love, let it be Jonathan's turn."

"Well, when you put it like that, I have to raise a glass, too." Jack gazed at Joanna and raised his cup with both hands.

Joanna followed suit, laughing and enjoying it all, now that she was no longer the target of her mother's matchmaking.

Everyone turned their attention to Jonathan.

Was he interested? Or would he politely decline, like I tried to do? Joanna wondered.

Pausing for just a second, a glint in his eye, Jonathan lifted his teacup as well. "Sure, why not?" he said, as the others all leaned in to clink their cups together in a big group toast. "Let's see if Carol can work her magic for me, too!"

Joanna clapped her hands, tickled that Jonathan was such a good sport, when she heard Jack clearing his throat. She turned to find him down on one knee next to her, a shining diamond ring between his fingers. "Oh my god! Jack!" she gasped.

"Now that our careers are secure and families all together in one place, I thought it would be a good time to ask. Joanna Lin, will you marry me?" he asked, flashing her that dazzling, double-dimpled smile.

Could he be any more handsome?

"Yes, Jack Sun, yes!" Joanna answered, pulling him up from bended knee. She threw her arms around him and kissed him. "I love you, Jack," she said.

"I love you more, Joanna."

"Congratulations!" Jack's mother and brother both called out.

"I'm so happy for the both of you," Carol said, wiping a tear from her eye. "Now, do I get credit for this match?"

"I'll give you partial credit," Joanna laughed,

giving her mother a hug, and then turning back to Jack. "But I think we have to credit ourselves, too, for making our own match!"

"And a perfect one it is," Jack agreed, pulling her in for another lovely kiss.

* * * * *